Desperate
MEASURES

Also by Phyllis Eickelberg:
Bearly Hidden, 2012

Desperate
MEASURES

A BRAIN TEASER MYSTERY

Phyllis Eickelberg

abbott press®
A DIVISION OF WRITER'S DIGEST

Desperate Measures
A Brain Teaser Mystery

Copyright © 2012 Phyllis Eickelberg

Abbott Press books may be ordered through booksellers or by contacting:

Abbott Press
1663 Liberty Drive
Bloomington, IN 47403
www.abbottpress.com
Phone: 1-866-697-5310

ISBN: 978-1-4582-0566-7 (e)
ISBN: 978-1-4582-0567-4 (sc)

Library of Congress Control Number: 2012914851

Printed in the United States of America

Abbott Press rev. date: 08/28/2012

PUZZLE MENU

Let's Start with a Big Clue.................................ix
What Should be Avoided? 2
Discover a Clue 10
A Bit of Philosophy 16
The Stage is Set.. 26
Watch Out, Heather!..34
Synonym Finder.. 39
Oh! No!.. 43
What's in Store for Aunt Myrtle? 49
Who is Not Going Away?................................... 53
What's in a Word?... 60
Silly Sense 67
What's Going On? 75
A Look Ahead... 82
Watch Out, Lewisburg....................................... 89
Dinner's Ready 96
Stair Steps 106
Story Stew..116
The Search Continues...................................... 124
Identify the Heirs... 130
Ask the Right Questions................................... 144
Watch Out, Vern.. 152
What Time Is It?.. 164
Where is Oliver's Missing Fortune? 174
What's Ahead? 183
Coffee Break! Sharpen Your Wits Time!......... 192
Puzzles Remaining 198
Not Enough Puzzles? 211
Puzzle Solutions 213

ACKNOWLEDGEMENTS

The author wishes to express a special debt of gratitude to her husband Jim, who has been patient and helpful throughout.

Thanks too, to manuscript proofreaders and consultants Lezli Weeden, Anne Chaimov, Carolyn Hegstad, Jan Fisher, Rosemary Cunningham, Susan Pachuta, Katie Cooper, Stacy Mellem, Frank Yates, Sam Hall, Doris Cameron-Minard, Peter Saunders and Dr. Steven Eickelberg.

Exotic herbs, hidden treasures and murder

Desperate Measures is a story about greed, bomb threats and an heir with special vitamins for the relative whose assets she expects to inherit. What's really in those *special* pills she's feeding him? Are they meant to ensure good health or are they meant to ensure the heir gets the fortune before the will can be changed?

And what happens if the will is no longer legal, or the jewel thief has hidden his loot in someone else's house, or there's a fiancé with debts that need to be paid?

Will someone resort to desperate measures to get what he wants?

Join Heather Samuelson in her pursuit of a missing fortune, stolen jewels, and a killer so clever there seems to be no way to connect him to his crimes.

LET'S START WITH A BIG CLUE

	1	2	3	4	5	6	7	8	9
A	K	O	L	R	H	D	B	L	C
B	F	E	M	A	O	A	R	T	T
C	S	T	H	E	I	N	L	G	E

Find all the killers

B1	B4	C2	A1
C5	A3	A5	C5
C6	C7	C9	A3
A6			A8
			C9
			A4
			C1

CHAPTER 1

The thief knew what to do and how to do it. With closing time only minutes away, no one would notice items surreptitiously removed from stock. An inventory would eventually disclose the inaccurate count, but it wouldn't arouse suspicion. Small counting errors happened all the time.

"Besides," reasoned the thief, soon to become a murderer by proxy, "I need to protect my investment."

When it came to safeguarding one's interests, desperate measures were often necessary. What did it matter that they included cold-blooded murder?

"It's all ours!" Heather Samuelson jammed a slim key into the lock of the townhouse she and her sister Sally had purchased in Lewisburg, Oregon. Moving-in day had arrived. She twisted the key once, then twice.

"Hurry up. This is heavy." Sally shifted the weight of a box she was holding.

"The lock won't turn," Heather complained, twisting her key a third time. She brushed damp curls from her forehead, eager to get out of the hot July day. "My key worked yesterday. Do you think we need to call a locksmith?"

"It's not the door or your key. It's you. Try again." Sally shifted the heavy load once more.

"Maybe it's that ghost our realtor was telling us about." Heather paused reflecting on their realtor's parting comments once the sale closed.

"You told me to wait until you'd signed the final papers before I got specific about ghosts." The realtor waited until both Sally and Heather nodded. Then she continued, "I've never seen one. That's the good news. The bad news is, strange things happen here. Your new home has an interesting history. Should I continue?"

The sisters had nodded, eager to take possession of the two-story townhouse. It had been affordable, the bank had been eager to get rid of it, and the timing was perfect for two young women concentrating on their careers.

With a sigh the realtor continued, "Neighbors complain of doors slamming when there's no wind, and they told me no one has lived in the house for ages. They also said children have avoided it for generations, but of course we know that isn't true."

The sisters laughed, waiting for the punch line.

Only there hadn't been one.

The realtor wished them well, promised to handle the sale if they decided not to stick around, and with a wave, hurried to her car.

WHAT SHOULD BE AVOIDED?

Add one letter to each of the words below to form a new word. The addition may be at the beginning, end, or within the word. Place the added letter on the line below the boxes. The added letters, reading from left to right, will form two 6-letter words that answer the above question.

G, H, I, N, O, O, O, R, S, S, S, T

ore	tree	curt	care	here	tore
gore	three	court	scare	there	store

G hosts

rank	fur	ran	talk	bard	the
prank	four	rain	stalk	board	then

poison

Heather jammed her key in the lock once more. "Either there really is a ghost and he wants us to stay out, or we need a locksmith."

"More repairs?" Sally sighed. "The next house we buy better not come equipped with a ghost and things that don't work. Hold this." She pushed the heavy box into Heather's arms and fished in the pockets of her shorts. "I'll bet you're planning to add our ghost to your next computer game."

"Good idea," Heather nodded. As a successful computer game developer she was always looking for story ideas.

"Got it!" Triumphantly Sally displayed a slim key and shoved it in the keyhole. When the lock turned she pushed the door open and took the heavy box from her sister. As they stepped into their barren living room, they heard an unfamiliar burring. "Is that a telephone?" Sally set the box she'd been carrying on the floor.

"I'll get it," Heather said, racing to the kitchen. "Hello?" she gasped when the receiver was in place.

"Did I catch you at a bad time? You sound out of breath."

"Aunt Myrtle?" Heather smiled and settled down to talk to her absentee relative. She glanced back at Sally, amazed to see her tall blond sister standing beside a frail-looking woman who seemed to have materialized in the center of their living room. Heather shivered. Was she one of the spooks?

"Heather? Are you there? Answer me. What's wrong?"

"We're fine, Aunt Myrtle. Sally and I just came in the door with our arms full. You're the first person to call our new phone number."

"Do I win a prize?" Myrtle Wilson was always optimistic.

"No prize. It just means the phone is working."

"No prize, huh? We'll have to see about that. Now then, the reason I called is to tell you I'm moving to smaller digs. I thought you'd want to know. Since my furniture has been handed down from your great-great-grandparents, I'm passing some of it on to you girls. For your new home."

"Thanks, Aunt Myrtle, but..."

"Don't interrupt, Dear. That's bad manners. I've already shipped some nice pieces. They're promised for delivery at noon tomorrow. I'm arriving in Portland in the morning at eight. On United. Make sure someone picks me up."

"But..."

"You're doing it again, Dear. Stop interrupting. As I was saying, after I help arrange your new furniture and tell you its history, I'll get out of your hair and go home. That's a promise. See you in the morning, Darling. Be on time. Bye now."

"Wait a minute, Aunt Myrt!" Heather raised her voice and leaped to her feet. Ordinarily she never shouted. "Aunt Myrtle?"

The dead phone buzzed in response.

"Aunt Myrtle hung up on me," Heather complained as Sally entered the kitchen with a plate of cookies. "Where did those come from?" she asked, slamming the receiver into its cradle.

Sally thrust the plate into her sister's hands and helped herself to a cookie. "The old lady who brought them said her name is Laura Bender. She lives on the west side of our living room wall. I suspect she's the one who's been leaving cookies on our doorstep all week."

The sisters had purchased the center unit in a triplex. During the week, as new carpet was being laid and a new furnace installed, pastries had mysteriously appeared on their doorstep.

Sally moved to the refrigerator. "Do you want something cold to drink?"

At Heather's nod, Sally handed her a bottle of cold water, and continued. "That old girl walked right in our door like she owned the place. Didn't even knock."

"We'll turn Aunt Myrtle loose on her." Heather selected a cookie and took a generous bite. "These are pretty good." She licked frosting from her fingers.

"What did Aunt Myrt have to say?"

A slight flush colored Heather's face as she frowned, wrinkling her forehead.

Sally laughed. "Something upsetting, I take it?"

"Right on," Heather confirmed.

"Aunt Myrtle lives on the other side of the continent. It's not like she can drop in unannounced and stay for a week."

"No?" Heather slumped in the chair beside the phone. "If you think she can't drop in unannounced and stay for a week then you get up tomorrow morning and meet her plane when it lands in Portland at eight A.M."

"You're kidding. That's a two-hour drive. I'd have to get up at five."

"My point exactly."

"You got the stuff, right?" The voice on the telephone sounded concerned.

"Of course I got it. Nothing to it. No one noticed. And it's already on its way. Before long, we'll be very, very rich."

"You'll keep in touch while you're gone, won't you? If something goes wrong, I'll need to disappear in a hurry."

"Nothing will go wrong, Chris. How often do I have to tell you? And if you disappeared, I'd find you."

"I'd count on that, sweetheart. It's the authorities I don't want finding me. My DNA would tie me to Pamela's murder. For my sake, could we go over everything one more time?"

"All right. Once more, but that's it. I have to catch a plane. Like I said, no one will suspect anything is wrong until it's too late, and then…."

"Where's our cookie plate?"

Heather and Sally nearly dropped the bookcase they were struggling to place against their living room wall.

The question came from a white-haired woman standing in their entryway, a plate of chocolate cookies resting precariously in trembling hands.

"I'll be right with you, Laura," Sally said. She settled her end of the bookcase, leaving Heather to swing her end into position. "My sister and I were so busy arranging furniture we didn't hear the doorbell." Sally grabbed the empty cookie plate from a nearby chair.

"Take these first," the woman gasped. Chocolate cookies were about to slide from the plate.

Sally rescued the treats.

"I don't use no doorbells." The woman snatched the empty plate from Sally's hands. "And you got it wrong. I'm Baby Bender. Laura's my twin. She's fourteen minutes oldest." Baby smiled and nodded at the chocolate cookies. "You'll love them there cookies. I made 'em for you girls as a going away present. They've got melted marshmallows down under all that nice gooey frosting I heaped on them. Try one."

"Heather, this is our neighbor," Sally said, beginning introductions. She paused, then looked back at Baby, realizing what she'd said. "We're moving in; not out."

"This house ain't yours," Baby snapped. "You don't belong here. You gotta leave. We told them real estate people about the ghosts. They shouldn'ta sold this spooky old place. You'll be sorry if you don't leave."

The sisters looked at their guest, then at each other. When the kitchen phone rang, Heather hurried to answer it, leaving Sally to usher Baby Bender from their house. When she slammed the door behind their guest and locked it, Heather laughed.

"Hello?" Heather was still chuckling as she answered the phone.

"Welcome to Taborhill Garden Estates," boomed a man's voice.

Heather moved the receiver away from her head.

"It's time we had young people moving in. Most folks here are like me, over sixty." The caller chuckled. "I'm Oliver Lloyd. Is this a good time to drop by with sandwiches? I figured moving in and all, you'd forget to eat lunch."

Heather shook her head. They'd been in their new home less than three hours. Myrtle called, the Bender twins had each delivered cookies, and now someone named Oliver Lloyd was offering sandwiches.

"How did you get this phone number?" Heather asked.

"I visited with the lineman when he hooked you up. Are you disappointed?"

Heather laughed. "Come ahead. The more the merrier. But bring enough so you can join us. Will iced tea suit you?"

"Perfect. I'll be there in a few minutes. I only live a couple doors away."

Sally walked into the kitchen as Heather hung up the phone. She was carrying chocolate cookies. "Are we having company for lunch?"

Heather nodded. "We have a neighbor named Oliver Lloyd. He's bringing sandwiches." She ran her fingers through her short auburn curls. "Is it just me or is our cooling system letting us down?"

Sally walked to the thermostat in the hallway, and groaned when she saw it. "It's not you. We need that installer back. His New Miracle Cooling System isn't cooling." The ringing doorbell interrupted her. "Hot damn! This place is in the middle of Grand Central Station, not Lewisburg, Oregon."

Laughing, Heather went to the door to admit a tall, rangy man with beautifully groomed white hair and twinkling brown eyes. Gaunt lines ran vertically down his leathery face, stopping just below a dense mustache.

"Oliver Lloyd, I presume?"

"That's me!" Oliver handed Heather a tray of sandwiches. "Some of those are peanut butter and some are tuna." He stepped into the house, walking stiffly. Heather closed the door behind him, and locked it.

"I'm Heather." The hand not holding the tray of sandwiches stretched toward Oliver to shake hands. He clutched her fingers and planted a wet kiss on them. Heather smiled uncertainly, continuing introductions. "The tall lady across the room is my sister, Sally. We're co-owners of this townhouse."

"No kissing," Sally cautioned, waving her fingers at Oliver. "Have a seat over here." She gestured toward one of four kitchen chairs surrounding a collapsible card table. "For dessert we can have cookies supplied by Laura and Baby Bender."

Oliver laughed. "No one calls Laura by her given name. She's Binky." He shuffled toward one of the chairs. "Binky's been on a tear for a week. Her only son is due home any day and she wants to serve his favorite dessert. The trouble is, he's been gone so long she can't remember what it is that he likes." He chuckled. "She's been making every dessert known to man, and unloading them on the neighborhood."

"Are you saying we should expect more pastries?" Heather removed a pitcher of iced tea from the refrigerator and brought it to the table.

"Those old babes creep me out," Sally added with a dramatic shiver. "They walk in without knocking. One minute I'm alone and the next minute one of them is at my elbow pushing cookies at me."

Oliver laughed. "They walk in on all of us." He patted his belly. "As for the desserts, I've learned to say 'thanks' and toss them in the garbage when they leave."

Heather glanced at her sister, aware of Sally's sweet tooth. Any desserts that showed up at their house were not apt to be tossed out.

"Sorry about the small table," Sally said. "It's temporary. We're buying furniture next week."

Heather cringed. She'd forgotten to tell Sally that Aunt Myrtle was planning to fill their house with her castoffs.

Oliver slowly eased onto a chair.

Sally asked, "Will this table arrangement suit you?"

He laughed. "Not to worry. It's my arthritis slowing me down. I'm headed for our community swimming pool after lunch. The eighty-five degree water helps my aches and pains go away."

Sally sat down and reached for a sandwich. She took a large bite. "These are good," she said. "I didn't think I could eat lunch I was so full of cookies." Sally picked up her napkin and wiped tuna from her lips.

Oliver laughed. "Tell me about yourselves," he invited, draining his glass of iced tea and motioning for more.

Sally took another bite, nodding at her sister to begin.

Heather smiled and refilled Oliver's glass. "I'm the oldest. I operate a desktop publishing business from home, do design projects for websites, and develop computer games."

Oliver studied Heather's green eyes and short red hair. "I think you're about the age of my niece Olivia. I expect her in a few hours. She's visiting for a week." He turned to Sally. "And you?"

Sally swallowed. "I work for the Lewisburg Police Department, and I'm the youngest of three sisters." Sally's light blue eyes crinkled when she smiled and added, "I outgrew the others." She was five-ten while her sisters were both five feet two inches. Sally pushed at blond hair cut in a no-nonsense style and added, "And that's it."

"There's another sister?"

Heather nodded. "Rachel lives in town with her librarian husband and twin boys who are ten or eleven. I forget which." She reached for a sandwich.

"Now," suggested the professional detective. "What about you?" Sally grinned at Oliver and added, "If you can tell us why this house is supposed to be haunted, we'd appreciate it."

Oliver returned her smile. "I haven't heard about any haunting, but this place does have an interesting history. Maybe that's where you got the idea it was haunted. I'm a retired antique dealer who's headed to the hospital day after tomorrow. My pacemaker batteries need to be replaced so my ticker doesn't forget to tick." Oliver's smile lifted his mustache.

"Is the surgery complicated?" Heather asked.

"It's not like an office visit, but the recovery time should be quick." He took a sip of tea before adding, "I have to stick around the hospital until the doctor is sure everything's connected properly. Then I can come home."

"Do you need help? Someone to drive you to the hospital? Someone to water plants?"

"Thanks. That's what my niece will do." Oliver smiled at the sisters. "Olivia's a pharmacy student in Rhode Island and works part time at a drug store. She comes to Oregon one week every summer to lend me a hand—usually with gardening. She'll drive me to the hospital and take care of Max while I'm gone."

"Who's Max?" Sally asked.

Oliver said, "He's my pal, and he hates going to kennels."

"I have an idea," Heather said, thinking of a new drugstore client whose website she was developing. "Why don't you and Olivia have dinner with us tomorrow? Our Aunt Myrtle will be here and we can all get acquainted." Interviewing Oliver's niece might give her new ideas for her client's website.

Oliver glanced at their small table and frowned.

"Don't worry," Heather laughed. "I think that's going to change sooner than we planned."

Sally began to clear lunch plates. It was an excuse to get up and wipe beads of perspiration from her forehead. "I hope we can get that repairman here before then. As you can tell," she nodded at Oliver, "our new cooling system isn't working as it should." She turned to Heather. "Did you phone them?"

Heather nodded. "He promised to come tomorrow."

"Another day in this heat?"

"You could join me in the swimming pool," Oliver offered. "It would give you a little relief." He eased out of his chair. "I'll fill you girls in on the history of this place at dinner tomorrow. Then we'll see if you still think the place is haunted."

###

DISCOVER A CLUE

Someone has already been murdered.
Cross out the words below to discover the victim's name. It's one
you've heard and should remember. It's not in the list.

Discovery   Max   Oliver   Run

Fortune   Money   Out   Seek

Green   Motive   Pins   Victims

Lies   Murders   Plot

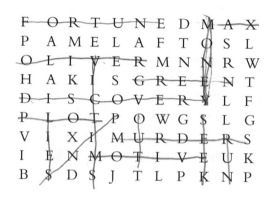

```
F O R T U N E D M A X
P A M E L A F T O S L
O L I V E R M N N R W
H A K I S G R E E N T
D I S C O V E R Y L F
P L O T P O W G S L G
V I X I M U R D E R S
I E N M O T I V E U K
B S D S J T L P K N P
```

CHAPTER 2

The intruder entered the house after everyone left on various errands. He hurried to the refrigerator and removed bottles of cold water and leftover sandwiches. Then he climbed the stairs and opened the door to his special hideout where he settled down for lunch and a nap. With luck he'd have one more night alone in this house before its new owners moved in. Hopefully that would give him enough time to finish a job begun years earlier. He'd finally be wealthy beyond belief, and able to travel around the world.

Lunch finished, he settled down to wait for nightfall.

"Uncle Oliver, I'm here." It was late afternoon when Olivia Lloyd dropped her suitcase inside her uncle's front door. She was greeted by an exuberant Max.

"Down, boy," cautioned Oliver, shuffling to his niece's side. "Me first." He pushed the golden retriever away and stepped into a hug with the dark-haired Olivia. Her pointed chin, deep dimples, and dark brown eyes reminded him of his brother Edwin each time he saw her.

"Maybe I shouldn't hug you," she said, still clinging to him. "I might be coming down with a cold. We need you to stay healthy for your surgery."

"Hug away," Oliver assured her. "Don't stop." He laughed as the gentle embrace became more intense.

He loved this niece and it delighted him that she was willing to help when he needed it. During each of the last four years, at his expense, she had flown from Rhode Island to Oregon to help with spring housecleaning and gardening. Like the Samuelson sisters, Oliver lived in a two-story townhouse triplex among groups of similar townhouse clusters. His had a fenced back yard in which he occasionally grew a few tomatoes and cucumbers.

"Okay! *Now* Max can have a turn." Oliver released his niece.

"Good boy, Max," Olivia laughed, enduring the dog's enthusiasm. "What do you want me to do first, Uncle Oliver? Should I start dinner or weed the garden?"

"First," Oliver replied, "let's have a cup of tea and get caught up with what's going on in our lives." He had some news for his niece, and he wasn't sure she'd be happy with it.

"Good idea." Olivia hurried to the kitchen just as the doorbell rang.

Oliver opened the door. "Heather! What a nice surprise."

"You forgot your sandwich tray, and Sally and I are leaving for another load of things from our apartment."

"Come in a minute. I want you to meet Olivia. She just arrived."

Heather stepped into the cool interior and gasped. Expensive paintings hung on every wall, and below them were clustered tasteful groupings of antiques. "Wow," she said. "Leftovers from your antique stores?"

Oliver nodded, and stepped into the kitchen to beckon Olivia. She was digging frantically through the contents of her purse. "Lose something?" he asked, putting the sandwich tray on the counter.

"I brought some special vitamins," she muttered, removing things from her purse. "Oh, here they are." She held up a lidless, unlabeled plastic container. "The lid came off. I brought these for you to take so you'd be ready for surgery. I already took some to keep my cold at bay."

"Step into the living room a minute. I want you to meet our neighbor, Heather Samuelson. She and her sister are moving in down the street, and they've invited us to have dinner with them tomorrow." Oliver ushered his niece into the living room.

"Hi, Olivia," greeted Heather.

"It's nice meeting you, Heather. Thanks for the dinner invitation." The teakettle in the kitchen whistled. "Won't you stay for a cup of tea?" Olivia was already heading for the kitchen.

"I wish I could, but I'm in a hurry. My sister Sally and I have more things to get moved before our aunt arrives in the morning."

"I look forward to meeting your aunt," Oliver said. "I suspect she'll be closer to my age than you and your sister."

Olivia returned from the kitchen and handed Oliver a steaming cup of orange pekoe along with two of the tablets she'd fished from the bottom of her purse.

"You'll be meeting Aunt Myrtle tomorrow at dinner." Heather smiled. "See you both then."

Oliver and his niece moved to the living room, stirring their tea in delicate bone china cups.

"These vitamins you gave me have numbers on them," he said, settling on a 19th century Victorian sofa. "They say *ten*. Is it okay to eat two tens before I swallow numbers one through nine?" Without waiting for an answer Oliver plopped the white tablets into his mouth and washed them down.

"I never noticed the numbers," Olivia commented, checking those she was preparing to swallow. Hers also had a *ten* on them. "Taking two of these shouldn't be a problem. I swallowed a couple on the plane, trying to make sure I wasn't coming down with a cold." She swallowed the pills.

"Now then, Namesake. You start. What's going on in your life?"

"To begin with," Olivia replied, "now that I've been admitted to the master's program, it's been easier to find part time work. A drugstore near the campus needed help so I do a few hours there after school weekdays and all day Saturday."

"And school?"

"It's about the same. My grades are good enough for a small amount of scholarship help."

"Hard work will make you appreciate your education more than if it was handed to you." Oliver looked at his niece's doubtful expression and laughed. "You don't look like you agree, but it's true. I could make the financial arrangements easy for you, but it wouldn't be as good a lesson as what you're getting on your own."

"There are times I wish it was easier. Now that Dad's insurance money is gone, I have to work longer hours to cover expenses."

ver nodded. "How's the search for a boyfriend? Are you still

Robert?" He'd been hearing about Robert since Olivia's freshman year.

Olivia blushed. "I thought I was getting serious about him, but I'm not sure now. There's a handsome pharmacist at the drugstore who's been paying me a lot of attention." She twisted an onyx ring on her right hand. "Vern gave me this friendship ring so I'd think about him while I was here. He wanted to come with me, but Mr. Breeze couldn't let both of us have the week off."

"I'd like to meet him before you get too serious," Oliver said. "Does Robert still operate a car shop?"

Olivia hung her head. "He's having financial troubles and could use a shot in the arm." She glanced at her uncle, and laughed when she saw the expression on his face.

"And he'd like you to furnish that financial zinger?"

Olivia nodded.

"How's the pharmacist fixed for cash? At least he's in a field that should provide a good living if he turns out to be your true love."

"Vern seems to have enough money. He takes me to expensive places. Robert is my fast-food and corner movie date, while Vern always goes first class. He was married to his high school sweetheart, but that ended tragically. I think she was murdered. It broke Vern's heart, so he moved away from Kansas and came to Rhode Island to start a new life. I suspect there was some insurance money when Pamela died."

"That brings us to the subject I want to talk about." Oliver leaned toward his niece. "I appreciate you helping me each year and staying in touch. Your cousins don't give me the time of day. This year I'm especially thankful you've come because of my hospital stay. You've saved Max from going to a kennel."

"Are you worried about getting those pacemaker batteries replaced?" Olivia patted his arm. "That should be simple. I looked it up on the internet."

"Smart girl. That's isn't what I want to talk about. I want to talk about my will."

"You said you'd be making some changes."

Oliver heaved a sigh. "I intend to give ten percent of my assets to each of two long-time friends. I just wanted to make sure you understood that the eighty percent you'll inherit will still make you very rich. Every unmarried man in six states will be asking for your hand in marriage."

Olivia giggled. "I'm glad you're remembering your friends. It's not as if I had grown up thinking whatever you had would all be mine. I'm only one of your three nieces. I always assumed the others would be mentioned in your will."

"I don't intend to leave Sharon or Marilyn anything and I never knew if my sisters, Isabel and Evelyn, had children. You and a couple of my best friends will get it all. I've written instructions for my lawyer and have an appointment to see him day after tomorrow, before I check into the hospital. The new will should be ready to sign when I get out. I'll give you a copy to take home with you."

"You've been very good to me since Dad died."

"I miss Edwin. All of my siblings are gone now. After Milton's death Sharon and Marilyn still had a mom, but after Edwin died and your mom ran off with that salesman, you didn't have anyone except me."

"I was lucky to be nearly finished with high school." Olivia paused and got to her feet. "If tea time is over, I'll work in the garden, then whip up something for dinner."

"Forget about dinner. There's enough food in the refrigerator. We'll eat that."

"Perfect. I'll unpack then."

Oliver moved slowly to his feet. "If a couple of old duffers show up while I'm napping, invite them in. It'll be Arlyn and Jerry, checking up on you."

"Whatever for?"

Oliver laughed. "They're the ones looking after me when you aren't here. They'll want to see if you look able to handle an old guy with a battery-powered implant that keeps him breathing."

"Bring 'em on," Olivia laughed. "But you better warn them. I'll be doing a little inspecting of my own."

She grabbed her suitcase. "I noticed your new Oriental carpet in the dining room. It's lovely."

"The floors in that room are always cold. I was trying to solve the problem."

###

"Thank goodness you're back," Sally greeted Heather.

"What's the matter?"

"One of your clients called. Twice." The phone rang again and Sally cast a helpless look at her sister. "Your turn."

Heather rushed to the phone. "Hello," she said. "This is Heather."

"Well, this is Abe Coffman. You've got to make some changes to my website. The only people calling me are those who want cheap jewelry. It's the high rollers I want checking me out."

"I can see you later in the week, Mr. Coffman. I haven't been at my computer for two days. My sister and I just moved into our new house. We've been very busy."

"Well hurry up and get UN-busy. I want those changes now!"

###

A BIT OF PHILOSOPHY

ALL fairy tales come to an end

D – 3 = A	D + 2 = F	P + 4 = T	A + 2 = C
J + 2 = L	E – 4 = A	C – 2 = A	L + 3 = O
N – 2 = L	G + 2 = I	K + 1 = L	L + 1 = m
	P + 2 = R	H – 3 = E	I – 4 = l
	V + 3 = y	P + 3 = S	

W – 3 = t	D – 3 = a	A + 4 = l
Q – 2 = O	K + 3 = n	J + 4 = n
		G – 3 = d

ABCDEFGHIJKLMNOPQRSTUVWXYZ

16

CHAPTER 3

As Heather drove to the Portland airport the next morning she filled the two hour drive thinking about unanswered questions that surfaced after her mother's sudden death in February. Mattie Samuelson's car had been struck by another and pushed into flood waters of the Lewis River. Unable to get her seatbelt unbuckled, Mattie had drown.

After her death her daughters searched the desk that had been so important to Mattie. She'd always said anything of real value was in it. But after her death what her daughters found were puzzles.

First had been a collection of birthday cards Mattie received from various locations around the states, each written in a style very like her husband's, but since Charlie had been dead for eight years, the girls were left wondering who sent the cards. Could their mother have had a lover?

In addition to the cards, Mattie left behind a scrapbook with newspaper clippings and obituaries for people none of her daughters had ever heard of. The final puzzle Mattie left had been a sealed envelope her attorney turned over to Heather. It contained a letter with additional puzzles. The letter had said:

"My Darling Girls:

"If you are reading this it means you've saved the desk, and I'm not around to explain any of its contents, or to tell any more grandbabies those wonderful puzzle stories that young Tim and Tom have loved to hear me invent. I'm sorry. I wish I was still with you. Instead I will leave you with my newest and last fairytale. Your puzzle satisfaction will be based on your own inventiveness, but then that is Heather's hobby, isn't it!

And if Sally will quietly do nothing, then Rachel can take up the telling of this story to any new grandbabies. I send you love.

"Once upon a time in the land of long ago,
Lived a grownup Cinderella whose story you should know.

"After Cindy's shoe was restored, she and Prince Charming married and were living happily ever-after with the sweetest babies any parent could hope for. Prince Charming was ruling his divisional kingdom of the faithful and the truthful, lending others his skills as they had need of them.

"Unfortunately, Prince Charming discovered he was sharing his skills with the Big Bad Wolf.

"It turned out that BB Wolf wasn't just huffing and puffing on the doorstep of the three little pigs; he was hurting everyone in the forest except himself. The Prince talked the matter over with the Game Warden who promised to put Big Bad into a cage so others would be safe. Of course the Prince would have to tell the whole world about Big Bad's treacherous ways.

"To everyone's chagrin Big Bad had evil friends and he had wonderful gifts for those friends, if, while he was trying to get his cage door open, they would do away with the Prince as punishment for tattling. He also wanted bad things to happen to anyone who had a hand in putting him in that cage even though it was his own evil deeds that caused him to be there.

"To save Prince Charming, the Game Warden sent him to a safe tower where he couldn't be found. If Big Bad got the cage open, the Prince would again have to help cage him. Big Bad's evil friends were frustrated when they couldn't find Prince Charming, so they decided to do away with Cinderella. They knew *that* would bring the Prince out of hiding.

"And for a brief moment, it worked.

"Soon after that Big Bad heard that Prince Charming did a 'Humpty Dumpty.' It satisfied Big Bad's urge to kill him so Cindy and the babies were left alone and Big Bad's evil friends chased after the others on the hit list.

"Most of Prince Charming's family learned to live happily ever-after without him because they were adults, finding their own way through the forest.

"Now then, whether the Kings Men are successful in putting the egg shells back together, is yet to be seen. Whether the grown babies get to applaud and view the completed eggshell puzzle is also undetermined.

"May you all live Happily Ever After!

"PS: On a lighter note, I recommend some of the vacation locations I visited over the last few years. They are not the usual places to visit, but each has its own charm. These were Montgomery, Juneau, Phoenix, Little Rock, Sacramento, Denver, and Hartford."

"I'm so glad you were able to join me, Vern." Olivia smiled as she greeted the handsome pharmacist. His coal black hair, dimples, and dark brown eyes made him the handsomest man she'd ever known. "It was a nice surprise having you call last night." They were at an airport south of Lewisburg where Vern had just landed. "How did you get Mr. Breeze to give you the time off?"

"I have my ways," Vern replied, not admitting that when the old man refused to give him the week off, he'd quit.

"I'm eager for you to meet Uncle Oliver."

"I came out here to be with you, Olivia. I want to keep you company while your uncle is in the hospital. He and I can get acquainted when he comes home." Vern climbed into Olivia's rental car.

"But I told Uncle Oliver I was picking you up and he said to bring you around. He's never known any of my friends."

"What I want to do is buy a new car while I'm out here," Vern said as they headed north. "This state doesn't have a sales tax so cars are cheaper. Maybe you and I will consider driving it back to Rhode Island. We might make it a honeymoon trip."

"You mean get married here where Uncle Oliver could give me away?" Olivia smiled.

"We'll have to see how things go," Vern replied. "Wait! Stop! Pull over. That's where I want to start looking." Vern pointed to a Lexus dealership. "Let's see if they have any hardtop convertibles we can test drive."

"But those are expensive," Olivia cautioned. "Can you afford that?"

"We want something dependable for the trip home, don't we? Come on. Let's take a few spins in some fine wheels."

At Portland International Heather located her aunt standing at the curb. Myrtle's graying hair was pushed behind her ears as she dabbed a tissue against perspiration dotting her forehead. She looked fatigued.

"Hi, Aunt Myrtle."

"What kept you? I've already got my luggage."

"Traffic is terrible today." Heather hugged her aunt, then grabbed her luggage handle.

"We better hurry," Myrtle said. "Your new furniture is promised for noon. Where's your car?"

Heather frowned at her watch, still appalled at the idea that a truckload of furniture neither she nor Sally wanted was arriving at their doorstep in three hours. What would they do with it once they found furniture they liked better?

Two hours later Heather pulled into her new housing complex. The collection of sixty two-story townhouses more or less surrounded a private swimming pool.

"I can't believe this is where you girls decided to invest your inheritance." Myrtle's critical observation referred to the insurance settlement her nieces received after their mother's untimely death. "Why buy a house in a community of old geezers instead of some place where men your own age hang out? What were you thinking?"

Myrtle was out of Heather's car in a flash, still frowning at the gun-metal gray triplexes making up the complex where two of her three nieces now lived. "Good grief. These places are hooked together," she moaned. "You've bought a blooming row-house. You don't even have your own yard. You might as well have stayed in an apartment."

"The houses are individually owned," Heather explained. "The reason Sally and I decided to live here is because we wanted more space and more privacy. We're busy with our careers. We don't want to mow lawns and dig weeds. Now we own a house where gardeners do the work, leaving us time to swim in the pool."

"You don't say," commented Myrtle, sounding more agreeable. "Let's get my luggage inside before the moving van arrives. I should be able to help you arrange the furniture by dinnertime, tell you the history of the various pieces, and be gone in a day or two." She smiled at her niece. "I brought a bathing suit. Can I use the pool? A warm swim after my all-night flight would be relaxing."

Myrtle pushed past Heather as the front door was unlocked. "What a lovely room," she said. "It's dark, but it's bigger than I expected. I think we'll be able to fit everything on the truck into it quite nicely. Where do I sleep?"

"Could I get my cookie plate back?" The voice came from behind Heather and her aunt. "I brought you this here coconut cake, but I want my plate back." The speaker's hands trembled, causing white coconut to settle around the bottom layer like aspen leaves settling on the ground in October.

Myrtle studied the white-haired woman as Heather replied, "I'll get your plate, but please, no more desserts." Heather headed for the kitchen.

"Who are you?" asked Myrtle, moving closer to the intruder. "And why didn't you ring the doorbell?"

Baby said, "I live next door and I been walking into this here house without knocking for more than a decade. If you don't take this cake, I'm going to drop it on the nice new carpet these girls installed."

Heather returned with the cookie plate as Myrtle rescued the coconut cake. "I can see I'll have to train my nieces to lock their doors."

"Well," huffed Baby, grabbing the dish Heather held. She headed for the door. "I hope the ghost gets both of you." As Baby left she kicked at the front door, thumping it against the wall so that it slammed shut behind her.

"What ghost is she talking about?" Myrtle asked.

Heather locked the door. "We haven't seen one, but when we do, I'm putting it in a role-playing computer game, and selling it. I wish you hadn't accepted that cake. Yesterday she and her sister delivered two kinds of cookies. And while Sally and I were painting walls last week, another ton of goodies showed up. I've gained three pounds in the three days since we started painting in here."

"That woman will be a pest if you don't get her stopped." Myrtle dipped a finger into the frosted perfection. "If the pastry chef lives on one side of you, who's on the other side?"

"That's a nice young family, a single mom and two boys about ten or twelve. So far they're quiet, well-behaved, and they don't spend every waking minute baking something they want Sally and me to eat."

"Maybe you should consider sending the cookies their way."

"Good idea." Heather reached for the cake. "I'll start with the cake."

"No way. Coconut cake is my favorite. This dessert is staying right here. Now where were we?" Myrtle took the cake to the kitchen, set it on the counter, and dipped another finger into the frosting. "Mmmmm," she hummed. "I think you were going to show me to my room."

The second floor of the Samuelson townhouse held three bedrooms, one bathroom and a waist-high door leading to the unfinished crawlspace where the new heating and cooling system had been installed. Sally and Heather each had their own bedroom and the third bedroom held Heather's desk, her computer, and dozens of packing cartons waiting to be unpacked.

"I take it this will be my room?" Myrtle had stepped into the third bedroom.

"We've rented a cot for you. It will come this afternoon." Heather lifted a carton from the collection and set it on her desk. It contained the puzzling items from her mother's desk. "We don't plan to put a permanent bed in here for years. This is going to be my office." Heather reached into the box and removed a calendar she hung on the wall in front of her desk.

Myrtle slipped out of her shoes. "There's a nice twin bed in that load of furniture that's coming. It should fit in here once you get all these cartons out. Where are your sisters?" Myrtle dropped her cosmetics case on top of one of the cartons and hung her jacket in the closet.

"Rachel is home with sick boys," Heather replied, trying not to groan at the idea of moving two dozen heavy cartons so that a bed she didn't want could be substituted. "She thinks the boys are getting summer colds, but it might just be allergies. As for Sally, she was going to get groceries after she hung the drapes in the living room. Since the drapes are up, she must be at the grocery store. We have neighbors coming for dinner tonight and if the twins are better Rachel will bring them over to greet you."

"I'm anxious to see those twerps. I bet they've grown a foot since I was here in February." Myrtle removed her slacks. "I'm surprised you're entertaining so soon. You haven't finished moving in."

"Our neighbor goes into the hospital tomorrow and his niece is visiting. We wanted to get better acquainted with him and I wanted to ask his niece some questions about the drugstore where she works. Having them come for dinner seemed the best way to accomplish it all."

"Why did you lock the front door?" grumped Sally. "And don't tell me the ghost did it." She had returned from the store with sacks of food clasped in both arms. Locating her house key had been an act of desperation.

"Baby Bender made herself at home again," Heather explained, taking one of the grocery bags. "You and I will have to keep that door locked or set a third place at our dinner table."

"What a bother," Sally agreed, setting groceries on the kitchen counter. "I suppose that luscious coconut cake is her latest gift?"

Heather nodded. "Aunt Myrtle said she'd eat the whole thing, but it beckons me. I've got to resist or buy a new wardrobe in larger sizes."

Sally scooped frosting with a finger and moaned with pleasure at the flavor. "Where is our auntie at the moment, or is she that sexy babe at the swimming pool?"

"That's Myrtle, all right. For someone her age, she's wearing a very skimpy suit. I think she's not swimming as much as she's flirting with Oliver."

"That should get his pacemaker ticking faster, even without new batteries." Sally laughed and reached for the newspaper she'd brought home. "Myrtle will make tonight's party interesting. Do we have five lap trays?"

"Apparently there's a dining room table in this truckload of furniture that's due any minute."

"It's a good thing we don't have much furniture of our own. I hope Myrtle leaves some space for us to add pieces we select."

"I'm eager to talk to Oliver's niece," replied Heather. "I think she can give me some ideas for a website I'm working on."

"Olivia left soon after you headed for Portland this morning," Sally said. "And as I left the grocery a few minutes ago I saw her in a nifty little Lexus convertible being driven by an extremely handsome man."

"Are you sure?"

Sally nodded. "Would I kid about seeing a handsome man in an expensive sports car? I thought helping Oliver was the reason his niece made the trip. In fact, I thought she didn't know anyone else in town."

"Who do you suppose she was with?" Heather was flipping open various cupboards, deciding where to store the food.

"You're asking the wrong person. By the way, if the rental cot arrived, I'll make Aunt Myrtle's bed."

"It's not coming," Heather replied. "Myrtle cancelled it."

"Is she going to a motel?"

Heather shook her head. "Apparently there's a bed on the van. She's having it set up in *my* office as soon as the cartons in there are moved out."

"Moved out where?" Sally asked in alarm. She was scanning a newspaper story about a trial judge who had gone fishing while wearing hip-length waders. He'd stepped in a deep hole, the waders had filled with water, and he'd drowned. "There's no other place to put all those boxes."

"I think our choice is to either solve that problem, or have Aunt Myrt set up her bed in the hallway."

Before Sally could comment the doorbell rang. A large moving van had backed up to their carport and a crew was laying ramps to their front door. Myrtle, dripping wet, was giving the movers directions.

###

A short distance away a curious individual watched the activity at the Samuelson residence. It looked like expensive furniture being moved into the newcomer's house. Expensive furniture represented money, and people with money were always of interest.

Perhaps it was time to call on them. Again.

###

THE STAGE IS SET

Characters introduced so far are lovers, murderers, thieves, victims, and sisters. Some assume more than one role. Assign the characters below to the proper role or roles.

Oliver, Olivia, Vern, Binky and Baby, Stranger, Chris, Myrtle, Pamela

VICTIMS: _____

MURDERERS: _____

LOVERS: _____

THIEVES: _____

SISTERS: _____

BYSTANDERS: _____

CHAPTER 4

Myrtle joined her nieces in the kitchen, still wearing her damp swimsuit. "Your neighbor is quite impulsive and charming. I'm sorry he's headed for the hospital so soon. It would be fun to spend more time with him."

The furniture that traveled from Boston to Lewisburg had been unloaded and the movers were gone.

"You did seem to hit it off," commented Heather, licking a telltale flake of coconut from one corner of her mouth. A generous slice of cake was missing.

"Oliver's a flirt and he's very proud of his niece. I think he told me her life history at least twice. He's been like a father to her since his brother Edwin died and his sister-in-law ran off with the milkman."

"The milkman?"

"Some salesperson. I've forgotten what he sold. I'm going to change now. I'm invited for afternoon tea. You won't mind if I skip lunch with you girls, will you?"

"Go ahead," laughed Sally.

Heather agreed, "Enjoy tea with the Lloyds. Sally and I have a few things to do before we start dinner, like move boxes out of the guest room."

Sally groaned.

Myrtle said, "I had the movers put them in the hallway."

"You did?"

Myrtle nodded. "All except that box you had on your desk. All you need to do is get the bed dusted and made up. By the way, please don't try to rearrange any of your new furniture. It's too heavy for you girls." With that Myrtle headed up the stairs to change clothes.

A short while later she was back, sporting a low-necked sundress and clutching a scrapbook.

"How do I look?" she asked, reaching up to fluff her hair. "I thought I'd do my best to give Oliver a nice send off." Myrtle winked and adjusted her neckline a bit lower. "How's that?"

"You're more apt to give him a heart attack," Heather said. She and Sally were seated at a large table that arrived with their new furniture. "Why are you carrying Mom's scrapbook?" Heather had just recognized what Myrtle was holding.

"I brought it down so I'd remember to ask if you ever made any sense out of it."

The scrapbook Myrtle held contained obituaries and newspaper stories of a jury trial that had taken place eight or nine years earlier. The millionaire defendant had been found guilty of brutally murdering four people, and once the jury unanimously agreed he deserved the death penalty, he was escorted from the courtroom screaming, "You're all dead."

"So far I haven't had time to figure out why Mom saved those clippings," Heather said. "I hope to get started on it now that Sally and I are settled."

"Okay. I'm off to enjoy a cup of tea," Myrtle said.

"Be on time for dinner," cautioned Sally, reaching for the scrapbook. "Don't make me come after you with handcuffs."

"I can go along with handcuffs," giggled Myrtle, heading for the door. "But no guns. Guns aren't any fun at all." She paused at the door. "You better lock this behind me or you'll have uninvited company." With that, she headed for Oliver's house.

"This is interesting, Heather. Take a look." Sally passed the scrapbook to her sister. "The judge mentioned in Mom's scrapbook is the fisherman who drowned yesterday."

"That is interesting. After Aunt Myrtle leaves I intend to get mom's puzzles solved. Save the drowning story. For now let's put it in the scrapbook."

###

"Come right in, Myrtle," Oliver greeted, a cup of tea in one hand. "Meet my namesake. Olivia, this charmer is Myrtle Wilson. She's the aunt of those nice girls who've invited us to dinner tonight."

"I'm pleased to meet you, Myrtle. Sit down and I'll get you a cup of tea." Olivia headed for the kitchen in search of another bone china cup.

Oliver escorted Myrtle to the loveseat near the fireplace, and sat down beside her. "Take this cup," he said, gallantly handing her the one he'd been holding. "It was just poured and I haven't touched a drop. Today's flavor is peppermint. I hope you like it."

"I like anything with a bit of a bite to it," Myrtle responded, taking the cup and nearly draining it. "What a lovely room." She was looking at the painting over the fireplace. "Those flowers look real enough to pick. The painting looks like it was done by one of the Dutch masters."

"It's a still life painted with the Dutch influence. It was done by a well-known English painter."

"One seldom sees such vibrancy in a still life," Myrtle continued. "Look how he's captured the light and the shadows."

"Here's your tea," announced Olivia, returning to the living room. Max was at her side. She started to hand the cup to Myrtle then realized she was already holding one. Olivia looked perplexed until Oliver reached for the cup she was carrying.

"I'll take that one," he said.

"You gave our guest your tea? Your cold cup of tea?" Olivia sounded aghast.

"I thought she should have the first cup and I hadn't tasted it yet. Come here, Max. Meet Myrtle." With tail wagging, Max greeted the newcomer.

"But your tea must have been cold and I had already dissolved two vitamins in it." Olivia was still complaining.

Oliver looked at Myrtle and smiled. "Feeling better already, aren't you, Myrtle?" He laughed. "Olivia isn't really upset about the temperature of the tea or the vitamins," he said. "Her sweetheart is in town and won't come for introductions until after I get home from the hospital. She's anxious to leave us and get together with him."

"Uncle Oliver," Olivia groaned.

"Just pour our guest a bit of fresh tea, Sweetheart. Then take a seat while we all get better acquainted." He batted his eyes at Myrtle, watching her hug Max. "I suppose it's too soon to propose."

"It depends on what it is you want to propose." Myrtle smiled, not entirely convinced Olivia understood how teasing went between people of their age. Was she taking the exchange seriously?

"You stick around until I get home from the hospital, Myrtle, and I'll propose enough activities to…"

"To do what, you silly man?" Myrtle released Max so he could investigate noises he'd heard outside. "…test your new batteries?"

"Something like that." Oliver smiled first at Myrtle, then at Olivia. "Here I am, surrounded by my two favorite ladies in the whole world. What do you think of that, Max?" He ruffled the dog's fur. "How lucky can one guy get?"

Myrtle raised an eyebrow, and considered the casual way Oliver assumed a relationship existed between them. She enjoyed a little flirtatious hanky-panky, but that didn't constitute a serious relationship. After he came home from the hospital, she'd have to make sure he understood. As interesting as he was, and as many interests as they shared, she was quite content with her single life.

"While I'm recuperating," Oliver continued, stroking his mustache. "You two ladies can keep an eye on each other. Myrtle, I'm sure that if you'd like to walk Max now and then, Olivia would be glad to hand over his leash. Right, Ollie?"

"Not your childhood nickname." Olivia shook a warning finger at her uncle. "Of course Myrtle can walk Max. That way I'm free to work in the garden and do housecleaning. By the time you get home, Uncle Oliver, we'll be the best of friends." Olivia nodded at Myrtle and whispered loudly, "I have some stories to share with you, Myrtle. Some you'll get a big kick out of."

"No you don't," Oliver warned. "No Oliver stories. Promise. If you tell Oliver stories, I'll write you out of my will."

The two women laughed at his threat.

"Okay," giggled Olivia. "No Uncle Oliver stories. At least," she lowered her voice, "not while he's sitting in the same room."

"Aunt Myrtle," exclaimed Heather in alarm. She had answered her doorbell and found her pale aunt leaning heavily on the arm of Oliver Lloyd.

"She felt dizzy," Oliver explained as Myrtle stepped into the house, stumbling.

"I don't know what's come over me," she whispered, reaching for Heather's arm. "I guess I should rest a while before dinner. Maybe I'm not as young as I thought."

Heather put her arm around Myrtle's waist. "Thanks, Oliver. I'll take care of her. We'll see you and Olivia in a couple of hours."

Oliver had an impish grin. "Myrtle's going to run an important errand for me tomorrow. Make sure she's well enough to do that." He gave Myrtle a conspiratorial wink, then headed home.

"I feel so shaky." Myrtle bumped against one of the newly arrived end tables. "I don't think I can make it up the stairs." She patted the arm she'd just bumped.

"Sit here." Heather ushered her aunt to an upholstered chair. "I'll make up the hide-a-bed and you can lay down for a couple of hours. You've had a busy day traveling all the way across the country, swimming, and then directing the movers. I'd say that's a good reason to feel unsteady."

"Maybe it's the weather," Myrtle suggested, trying to reassure her niece. "It might even be hotter inside your house than it is outside."

"I wish that installer would get his cooling system working. He can't come until tomorrow." Heather whisked open the hide-a-bed, applied two sheets she'd recently unpacked, and added a soft pillow. Soon she had her aunt resting. "Can I get anything for you? A light lunch? A cold drink? How about some coconut cake?" She was trying to tempt Myrtle with something nourishing, refreshing, or packed with sugar.

"I just feel achy," Myrtle whispered, shutting her eyes. "I guess my arthritis is flaring up more than I thought. It's hot in here, but I think I'd like to have a light blanket anyway."

Heather provided an afghan and tucked it around Myrtle. "Are you on any medication I should know of?"

"You're sweet, Heather. We'll talk about my medications later. I think I'm ready for a little nap."

"I'll be in the kitchen. Call if you need anything." Heather kissed Myrtle's cheek, but as she moved toward the kitchen, the doorbell rang. She turned to answer it, noting Myrtle was already asleep.

"Hi Beautiful," said the handsome man who moments before had coasted to a stop on a big motorcycle now parked in the Samuelson carport. He was unbuckling his helmet as he greeted Heather. "Want a strong arm to help move furniture or hang drapes? I've got a couple hours of free time."

"Jazz," Heather whispered in a happy sigh. "You're just in time." She stepped outside, closing the door behind her.

"What's going on?" Deputy Jazz Finchum had come into Heather's life earlier in the year when he'd assisted the Samuelson sisters in bringing to justice criminals stealing from residents of an assisted living facility. He was a well-built man whose six-foot-two stature was exactly a foot more than Heather's. While Heather had deep green eyes, his were such a vivid blue they sometimes appeared to be black. At times he let his beard grow to a lush red-gold that matched the color of Heather's short curls.

"It's Aunt Myrtle," Heather responded. "She arrived this morning along with furniture she's passing on to Sally and me. At the moment she's not feeling well. I've got her resting on the hide-a-bed in the living room." She smiled shyly. "If we're quiet, we should be able to get past her and into the kitchen. That's where I could use some help."

A door slammed. "What's going on?" asked Mrs. Bender, dashing from her house with a plate of peanut butter cookies. "These are for you." She pushed the plate at the astonished Heather and turned an eye of appreciation on Jazz's motorcycle. "Great bike you've got, mister. Do you take people for rides?" Seeing Jazz shake his head she continued. "Could you make an exception and give me a ride anyway? I could be ready in five, maybe ten minutes."

"Can't do it," Jazz said, turning back to Heather.

"Nice seeing you again, Mrs. Bender," Heather greeted insincerely, about to explain why the mouth-watering cookies could not be accepted. "Please understand that we can't accept any more cookies or cakes." Heather tried to give the plate of pastry back to her neighbor. She could see Jazz looking like he'd be more than willing to take charge of it.

"Are you saying you don't like peanut butter cookies?"

"No, I'm saying we can't keep eating your wonderful cookies and cakes without gaining weight."

"It's not fair. You accepted Baby's chocolate cookies and coconut cake." She pouted. "You can't refuse my peanut butter cookies after accepting Baby's things."

"Aren't you Baby?"

"Of course not. I'm Binky. I was counting on you helping me. I've got to practice my baking. My son Tommy is due here any day now. I don't want him thinking his mom is getting old and has forgotten how to bake his favorite dessert." Under her breath she added, "I just can't remember what his favorite dessert is, he's been gone so long."

Heather sighed. "Okay. Thank you, Binky. We'll take this one last batch of cookies, but please, no more." She nodded at her neighbor, then opened the door and pulled Jazz into the house behind her. She handed him the cookies while she locked the door.

As they tiptoed past Myrtle's sleeping form, he whistled silently, impressed by the antiques filling the rooms. "Lovely furniture. You made a good haul, but that's some bruise Myrtle has on her arm." He stepped close to whisper his observation in Heather's ear. His big hands were measuring a space the size of a saucer.

"She was in a skimpy swim suit just a few hours ago," Heather responded as they entered the kitchen. "I didn't notice any bruises then and her suit didn't leave a lot to wonder about."

Jazz smiled, picturing the older woman in a skimpy suit. "Maybe it was a shadow I saw." He looked at the signs of chopping and stirring that made Heather's kitchen a wonder to his bachelor eyes. "Want help preparing tonight's feast?"

"Spoken like an experienced kitchen assistant." Heather handed him a cutting board, a sharp knife and a freshly washed head of lettuce. "Sally went to the store for some fresh herbs. You can help with the salad."

Jazz checked the pot simmering on the stove, sending up mouth-watering fragrances. Then he washed his hands and started chopping lettuce. "Spaghetti sauce?"

"Right." Heather's eyes twinkled. She handed Jazz a mixing bowl for the lettuce. "We're having vegetable salad, and spaghetti with both meat sauce and vegetarian sauce."

"And?"

"And the pesto I made last week."

"Followed by?" Jazz prompted again, salivating as he anticipated her response. He put the last of the lettuce in the bowl.

"Followed by chocolate cake," she announced.

"My favorite." Jazz swung Heather around and planted an excited kiss on her forehead.

She plucked his fingers from around her arms, "Who do you think you're kidding? There isn't a dessert made that isn't your *favorite*." She smiled fondly at him. "Now chop some tomatoes, please."

"I see you have your mom's scrapbook out. Ever figure out what that was all about?"

"Not yet. Ask me again in a week."

Jazz looked sharply at Heather. "Are you close to figuring out what the scrapbook has been tracking?" He had borrowed the scrapbook soon after Heather found it, and shared it with his partner. If their conclusions were correct, it was only a matter of time before the Samuelson sisters' lives would be in grave danger.

WATCH OUT, HEATHER!

	1	2	3	4	5	6	7	8
A	Y	M	T	S	D	V	O	I
B	R	C	P	B	M	G	K	E
C	G	W	T	E	N	N	H	A
D	R	E	R	D	O	L	U	R

A1, D5, D7   C8, D1, B8   B4, D2, A8, C6, C1
C2, C8, A3, B2, C7, D2, A5

Y O U   a r e   b e i n g
w a t c h e d

CHAPTER 5

"Are you sure you shouldn't be resting?" Sally studied her aunt's movements as they set the table. "Heather said you were pretty unsteady this afternoon."

"I'm fine now that I've had a little nap and a shower."

Sally viewed Myrtle's answer suspiciously. The house was almost too warm, yet her aunt had changed from summery clothes into slacks and a turtle-neck blouse with long sleeves. "What is this errand Oliver wants you to run for him tomorrow? Anything we can help with?"

"I'm to take some notes to his attorney. Something about making changes to his will. I agreed to keep the appointment and hand over his instructions so he could go to the coast with his niece."

"If Oliver's attorney has questions," Heather tested the spaghetti sauce as she spoke, "you won't be able to answer them."

"He assured me everything is written out clearly so there won't be any questions. All I have to do is deliver his instructions. Oliver gets out of town so seldom he was eager to take advantage of Olivia's offer. Since I was willing to keep his appointment, he felt like he could go."

"I wish you hadn't gotten involved in his legal activities," Sally said.

"It's not like I'm signing anything. I'm just delivering an envelope. A messenger service could do that. Oliver wants to sign his new will when he gets out of the hospital."

At that moment the doorbell rang and the unlocked door flew open. Rachel could be heard calling to her boys to wait until they were invited in.

They weren't waiting.

"Hi Aunt Sally, Aunt Heather, Great-Aunt Myrtle." Tim put a large bowl of grated Parmesan in Sally's outstretched hands. "Wow. You got a lot of neat old furniture. I want to look at everything. Does any of it have secret compartments?" Before anyone could answer, he'd rushed back into the living room to hunt for hidden openings.

"Hi everyone," Tom greeted. "Quick! Take this!" He handed ice cream to Heather. "Aunt Heather, Tim and me...I, Tim and I need more puzzles. And make them harder. The last one was too easy." The boys were enthusiastically testing puzzles Heather created for her business.

"Your boys have grown a foot," Myrtle congratulated Rachel. The slim, red-headed twins could be heard opening and closing drawers in the antique furniture.

"They're almost as tall as I am," Rachel laughed. "Can I help, Heather?"

"We're doing just fine," Heather replied as a crash came from the living room.

"Boys," yelled Rachel, rushing to calm her sons before too much damage could be done.

The doorbell sounded again. "Got it," yelled one of the boys as they both raced for the door.

"No running in the house," called Rachel. To her sisters she said, "I had to give them allergy medicine. It makes them hyper." She hurried after the twins.

"Jazz," the boys shouted once they'd opened the door to him.

"Two of my favorite redheads," Jazz responded, handing two bottles of wine to Rachel. He captured the boys and with one twin tucked under each arm, headed for the kitchen.

"No, put us down," begged Tom wiggling frantically as he tried to escape the firm grip on his thin body.

"We're supposed to stay out of there. They'll put us to work." Like Tom, Tim didn't have any better luck escaping.

Jazz arrived at the kitchen door with the giggling, wiggling boys. "Howdy, everyone. Need another body or two jammed into the kitchen?"

"Jazz!" Myrtle grabbed the deputy's shirt front and pulled him toward her.

Jazz allowed the boys to escape so he could embrace the delightfully outspoken woman he'd met in February. "I'm indebted to you, Aunt Myrtle. If you hadn't trained your nieces so well, I'm sure they'd have left me home eating cold beans out of a tin can."

"What tales you tell," laughed Heather. She'd been more or less dating Jazz during the past few months and she knew how few cold meals he ate.

Again the doorbell announced visitors. Oliver and Olivia entered and were introduced, then settled in the living room while finishing touches were made to the meal.

"I don't believe it." Oliver was sitting on a Victorian sofa centered on one wall. He ran his hand over the satin mahogany finish that sculpted the sofa's back.

"Uncle Oliver was an antique dealer," Olivia explained.

"Look at this, Olivia." Her uncle turned to the mahogany occasional table next to the sofa. "It's the mate to one I have upstairs." He looked at Myrtle. "It's late English Regency. From the Victorian period, you know."

Myrtle smiled and nodded. "The top is inlayed with rosewood, satinwood, and mahogany. My great grandparents brought it from England more than a hundred years ago."

"They had a good eye for pieces that would appreciate. The brown and black striped wood that's been used for cross-banding is kingswood."

"Uncle Oliver," cautioned Olivia. "You're getting carried away. You asked me to remind you, if you did."

"Oops," he admitted. "It's seldom I find someone knowledgeable regarding antiques. Myrtle, I must show you my collection of lovely pieces."

"Thanks, Oliver. I'd love to see them. Perhaps we could do that after dinner."

"Perfect. It's a date."

"Oh dear!" The exclamation was a voice Heather and Sally were beginning to recognize and dread. "I didn't realize it was such a big group or I'd have brought a larger plate of brownies."

"Someone forgot to lock the door," whispered Sally. "You finish cooking, Heather. I'll get rid of the cookie lady."

"Hi, Oliver," the uninvited guest greeted.

"How are you doing, Binky?" Oliver answered politely.

"My Tommy's home for a few days," Binky announced. "You haven't met him 'cause he's been at that academy for so long, but Baby and I are excited to have him back with us. Her Jimmie Joe graduates from his academy and will visit in a couple of weeks."

"I'm glad the boys are visiting. Why don't we talk about it later, Binky?"

"You promise?" she asked.

"I promise," Oliver replied.

Sally thanked her neighbor for the treats, and saw her to the door. Once the door closed, she twisted the lock. "What's the story, Oliver? I thought that was Baby?"

"Laura and Victoria are identical twins. Victoria, known as Baby, is the youngest. Laura, called Binky, is older by a few minutes."

"Are they both Benders?"

Oliver nodded. "They married the same man, but at different times."

"How can you tell them apart?"

"Baby's hands tremble. That's how I can tell. If she ever gets that shaking under control, I don't know how I'll know the difference."

Pounding erupted at the front door.

"For goodness sake," complained Sally, rushing to the door to open it.

"You've got kids here," rejoiced the tallest of two young boys standing on the Samuelson doorstep. "We live next door and there aren't any kids around here to play with. Can your boys come out to play?"

Sally laughed and turned to her sister. "It's for you, Rachel."

Rachel smiled at the eager boys waiting for a response. "Tim and Tom are about to eat dinner. They can join you when they finish. Is that okay?"

"Sweeeet," responded the youngest of the brothers. He appeared to be eight or nine, and wore his blond hair in a buzz cut. "Have them come next door. We're Johnny and Joey Corbin. Our mom said to tell you we get along real good and we're polite."

"Yeh," agreed Johnny, "'cause if we aren't, we'll be grounded until it's time for us to collect Social Security. At least that's what our Mom always says." The ten-year-old giggled. Like his brother he had a buzz cut.

Rachel laughed. "Tell your mom I'll meet with her in an hour."

SYNONYM FINDER

Fill in the missing letters on the grid.

Letters can only appear once in a row, column or nine-box square.

The murderer is deadly, unfeeling, remorseless and _____.

ORAUSENGD

		N				O		
U	E		S	A	O		N	D
		S	D	N	U	G		
		A	O	R	D	E		
E		D	A	S	G	U		O
		O				D		
S		U				A		G
	G			D			O	U
A			U	G	S			R

Dinner was almost finished before Heather found an opportunity to ask Olivia about her job at the drugstore. The aloof feedback was not what she'd hoped.

"Sorry, I only stock shelves and help with cash register sales." Olivia changed the subject, "It's kind of your aunt to keep Uncle Oliver's appointment with his attorney. He's really looking forward to a day at the beach. I've promised to have him back in town in time for his hospital admission. It's set for late afternoon."

"You're being admitted to the hospital?" Rachel hadn't heard that before. "Nothing serious, I hope."

"It's a simple surgical procedure. I'm getting new batteries in my pacemaker." With one finger, he drew a little square over his heart. "I'll have such a small incision it won't be worth showing off."

"Wow," chirped Tim. "Can Tom and me see where you have a battery inside of you now?"

"Yeh," agreed Tom. "Are you like our electronic cars? Can we click a remote and make you dance or something?"

"Not with this older model, you can't," laughed Oliver. "But I'll check with my doctor. Perhaps he can put in something more up-to-date that will work like that."

"Sweeeet," the twins chorused.

"That's enough out of you two," cautioned their mother. "Finish your dinner and go play with the boys from next door."

"When I get home," continued Oliver, "I expect to be in top form with all the high-powered vitamins Olivia's been feeding me. Maybe Myrtle and I can figure out something two old people can do together."

"Old people?" exploded Myrtle. "Speak for yourself. I am *not* old. Ripening, perhaps, but not old."

"That's what I'm counting on," laughed Oliver. He turned to Jazz. "If you're a cop, do you patrol our highways?"

"Not at the moment. Generally that's more of a municipal function and belongs to Sally's city police. I deliver civil papers, supervise parole and probation clients, or organize search and rescue operations."

Oliver laughed. "You'd never get a television series based on that."

Jazz smiled. "What if I tell you I also solve crimes?"

"What are you working on now?" Olivia asked. "Can you talk about your work?"

"Not usually. I help get cases ready for trial and we like to keep some surprises back so the other side is caught unaware."

"Did you ever meet up with Thomas Fuely?" asked Oliver.

Jazz nodded, a grin on his face. "In our department he's known as Tom *Foolery*? What a character."

"Who's Tom Fuely?" asked Heather.

"He was a cat burglar with an interesting signature to his crimes," replied Jazz. "He not only robbed houses of whatever he could carry off; he also took time to dine."

"Dine? As in 'eat a meal?' In the house he was robbing?" Heather looked at Jazz to make sure he wasn't joking.

Oliver chuckled. "Jazz is exactly right. He'd make himself a sandwich or heat a can of soup. He lived here."

"In Lewisburg?" Aunt Myrtle's eyes were wide.

Still laughing, Oliver repeated himself, "He lived here. In this house. This was his home until he was tossed in jail and couldn't keep up the mortgage payments."

"That sends shivers up my spine," Heather gasped.

"Me too," chorused Myrtle. "I hate to think of my girls camping out in a robber's hideaway."

Jazz smiled. Tom Foolery's arrest had been his second brush with the law, causing his probation to be revoked. They'd sentenced him to the state's overcrowded prison for a term of one to five years. Jazz surveyed the women at the table. If knowing they were living in a house once occupied by a burglar sent shivers up their spines, then knowing he'd been released after serving one year and one month would have them moving out, lock, stock and antique furniture.

"Do you think that bad guy hid any of his loot in this house?" asked Tim, swiveling around in his chair to check out the room behind him.

Jazz shook his head. "They searched this place pretty thoroughly because most of what he stole has never been recovered. An insurance company is still offering fifty thousand dollars for its return."

"Wow," exclaimed Heather. "Maybe Tim's right. Maybe he did hide the missing loot here."

"No chance of that," said Oliver. "This house was gone over with a fine-toothed comb. There were dozens of cops with special detecting equipment here for days. Maybe weeks. Your house is clean."

"Guess what," Tim shouted, rushing from the Samuelson house to join the Corbin boys shooting baskets in their carport.

"What?" Joey tossed the basketball to Tom who dribbled it a few times before he did some fancy footwork and shot a perfect basket.

"Wow," the Corbin brothers exclaimed.

"This house my aunts are living in," continued Tim, "was once owned by a robber."

"I don't believe you." Johnny took a shot at the basket and missed.

"You can check with the cops if you want," Tom stated, backing up his brother's claims. "We've got two of them inside. Want me to call them?"

"Naw. It's okay. We believe you. Was he a bank robber?" Johnny's second shot was a winner.

"Nope," Tim said, catching the ball on the rebound. "He didn't do banks. He broke into people's houses and stole their jewels." His shot at the basket hit the rim and bounced back.

"That's not interesting," chided Joey. "It would be more interesting if he emptied bank vaults or printed his own money."

"Joey and me tried printing our own money last year when we got a printing set for Christmas," Johnny volunteered. "But it looked more like Monopoly money than anything we could use for buying stuff."

"Robbing people of their jewels is pretty interesting when you know there's a great big reward for what wasn't recovered."

"Wow!"

"Tim and me," Tom paused, then started again. "Tim and I are thinking the robber might have hidden his loot somewhere around here. Maybe in your house, if no one lived there when he was *stashing the booty.*"

"Maybe the robber buried *the goods* somewhere outside," Tim added.

"Hey," shouted Joey laying the basketball at his front door. "Let's play pirates."

"Good idea," agreed Tom. "Get a shovel and we'll look for buried treasure."

###

The guests had gone and Myrtle, exhausted after her walk to and from the Lloyd residence to admire Oliver's antiques, was already in bed. Sally and Heather finished cleaning up and were examining their new furniture.

"What about this?" Sally picked up the scrapbook their aunt had asked about earlier. "Have you solved Mom's puzzles yet?"

According to their mother's attorney, her letter had been updated annually. After her death he delivered it to Heather with instructions not to open it until after her mother's memorial service. It had now been read so many times the sisters almost had it memorized.

"I hate unsolved puzzles," Heather said. "I hope to sit down with Mom's letter now that we're closer to being settled. I want to know what she was hinting at. One thing's for sure; Mom never invented stories for Rachel's boys." Heather went into the kitchen and returned with an article she'd clipped from the newspaper. "I think this belongs with Mom's scrapbook." She handed Sally the story of the judge who had drowned while fishing. "I think everything in this scrapbook relates to the trial of Joel Bishop."

"But there are so many obituary notices."

"I think we'll find every one of them is connected to that trial."

"As part of the jury, or witnesses? Let me research that," Sally volunteered.

"I think that's exactly what Mom didn't want. I think that's why her letter says you are to quietly do nothing."

OH! NO!

A   B   C   D   E   F   G   H   I   J   K   L   M
N   O   P   Q   R   S   T   U   V   W   X   Y   Z

If A = N and N = A
If B = O and O = B

JURER VF GUR SNVEL TBQZBGURE?

CHAPTER 6

Oliver and Olivia waved to the Samuelsons as they left for the beach early the next morning. With Max and an overnight case both tucked in the car, they planned to return only in time for Oliver's late afternoon admission to the hospital.

"Could you drop me off at that coffee shop on Kings?" Myrtle asked as Sally prepared to head for the police station. "Heather's working in my room, creating a cobweb for a client. I thought I'd hang out with the caffeine crowd until time to take Oliver's papers to his attorney."

"That's a web-*site* she's creating, not a cobweb," laughed Sally. "Jump in. I'll have you there in the blink of an eye."

Moments later, Myrtle entered the small, intimate coffee shop where Jazz waited at a table in the back of the room.

As the waitress disappeared with their order he asked, "What's with all the hush-hush?"

"There was too much going on last night and I wanted some time to talk with you privately." She seemed to be avoiding the handsome deputy's eyes.

"Rachel's boys were certainly hyperactive, weren't they?" Jazz laughed. "For her sake, I hope she's able to take them off that allergy medicine."

Myrtle nodded. "Are you still involved in undercover work that requires disguises?" Jazz had appeared to be a bearded biker when they first met.

"Why?" he asked. "Do you need help with a disguise of some kind?"

Myrtle hesitated. "I'll get around to that in a minute." She supported her head in her hands. "I'm a little dizzy. Could you talk about yourself for a while?"

Jazz studied the woman across from him, then said, "Okay." He drawled out his response. "I'm currently working on problems that lead me across jurisdictions. That makes my life a little crazy." He watched Myrtle suspiciously. "Is that enough stalling to get you started?"

"Almost. Keep going." Lattes had been served and she gulped hers as if she were dehydrated.

"Since I saw you in February, I have something of a personal life now that I'm seeing Heather. I like that a whole lot." The smile he wore mirrored his words.

"I can't tell you how glad I am that you two got together. I was hoping you'd discover each other."

"Okay. My turn. I have a subject I want to discuss while we're stalling around."

Myrtle looked up.

"I want an explanation," Jazz reached across the table to capture her left arm, "for the massive bruising on this arm."

Myrtle tried to pull away, forcing her sleeve toward her elbow. The action revealed a vivid bruise on her lower arm. "Let go," she pleaded. "I'll have more bruises."

Jazz released her arm and waited.

"I'm taking an anticoagulant."

"A blood thinner? Is that why you're dizzy and bruising so easily?"

She nodded. "My pills stop blood clots from forming. Of course I'm a candidate for such things or I wouldn't be taking medicine to keep it from happening."

"You haven't answered my question. Should you be bruising so easily? Does your dosage need regulating? Should I take you to a doctor?"

Myrtle looked at the serious expression on the young man's face. "Thanks, Jazz. I called my own doctor this morning. He told me to stop taking pills for a day, then break them in half for a few days. He wants me to go to a lab so they can check my clotting time. Dr. Fitzpatrick monitored my rates before I came on this trip and everything was fine. I suspect I overdid it yesterday. Stress alters how much of the drug stays in my body."

"If you need a ride to the hospital for lab tests, just say the word. I'd borrow a car." His eyes twinkled. "With a siren! We could leave it on the whole way." He looked to see if she was tempted.

"Nuts. I was hoping you'd offer me a ride on your motorcycle." She paused, "Let's give it a day or two before I go to a lab."

Jazz continued studying Myrtle, aware she was avoiding the reason she'd asked him to meet her.

Myrtle had closed her eyes briefly. "Okay. The reason I asked you to meet me is because I poked my nose into something I shouldn't have. I wanted to tell someone other than my nieces. They'd scold me. I thought you might go easier on me because we're not related." She opened her purse and struggled to remove an envelope.

"You brought the evidence with you?"

A sharp beeping erupted. Jazz pulled out his cell phone, looked at the number, and began counting money for the lattes. "It's an emergency. Duty calls. Can we finish this conversation tonight?" He got to his feet. "I'd like to help you, but I have to leave."

"It's a date," Myrtle replied, "although I intend to visit Oliver once he's settled at the hospital."

Jazz nodded. "Do you need a ride back to the house?"

Myrtle shook her head. "I'll stick around here. I can always take the bus or a taxi." She waved as he hurried to the door, and when the waitress returned to her table Myrtle asked, "Any chance I can get a great big decaf, skinny, white chocolate mocha?"

It would have been comforting to tell Jazz what she'd discovered, but it looked like she'd be confessing that to Oliver's attorney.

###

"Heather, I need help." Myrtle had returned to the townhouse and was clinging to the banister.

Heather dashed down the stairs. "What happened?" She put an arm around her aunt as they moved to the sofa.

"I didn't sleep well last night." Myrtle kicked off her shoes and lay down. "I thought coffee would perk me up, but it hasn't. I need to rest. I won't be able to keep Oliver's appointment with his attorney. Could you do it?"

Heather thought about the Coffman Jewelers website she'd been working on. The impatient Abe Coffman would have to wait one more day.

"I can leave in a few minutes. What is it I need to know?"

Heather entered the office of attorney Chance Hamilton, ready to explain why she was there. He had handled the closing of her mother's estate so was acquainted with the Samuelson family. "It's nice seeing you again, Heather, but why are you here instead of Oliver?"

"He's at the beach with his niece. He wanted to spend as much time as possible with her since he's being admitted to the hospital late this afternoon. He's getting his pacemaker batteries replaced."

"And?" Mr. Hamilton still looked puzzled.

"And he sent this." Heather fished an envelope from her briefcase and handed it to the attorney. "He apparently wants to make changes to his will. I understand he's written everything out so you won't have questions. I'm just his messenger service." She smiled and waited for a response.

"And this is what he sent?" The attorney removed the contents of the envelope and began studying pages of a legal-looking document.

"He's hoping you'll make the changes so he can sign the new will after he's released from the hospital in a day or two."

Looking up from the papers he'd been studying, Mr. Hamilton said, "Sorry. I didn't hear that last bit. You say he's going to the hospital to get new batteries in his pacemaker? Is that right?"

Heather nodded. "The procedure is little more than an office visit, but he has to stay overnight to make sure everything is hooked up and operating as it should."

"This office can certainly have the new will ready for him day after tomorrow, but that old man better make damned sure his medical procedure is a minor one." The attorney slammed his fist against his desktop.

Heather said, "Is something wrong? Does his request rush you?" She leaned forward. She'd never seen Chance Hamilton so upset.

"The problem, Heather, is that Oliver has written his instructions for the new will on the original copy of his present will. Writing on the original will voids it." He slapped the papers on his desk.

"I don't understand."

"The old will isn't legal any more. At this moment and until Oliver signs his new will, he doesn't have a will in force."

"Is that bad?"

"Only if he dies. If the doctor in charge of his wiring makes a mistake, Oliver's will won't be in effect and none of his wishes will be recognized. By law, all of his heirs will share his estate equally and anyone who is not a relative inherits a big fat goose egg."

When Heather returned home to relay the attorney's news to Myrtle, she found Heating System Specialists attempting to correct the problem causing their newly installed heat pump to heat but not to cool.

"You've been trying to solve the problem yourself, haven't you?" accused Bud Reeder, the HSS installer. He had already spent two full days under the Samuelson eaves installing a large appliance in a small space, and this was the third time they'd needed him to return for adjustments.

"Not me," laughed Heather. "I rely on your expertise because I don't have mechanical skills."

"Well, some folks think they're smarter than trained technicians and they poke around where they shouldn't. That's what's causing your problems." Bud didn't sound convinced that Heather wasn't one of *those folks*. "I found tin snips and a screwdriver up there." He handed the tools to Heather. "Someone's been messing around with an air duct."

"These aren't mine. You must have left them when you installed the furnace originally."

"These are *not* mine." Bud practically shouted his denial.

"Maybe they were left by the previous owner," Heather suggested, forgetting who had been the previous owner.

"They were *not* left by a previous owner. These tools were not up there when I installed your heat pump."

"I don't understand."

"Well," huffed Bud, "*someone's* been messing around up there. Your warranty won't be any good if you don't stay away from the system. Your only connection with it should be programming the thermostat. Let's check that out one more time." He walked with Heather to the thermostat in the hallway, ready to oversee one more lesson.

###

"Olivia just drove in," announced Myrtle as she left the dinner table that evening. "She has Max with her so she's already dropped Oliver at the hospital. Could I borrow your car, Heather? I'd like to see him tonight. His surgery is scheduled for early morning."

Heather examined her aunt's face. "Do you feel well enough to drive, because if you don't, I'd be glad to take you?"

"I'm much better this evening, especially now that the air conditioner is working."

Heather studied her aunt's face. "If you're sure you're better, then of course you may use my car."

"Thanks. I'll be fine." Myrtle caught the car keys Heather tossed to her. "By the way, if Jazz calls, tell him I'll be in touch later."

"Jazz?" Heather sounded surprised.

Without answering, Myrtle put on her coat and hurried out the door.

WHAT'S IN STORE FOR AUNT MYRTLE?

Cross out the letters relating to the list of words.
The remaining word, not on the list, answers the above question.

T	O	M	F	O	O	L	E	R	Y
B	E	U	Q	P	A	S	T	R	Y
L	U	R	E	T	R	I	C	K	S
O	G	D	E	A	T	H	L	T	A
O	I	E	N	P	O	I	S	O	N
D	A	R	K	X	W	O	K	R	V
T	Y	S	H	V	H	E	L	P	B
E	N	G	A	G	E	M	E	N	T

Blood, Dark, Death, Hosts, Help, Lure, Murders, Pastry, Poison, Tom Foolery, Tricks

"And who have we here?" Dr. Blair stepped into Oliver's room to check on his patient one last time before lights out. "Have you been keeping something from me, Old Man?" Oliver's long-time friend noticed how pale his patient was as he clutched the hand of the attractive woman standing beside his bed.

"Meet my fiancée," Oliver answered impulsively, winking at Myrtle. "Myrtle Wilson, this young whippersnapper is Doc Blair. He's the mechanic responsible for my wiring."

"Nice to meet you," answered Myrtle.

"I just had to wait long enough and the right woman finally showed up, Doc. I have some great plans for the two of us once you auto mechanics finish my oil and lube job."

"We leave the oil and lube work to our dieticians. My team and I just do front end alignments and battery replacements. Get a good night's sleep, Oliver. Tomorrow we'll install a zipper." Dr. Blair checked Oliver's charts one last time, nodding his approval.

"Make it a plastic zipper so I don't set off airport alarms," laughed Oliver. "I've got plans."

The doctor glanced suspiciously from Myrtle to his patient and back. "Do those plans include eloping once I leave the room?"

"It isn't that way," began Myrtle, ready to deny the label of fiancée.

"Don't spoil the doc's fun," Oliver said, his mustache twitching. "You can see he's enjoying all the visions dancing around in his head. Myrtle will be here in the morning, Doc. She'll wave me off and greet me when you wheel me out. You listen to her because I've put her in charge of all my affairs while I'm in your care. If she wants to be with me in recovery, you let her in."

"Talk about visions dancing around in one's head." Dr. Blair shook his head. "You know we can't let her into recovery. But when we get you closed up again, I'll be looking for her so I can warn her about what a cussed old guy you really are."

"You can't do that. Whatever you know about me fits under the heading of patient confidentiality."

"See what I mean, Miss Wilson. This is the patient from hell. I have to sedate him for a bit of minor surgery just so he won't be telling me how to do my job."

"If they'd give me a mirror I could do it myself," grumped Oliver, his brown eyes sparkling. "Somebody's got to be this whippersnapper's teacher." He waved to the doctor's back as the physician left the room shaking his head. Oliver turned to Myrtle, "Thanks for not saying anything. You can see how he enjoys thinking there's more life left in this old body than he guessed."

"I wouldn't consider spoiling your fun. I hope my news about your will isn't worrying you."

"I've already forgotten it since there's nothing we can do about it tonight. You will be here in the morning though, won't you? I'd appreciate it."

"Count on it. I want to be the first one to inspect this plastic zipper you're having installed."

"I'll feel better knowing someone's waiting to greet me."

"Won't Olivia be here?"

"I think she's planning on some housecleaning so she won't have to work around me when I'm taking little naps to regain my strength. As it is, Max is probably giving her a hard time. He's not used to having me gone. I hope he doesn't keep everyone in the neighborhood from a good night's sleep."

"I'll take him for a walk and wear him out. You're only going to be gone one night. Two at the most. Right?"

Oliver nodded. "Hand me my water, please."

"Of course." Myrtle handed Oliver his glass.

"Olivia sent along some last-minute vitamins for me to take tonight and in the morning. Doc doesn't believe in synthetic vitamins, so I didn't want to take them when he was standing around." Oliver popped two white tablets into his mouth and swallowed them.

"Since visiting hours are over, I need to leave." Myrtle moved to the door. "I promise I'll be here in the morning in time to plant a big juicy kiss on you so your doctor can continue his fantasies."

"How about a private smooch for me tonight?"

Myrtle laughed. "I'm already leaving you with fantasies. See you in the morning."

"Wait," Oliver called. "I want to give you something."

Myrtle turned back to see what he wanted.

"I'd like to give everyone a little something to consider and I'd appreciate it if you'd go along with me." His eyes twinkled with mischief.

"What do you have in mind?"

"Wear this." He handed her the ring he'd been wearing. "I want to enhance my reputation as a lady killer just a little longer. Bachelors have reputations to maintain, you know." Oliver's mustache twitched as he laughed.

"You are a flirt and a rascal, Oliver Lloyd. Promise you'll take it back as soon as you get home."

"It's a deal, as long as you promise you'll leave it on until then."

Myrtle nodded.

"Wait till my buddies get a load of my fiancée. How about a goodnight kiss now, you sweet young thing?"

"Don't you *ever* give up?" Myrtle clutched both of his arms firmly to the bed as she bent to kiss him on the forehead."

"Let loose of my arms," he pleaded, struggling to free them.

"I will, just as soon as I'm across the room." Myrtle hurried out of reach.

"What a spoil sport," Oliver pouted.

"See you in the morning, Oliver." Myrtle waved goodbye and tossed him a kiss from the doorway.

Oliver laughed. "You want to guess what I'm thinking?

"You're living in a fantasy world. I'll see you in the morning. Behave yourself."

"Sorry to bother you after business hours," Abe Coffman said.

Heather had been at her computer working on the jeweler's website when he phoned. "How can I help you," she asked. As clients went, Abe Coffman was turning out to be one of the most demanding.

"I've changed my mind about checking on the traffic statistics of visitors to my site. Can we still set it up like that at this late date?"

"No problem," Heather assured him. "I was just fine-tuning spam filters."

"Stop at the shop tomorrow. I have some new material to give you."

Heather sighed, wondering if she'd live to regret taking on Coffman Jewelers as one of her clients.

WHO IS NOT GOING AWAY?

Below are words with missing letters.
Supply the letters to find the answers.

a__tors	_C_	aw__ward	__		
hem__ock	__	he__rs	__		
po__son	__	b__ood	__		
myst__ry	__	trip__e	__		
unk__own	__	s__arch	__		
vic__ims	__	mu__der	__		
__tairs	__	invi__ible	__		

CHAPTER 7

Myrtle twisted Oliver's ring around her finger as she waited alone at the hospital the next morning. She hadn't slept well. One of her nieces had kept her awake wandering around the house, clicking latches as doors opened and closed. She stared at her watch. Oliver should have gone to recovery an hour after his surgery began, but two hours had gone by since then.

When the waiting room door opened and Doctor Blair entered, Myrtle hurried toward him.

"Sorry to keep you waiting," he greeted. "I had an emergency. Oliver's surgery went fine although the initial incision bled more than I expected. He's been in recovery almost an hour."

"Thank goodness. Can I see him?"

"Soon." The doctor started to say more, but was interrupted by an emergency page. "That's mine. Wait here. The nurse will get you when our patient is alert." Doctor Blair gave a little wave and rushed from the room.

Myrtle waited restlessly as the minutes ticked by, surprised when the door opened again, and Doctor Blair entered instead of a nurse. She smiled her greeting, then saw his face and reached for the arm of the chair in which she'd been sitting.

"Myrtle!" Dr. Blair sat beside her and reached for her hands.

"I'm not going to like your news, am I?"

"I'm afraid not. He's gone."

"Gone? Dead? He can't be dead. You said the surgery went well and he was in recovery. How could he die in recovery?"

"We don't have that answer yet, but it looks like he might have been bleeding internally. Oliver's never had clotting problems before, but it looks like he may have *bled out*."

"Dear God. What went wrong? What changed?" Myrtle tried to control hands that escaped the doctor's hold. They seemed to have a life of their own, clutching, then releasing each other.

"There'll be an autopsy as soon as the medical examiner can schedule one. Blood samples will go to the state lab for analysis. The hospital will need to make sure they aren't at fault."

"If there's a health factor of some kind, his niece will need to know in case she ever has surgery."

"You know, don't you, that as Oliver's fiancée, you have no legal standing in any of this. I don't suppose you actually tied the knot so you could make decisions for him, or claim his body?"

"No," Myrtle answered. She decided in that instant to keep her promise to Oliver and continue his engagement charade a bit longer. After all, she'd promised. "Oliver and I hadn't announced our engagement to anyone except you. We hadn't known each other long."

"I'm assuming you'll notify his family?"

Myrtle nodded and slowly got to her feet, satisfied the fiancée ruse would continue a while longer. Looking at Dr. Blair's sad expression, she knew it mirrored her own. "I'll take care of notifying the others," she said.

"Will you be okay?"

She nodded again and started down the empty hallway. Not only did she have to announce Oliver's death, but she'd agreed to enhance his reputation with a bit of chicanery. She was concerned with how things would go once she mentioned their engagement to the relatives, both his and hers.

"How did it go?" Heather asked, continuing to unpack a box of figurines she was distributing among various pieces of furniture. She didn't notice her aunt's face as Myrtle entered the house.

Myrtle tossed her purse on the sofa and plopped down beside it. "He's dead," she whispered. "That poor man didn't make it." Myrtle's face clouded with unshed tears.

"Oh, Myrtle." Heather rushed to her aunt and threw her arms around her. "How awful. What happened? Can you talk about it?"

"They don't know what happened. He made it into recovery, and died there. I promised I'd tell Olivia." Myrtle hiccupped and patted her eyes. "She'll have to claim his body, pay hospital expenses, and contact other relatives."

"I'll go with you," Heather said, noticing small hemorrhages around Myrtle's eyes. "You'll want to put on sunglasses."

As the two women made their way toward the Lloyd house, Heather noticed a sporty Lexus convertible in visitor parking. It sat beside a well-traveled panel truck.

"That convertible is the same make of car Sally saw Olivia in a couple days ago." Heather paused to admire the expensive vehicle before climbing the stairs to Oliver's front door. "Maybe we'll get to meet the gorgeous man she was with."

"That would be nice," Myrtle responded listlessly. "If he's visiting, she'll have someone to console her after I break the news." Myrtle pushed the doorbell and waited. Inside the house Max could be heard howling.

"It sounds like Max already knows of Oliver's death," Heather said.

At that moment the door opened and a portly woman with short gray hair and sunglasses emerged. She moved as if the weight of the world rested on her shoulders. After nodding to Myrtle and Heather she walked to the end of the street and got into the panel truck. A moment later she left.

"I wonder what Vivian Dexter was doing here," Heather said. "She owns a secondhand shop in town, one often under investigation for receiving stolen property."

"A secondhand dealer? When Oliver brought me here to look at his antiques he didn't mention selling any. He must have been interested in buying something." Myrtle stepped into the entry way and called Olivia's name.

"I thought I heard someone at the door." Olivia was coming down the stairs with a choke-hold on Max's leash. "I couldn't be sure with Max raising such a fuss. Sorry I took so long. Come in. He's going to the kitchen unless you've come to walk him, Myrtle."

Myrtle shook her head. "Not right now. Maybe later."

Myrtle and Heather moved into the Lloyd living room and sat down, each on the edge of her chair. Olivia joined them after putting Max in the kitchen. "Would you like some tea?" she asked. "It will only take a minute."

"What happened to the oil painting that was over the fireplace?" Myrtle suddenly asked. Two nights earlier Oliver had gone into detail about the expensive painting he was so proud of owning and now it was gone.

Olivia looked down at her hands and said, "I've been rearranging some of Uncle's art work. I guess that picture is one I took upstairs to his bedroom."

"It was quite lovely where he had it." Criticism edged Myrtle's voice.

"I thought Uncle Oliver might like a few changes. I assume you've been to the hospital to see him this morning. Did he tell you what time I should pick him up?"

"He's gone," Myrtle announced bluntly.

"Gone?" Olivia looked surprised. "How could he leave? Did you pick him up? The surgery must have gone a lot better than they expected if they've released him already."

"I'm afraid I didn't speak clearly," conceded Myrtle, annoyed because Olivia hadn't been at the hospital or asked about Oliver's condition sooner. "You're right that the surgery didn't go as planned, but it wasn't better than they expected; it was worse. Oliver didn't make it. He's gone. He's dead."

Olivia looked from Myrtle to Heather and back. "Is this some kind of sick joke?"

"It's no joke, Olivia," Heather said.

"Uncle Oliver is dead?"

"Yes."

"He can't be. He was in good health and taking all the right vitamins. What did that doctor do? The surgery was supposed to be a simple procedure." Olivia leaped to her feet and began pacing. "If Doctor Blair made a mistake that killed my uncle I'll sue him for every cent he and his stupid hospital can round up." She burst into tears. Her sobbing came in great gulps until she suddenly ran to the kitchen.

"I have more information for you," Myrtle called.

"Help me," yelled Olivia.

Myrtle and Heather rushed to the kitchen, where they found Olivia bent over the sink, trying to stop the flow of blood gushing from her nose. Max was running in circles around her feet.

"Tip your head back," Heather advised, grabbing a handful of paper towels to replace those Olivia was using.

"I'll get ice," Myrtle said, hurrying to the refrigerator.

"Id woan stop," cried Olivia through the cluster of towels clamped to her nose.

"Try this ice pack." Myrtle handed Olivia the towel with ice inside. "Keep applying pressure."

After a few minutes Heather said, "It seems to be slowing down." She gripped Max's collar, trying to calm him.

"Are you going to be all right?" asked Myrtle when they were able to escort Olivia back to the living room.

"I need to rest," Olivia said. She curled up on the loveseat, the compress still pressed against her nose. "Thanks for helping. I've never had trouble like that before."

"Is there a bleeding problem in your family?" Myrtle asked.

"Not that I know of." Olivia glanced at Myrtle, noticing her nervous hands. "You're wearing Uncle Oliver's ring."

Myrtle nodded. "He gave it to me as an engagement present last night."

"An engagement present?" Heather stared at her aunt.

"An engagement present?" Olivia echoed, glancing from the ring to Myrtle's face.

Myrtle nodded again. "Last night. At the hospital. Doctor Blair congratulated us and gave his blessings. We expected to break the news to all of you when Oliver came home."

"I don't know what to say," whispered Olivia, "except Uncle Oliver has always been quick to make decisions."

"I, for one, am speechless," contributed Heather, aware Olivia's phone had begun to ring.

"Could you answer that, Heather?" Olivia asked.

Heather nodded and picked up the receiver. "Lloyd residence."

"What's taking you so long?" a man asked.

"Just a minute." Heather handed the receiver to Olivia. "It's a man. He didn't give me his name."

Olivia accepted the phone. "Yes?"

"Olivia?"

"Yes, this is Olivia."

"What's going on down there? I thought we were going to spend time together today."

"Vern, this isn't a good time to talk. I've just learned that my uncle died in surgery. I'm resting."

"I'm so sorry," he said. "Let me know when your guests leave."

"Okay." Olivia handed the receiver back to Heather to hang up. "That's my boyfriend. He'll stay with me until I start feeling better."

"We'll be going then," Heather said, getting to her feet.

"Tell me, Olivia," Myrtle asked. "Did Oliver have other relatives?"

"As far as I know, there are just my two cousins, Sharon and Marilyn, and me."

"They might want to attend the funeral or memorial service, whichever you decide to have. I could contact them for you, if you like."

"Would you please? You can use Uncle Oliver's address book. It's in the top right-hand drawer of the desk in the study." She pointed toward a door leading from the dining room into an area with a small kneehole desk.

"It happened just the way I told you it would."

"No problems? No one's the wiser?"

"No, no one's the wiser. His death will look like it was due to natural circumstances."

"Perfect. When do we get the money?"

"Be patient, Chris. That part takes longer."

###

WHAT'S IN A WORD?

Below are seven little words that fit into ten larger words.
Two are used more than once.
The little word used three times has special meaning and preceded by
"don't," it is a warning.

DEN, EAR, EAT, EVE, LIE, RAG, RAN

D _ _ _ O N   C R _ _ _ E
S _ _ _ C H   H _ _ _ T
M _ _ _ S   N _ _ _ R
F _ _ _ R   S T _ _ _ G E R
D _ _ _ H   E V I _ _ _ C E

CHAPTER 8

"You realize of course that we didn't tell Olivia everything." Myrtle and Heather had left the Lloyd residence.

"What are you talking about? We told her Oliver was dead and that he'd proposed to you. What else was there?"

"We could have told her he wrote the changes he wanted for his new will on the original one, making it invalid. We could have told her that because he died without a valid will, none of his wishes will be honored. We could have said the amount of her inheritance will change considerably since all of Oliver's relatives will now split his assets equally."

"How do you know those details? I took the papers to the attorney and he didn't share all that information with me." Heather stared at her aunt.

"I read his will before I gave it to you. He was changing Olivia's inheritance. Instead of her getting one hundred percent, she was going to receive only eighty percent because he was giving ten percent to each of two friends. Of course that won't happen now."

"You read his will?"

Myrtle didn't answer.

"What am I going to do with you, Aunt Myrtle?" Heather's voice was sharp and emotional. "Telling Olivia about the will, or lack of one, is something Mr. Hamilton should do."

"You're right. I promised Doctor Blair I'd notify Oliver's relatives and I'll do that, but nothing more." Myrtle sighed.

Heather could see her aunt's weariness. "You look exhausted. Would you like me to make those calls?"

"Yes, please. I need to rest. Here's Oliver's address book with the numbers Olivia indicated."

Heather settled her aunt on the sofa with a warm afghan, then began dialing the first relative Olivia indicated.

"Hello?" The woman's voice was a whisper.

"Is this Sharon Bigelow?"

"Yes. Who's this?" The voice became louder.

"My name is Heather Samuelson. I'm calling on behalf of Myrtle Wilson, your Uncle Oliver Lloyd's fiancée. I'm sorry to report that your uncle died this morning."

"I thought that old geezer died years ago."

There was a moment of silence as Heather battled a sense of indignation. She counted to ten, then, unable to resist said, "No, the *old geezer* waited until this morning to die. We wondered if you wanted to be notified of his funeral."

"I only saw that man twice in my life. I won't be coming to any funeral for a man I didn't know." With that, Oliver's niece hung up.

Heather stared at the receiver in disbelief, then slammed it in its cradle. "She called Oliver an old geezer."

Myrtle laughed. "I guess that's one relative who won't miss him. Shouldn't we call his attorney?"

"Good idea. We need to let Mr. Hamilton know, but I've got to cool down first. The idea that Oliver's niece was disrespectful infuriates me. I think, now that he's dead and his will isn't any good, that Sharon has become an heir. I bet she'll be more receptive to inheriting money from a man she didn't know than she is of attending his funeral."

Myrtle started to get up. "Why don't you wait with the calls and I'll fix us a bite to eat?"

"You rest. I'll fix lunch. *Old geezer*, my foot." Heather stomped toward the kitchen just as her doorbell rang.

Reversing her direction, she headed for the front door.

"Mrs. Bender?" Heather checked her neighbor's hands for telltale trembling to see which of the twins she was addressing. It was a relief not to find a plate of pastry in the steady grasp currently clutching the sleeve of a tall, skinny, middle-aged man. "How are you today, Binky?"

"I wanted you to meet my Tommy." Binky pushed the man with short blond hair and pale brown eyes toward Heather. "He got here yesterday. You and Tommy are both single so I thought you two should meet."

Tommy ducked his head and stared at the ground.

After a quiet moment Heather said, "It's nice to meet you, Tommy and it's nice of Binky to let me know you'll be visiting. Will you be here long?"

"Don't know," he mumbled. "It depends."

"I'd invite you in, but my aunt's resting and I'm trying to keep the house quiet."

Binky nodded. "Just wanted you to have a chance at a handsome fellow, you being single and all."

"Thanks for thinking of me, Binky, and it's nice meeting you, Tommy. By the way, thanks for using the doorbell."

"Had to," Binky snapped. "You locked us out."

After a light lunch Heather went upstairs to her office to contact Oliver's remaining niece. She had regained her calm and notified Attorney Hamilton of Oliver's death.

"Jefferson residence." The woman responding to Heather's call was difficult to hear over the sound of children arguing in the background.

"Is this Marilyn Jefferson?" Heather asked, raising her voice.

"It is. Could you hold on a minute? Kids!" the woman shouted. "I'm on the phone. Stop fighting." In a quieter voice the woman said, "That's better. Who is this, please?"

"My name is Heather Samuelson. I'm calling on behalf of your Uncle Oliver's fiancée, Myrtle Wilson. I've called to let you know Oliver died this morning."

"Sharon called me after you talked to her. I'm sorry to hear of my uncle's death and I would like very much to be notified of his funeral. I might not be able to come because of the children, but I'd like the option. I'm a single parent with a full time job, so it isn't always easy to get away."

"I'll be glad to let you know times and places when they've been decided. Could you please tell me if you have other relatives? Aunts, uncles, cousins?"

"As far as I know, now that Uncle Oliver is gone, there's just Sharon, Olivia and me. What I can't tell you is what happened to my Aunt Isabel and Aunt Evelyn. None of the family heard from them once they graduated from high school."

"Marilyn, you've been a tremendous help. I'll call you as soon as funeral plans have been scheduled." Heather hung up the phone. "Now there's a lady who could use a surprise inheritance."

"Will she come for Oliver's funeral?" Myrtle asked, entering the room to sit on the edge of her bed.

Heather shook her head. "She'll try."

"Does it strike you as odd that Olivia's boyfriend is in Oregon? Do you think he flew here with her?"

Heather shrugged. "What I'm wondering, since the Lexus was in guest parking, is whether he's already visiting Olivia?"

"Do you mean already in the house? Do you think he was in the house when he phoned her?"

Heather nodded. "I'm betting he used his cell phone to dial Olivia's house phone. I suspect he was upstairs."

"Why wouldn't he come down and join us?"

Heather shrugged. "There's another aspect I'm curious about. Since the lady leaving the Lloyd house as we approached is a secondhand dealer, I'm wondering if she stopped in because Oliver asked her to appraise something."

"You mean instead of Olivia having called her? I'm afraid I'm not getting a good feeling for the dedicated Miss Olivia who gives up a week of her life each summer to help her rich, unmarried uncle."

"If you feel up to it, why don't we take a little drive and stop by Vivian Dexter's Treasure Trove?"

"And ask a few questions? See what we can find out? Do a little sleuthing?" Myrtle smiled.

"You've got it." Heather jumped up.

"This will certainly be an interesting way to spend a couple of hours." Myrtle pointed to the wall above Heather's desk as she got off her bed. "I noticed your calendar last night. It was Mattie's, wasn't it?"

"Yes. I used it as a guide for cancelling Mom's appointments, but. I thought I'd keep it because of the wonderful pictures of Connecticut."

"Whatever did my sister make that September reservation for?"

"What September reservation?" Heather grabbed the calendar and turned pages. And there it was! On September fifteenth a reservation number had been written without any identification. Heather said. "I didn't see this one. It hasn't been cancelled."

"Who are you going to call to get it cancelled?"

Heather started to laugh. "Mom is definitely still with us. It looks like she's left me one more puzzle to solve."

The Treasure Trove was an isolated little shop in the unincorporated section of Lewisburg. It crouched at the edge of a vacant lot being used as a dump-site for old appliances, old cars, and last week's garbage.

"May I help you?" The gray-haired Ms. Dexter wore tiny reading glasses resting on the tip of her nose. She ducked her head to look over them as she greeted Myrtle and Heather.

"Your shop always looks interesting," Heather began, looking around the room filled from floor to ceiling. "I wanted my Aunt Myrtle to see it before she flies home. Could we look around?" Heather noted her aunt already studying something on the wall behind her.

"Of course. Let me know if I can help." The antique dealer settled back at her desk.

"Do you see something you like, Aunt Myrtle?" Heather was aware that every word they exchanged could be overheard.

Myrtle grabbed her niece's hand and squeezed it until Heather almost cried in pain.

"I'm drawn to fine art and this floral painting intrigues me," Myrtle replied. Her eyes filled with sudden tears. The painting on the wall of the Treasure Trove had hung above Oliver Lloyd's fireplace two days earlier. "Could you tell me more about this work?" she asked Ms. Dexter.

"You have a good eye," the shopkeeper agreed. "That was done by an English painter in the style of the Dutch masters. His artistic family is well-known in England."

"One seldom sees such vibrancy in a still life," Myrtle added. "Look how he's captured the light and the shadows." Her voice caught.

"I don't expect to have that treasure long," Ms. Dexter added. "It only came into my possession this morning. I'm selling it on consignment."

"Who in our community is willing to part with such a fine painting?" Heather asked.

"I'm not at liberty to say," Vivian replied.

"Let's look around a bit more, Aunt Myrtle." Heather nudged her aunt toward the corner of the room where she'd spotted something of interest. "Look at this." She pointed to a small mahogany table near the window. "This is a mate to the table you gave Sally and me."

"That piece is late English Regency, from the Victorian period." Ms. Dexter jumped up again, ready to make a sale.

"We have one just like it," responded Myrtle. "The top is inlaid with rosewood, satinwood, and mahogany." Myrtle swallowed a lump in her throat, as she added, "and kingswood."

"I'd be glad to sell it for you," Ms. Dexter suggested. "Selling a pair will bring a much better price for both pieces."

"Ours isn't for sale," Myrtle replied, "but I do want to buy the painting, if you'll let me charge it to a credit card."

"That was quite an expensive purchase you just made," Heather commented as she and Myrtle headed back to the city.

"It has a special meaning for me," Myrtle explained. "You know, don't you, that it and the table both came from Oliver's?"

"I suspected as much. It means Olivia lied about what she did with the oil painting, and she was selling Oliver's things even before she knew he wasn't coming home. I'll call his attorney again. I want to let him know about this."

"I'll leave that to you, Heather. I'm feeling a little under the weather. Let's go to Rachel's. I'll leave the painting there for a while."

Heather nodded. "I'm going to call Dr. Blair, too. I think the fact that Olivia was selling her uncle's things before she knew he'd died might prompt faster work scheduling an autopsy and lab tests."

SILLY SENSE

Some answers below seem to fit more than one statement. But if you're being serious, there's only one correct answer for each situation. Find answers by making a one-word selection from each column and putting them together. Words are used only once.

When unwanted company arrives_____
You may be safe if you_____
When discovering a dead body_____
If you are allergic to the surroundings_____
When there is a thief in your midst_____

take	for	doors.
lock	and	help.
grin	far	often.
move	inventory	bear it.
call	your	away

CHAPTER 9

"Hi, Aunt Heather," greeted Tim when Heather and Myrtle arrived back at the townhouse. The twins and the Corbin brothers were playing a game of Crazy 8's in the Corbin carport. "Your new house has ghosts."

"Noisy ones," added Tom.

"Ghosts? What are you boys dreaming up now?" Heather smiled, but focused a suspicious look on her nephews.

"We're not dreaming," answered Tom. "You have ghosts." He pointed at Heather's house. "We heard them. They peeked through the drapes when we rang the doorbell. We thought it might be you or Sally, only it wasn't."

"No one opened the door and we had an emergency," continued Tim. "We needed to use your bathroom."

"Thanks for telling me about the ghosts." Heather smiled at their inventiveness. "Next time you come for a swim, borrow your mom's key so you can use my bathroom."

"You better tell her," Tim said. "She won't give us the key unless she knows it's okay with you."

"Come on. It's your turn," Johnny Corbin complained to Tim. "Lay a card down."

"Do you still need to use the facilities?" Heather asked.

"No, Johnny and Joey went swimming with us so their mom let us use their *faculties*," Tom announced.

"Not faculties, you dork," corrected his brother. "Facilities. That's a polite word for when you want to talk about the 'john' in public."

###

Dinner that evening with Jazz as their guest ended abruptly. Fresh blueberries scheduled for dessert had disappeared from the refrigerator.

68

Suspicion rested heavily on the heads of Tim and Tom because the sisters discovered a toilet seat up. It seemed obvious to them that the boys had been in the house.

Unless one believed their ghost story, of course.

Over coffee Heather related details of her conversations with Dr. Blair and Oliver's attorney. "Dr. Blair agreed to notify the medical examiner about the questionable aspects of Oliver's death," she said. "He expects an autopsy to be scheduled immediately. With Olivia selling things even before her uncle died it makes his death look more suspicious than it already is." Heather set her cup down and reached in her pockets.

"What about the attorney?" Sally asked.

"That turned out to be a rude awakening." Heather pulled a slip of paper from a pocket and handed it to her aunt. On it she'd written a time when Dr. Blair wanted to see Myrtle. "It turns out that Oliver hired Chance Hamilton to draw up his will and that's all. Mr. Hamilton isn't Oliver's personal representative."

"Who is?" asked Jazz. "I've never seen a will that doesn't appoint a personal rep."

"Oliver had appointed his brother, Edwin, but he didn't update the will once Edwin died."

"I'd guess," Jazz said, "that someone needs to hire an attorney to oversee things. As it is, there's no one to take inventory."

"Are you saying Olivia is free to sell everything she can get moved out?" Myrtle asked.

Sally interrupted, "You're Oliver's fiancée. Why don't you hire an attorney, Aunt Myrtle?"

"I asked Mr. Hamilton about that," Heather responded. "Myrtle can hire one, but Oliver's family members would have preference in handling his estate."

"That brings us back to Olivia, doesn't it?" Myrtle asked.

"I think we should contact Marilyn Jefferson and suggest she hire someone," Heather said. "She's the niece willing to attend Oliver's funeral."

"Would that stop Olivia from selling things?" Myrtle asked.

"Probably," offered Jazz. "Especially if the attorney inventories the contents of the house."

Aunt Myrtle caught her breath. "You call her, Heather. You have her number and you've already talked to her."

While Sally made a fresh pot of coffee, Heather called Marilyn Jefferson.

"Marilyn, this is Heather Samuelson again. We spoke this morning when I called about your uncle's death."

"I remember, but could you hurry, please? I have to leave for work or I'll be late. I'm a nurse and I have the night shift this week."

"Do you want to call me from work? It's important that we talk."

"I've got about five minutes before I have to leave. Is that enough time?"

"It is. Here's the problem. Your uncle died without leaving a will. As a relative, you are one of his heirs and entitled to divide his estate with the other heirs, when they can all be found."

"That's wonderful news. Why is that a problem?"

"It's a problem because your cousin Olivia is already at Oliver's and she's selling his antiques."

"You've got to get her stopped. That's not fair."

"Marilyn, you're the one who has to stop her. You need to hire a lawyer to take inventory, pay bills, and claim Oliver's body. You might consider hiring Chance Hamilton. He was Oliver's attorney at the time of his death."

"Give me his phone number. If I can reach him after hours, I'll call him from work. I think I'll also give Sharon a call. She's an heir, too, isn't she?"

"Yes, just like you and Olivia."

Jazz cornered Myrtle. "I understand you have a doctor appointment in the morning. I'll pick you up because I intend to go with you."

"There's no need for that. Heather's driving."

"Count me in. You and I need to ask Dr. Blair some pointed questions about what's going on with your health. I expect you to take good care of yourself so you can be around a long time."

"I'm not planning on going anywhere, and I'm certainly not planning to drop dead."

"That's my point exactly. We're going to make sure you aren't headed some place that doesn't have transportation back here."

"That's not true," Olivia complained when Chance Hamilton called her the next morning. "Uncle Oliver has a will. He was going to make some changes, but he has one."

"Actually he doesn't, Miss Lloyd. Once he wrote the changes he wanted on the existing will, it was no longer valid. His relatives will now share his estate equally."

"But I'm supposed to get it all. Uncle Oliver didn't plan to leave Sharon and Marilyn anything. That's why he left them out of his old will and the new one." In frustration Olivia kicked at Max as he bumped against her.

"That may be, but he also planned to remember friends who have been faithful. Now they won't get anything because it all goes to his relatives." Mr. Hamilton cleared his throat. "Are there more relatives besides you and the two nieces who've hired me to assist in settling the estate?"

"No," Olivia pouted. "There's no one else. At least not that anyone knows. We had two aunts, Isabel and Evelyn, but about twenty or thirty years ago they stopped contacting the family."

"I see." He continued reluctantly, "Your cousin Sharon has asked me to notify you that she will arrive in Lewisburg this afternoon. She expects to stay in one of Oliver's spare bedrooms."

"She can't do that. The house is mine. I won't let her in. Don't you understand? Uncle Oliver specifically said he wasn't leaving anything to her or Marilyn." Olivia pushed Max away. Her actions were greeted with a growl.

"But your cousins *will* get shares because that's the way the law works when there's no valid will. Since the house is now as much Sharon's as yours, you can't keep her from moving in."

Olivia slammed the receiver in the cradle and mumbled creative profanity under her breath.

"What was that all about," asked the man sitting across from Olivia.

"That was Uncle Oliver's attorney. He said Uncle Oliver doesn't have a will that's legal." Olivia leaped to her feet and pulled Max into the kitchen. She slammed the door and returned to her seat in the living room.

"It's this way, Vern. Uncle Oliver's old will isn't good anymore because he wrote on it, and since he hadn't signed a new one . . ." She let the sentence dangle, unfinished. "If he had signed a new will, he'd have included two friends for a pittance and I'd be getting eighty percent. Now his friends don't get anything and my two cousins each get shares equal to mine."

"Two cousins? That only gives you a third of the estate."

"What are we going to do besides get rid of that dumb dog? You and I were counting on that money so you could open your own pharmacy. With Sharon and Marilyn involved they can outvote me on everything."

"You need help, Sugar. Someone on your side to even up any voting." Vern's face lit up.

"Who's going to be on my side? You?" Olivia laughed. "My cousins won't listen to anyone without authority, and you don't have any."

"They'd listen to me if we were married. Let's get hitched now instead of waiting until we get back to Rhode Island. If we do, your cousins can't kick me out of *our* house."

"We'd have to get married at the courthouse."

"Righto. Let's get rid of that stupid dog, then say the magic words in front of a judge."

A short distance from the Lloyd house an interested observer checked out the neighborhood through a set of binoculars. Most of the morning's activity seemed to center around the house where a watchdog was now being led from the premises by two individuals in a hurry. After the dog was pushed in the back seat of a fancy convertible, the man and woman got in the car's front seats and drove away.

The observer examined a wristwatch, noting that lunchtime had arrived. The binoculars were laid aside while tired back muscles were stretched. Lunchtime seemed to be a perfect time to check things out.

"A three-day wait," grumbled Vern Higgins as he and Olivia stalked from the county courthouse a short time later. He was fumbling with the marriage license application packet they'd just purchased. "A three-day wait is unreasonable. I wonder if one of the neighboring states has a shorter waiting period?"

"We don't dare leave town to find out," Olivia announced, trying to keep up with Vern's strident pace. "Sharon will be on our doorstep in an hour or two, ready to claim her share."

"So? We don't need to leave town. We'll make some phone calls to find out. Come on, get in the car and let's get back to the house" Vern paused. "Whoa, I've got an idea. Let's rent a van and load things into it before your cousin gets here. We'll stash them in that storage locker we rented."

The outcome of Myrtle's appointment with Dr. Blair surprised both Heather and Jazz as they sat in on her examination.

Because Heather had been kept in the dark concerning her aunt's medication, all of the facts being discussed came as a surprise.

Jazz had known about Myrtle's blood thinning medication, but he hadn't known how much trouble she was having. Besides dizzy spells there were bruises and small hemorrhages plainly visible around her eyes.

"Once more," Dr. Blair asked. "Is there anything else? You haven't mention problems brushing your teeth. Any bleeding there?"

Myrtle nodded, staring into the doctor's concerned eyes. She didn't look at Heather in case she saw signs of panic. She had expected to tell her nieces about her health problems and medications later, but now it was too late.

Heather fidgeted. She didn't realize she was ringing her hands until Jazz reached over to rest his comforting palm on hers. What she wanted

73

to do was dash across the room and throw her arms around Myrtle, and then scold her for not sharing health information sooner.

"You must know," continued Dr. Blair, "that the excessive bleeding you're experiencing is probably due to some substance that has increased your anticoagulant's blood thinning capability." He made notes as he spoke.

"I've been on this medication for almost two years now," Myrtle complained. "I do *not* make mistakes in what I eat. I know exactly which foods contribute to thinning my blood and I avoid them as if my life depended on it, which, of course, it does."

Dr. Blair studied Myrtle as she sat calmly beside his desk. "And you've avoided all kinds of aspirin and vitamins?" He watched for her confirming nod. "And still you see blood when you brush your teeth?"

Another confirming nod. "Not as much as a couple of days ago, but it still happens."

"Are you taking your medicine at the same time each day?"

Another nod.

"If you have your pills with you, may I see them?"

Myrtle removed a vial of bright pink pills from her purse. They were all imprinted with the number one. She handed the vial to the doctor.

"There isn't a lower dosage than what you're taking, Myrtle." He handed the pills back to her. "But the fact remains, something has increased your medicine's blood thinning ability. Is there anything else I should know about? Nosebleeds for instance?"

"No," Myrtle said. "No nosebleeds."

"Excuse me for interrupting," Heather said. "You've just reminded me that Olivia had a serious nosebleed. I might be reading more into what I'm hearing, but it strikes me as odd that Oliver died because of excessive bleeding at a time when both Olivia and Aunt Myrtle began having clotting problems."

Dr. Blair nodded. "That gives me another direction to go with the toxicology tests the medical examiner will perform on Oliver's blood and stomach contents. Tell me, Myrtle, when did you have your first indication that something wasn't right? Was it while you were on the plane?"

"Actually my first dizzy spell happened while drinking peppermint tea with Oliver and his niece. He had to take me to Heather's because I was too dizzy to walk alone."

"Which day was this?"

"On Monday. Two days before Oliver's surgery."

"That's interesting." Dr. Blair made additional notes that he underlined several times. "For now, I suggest you continue your medicine at half-dosage. Once you no longer experience any signs of bleeding, bruising or dizziness, return to your previous level. I'm sending you to the lab for tests. If they indicate a problem, I'll be in touch with you immediately. Can I count on you to stay in town a day or two?"

Myrtle nodded. "I'll be here."

"If you have any symptoms that alarm you, call me immediately. We'll put you in the hospital and run more tests."

WHAT'S GOING ON?

Warning! Warning! Warning!

	1	2	3	4	5	6	7	8
A	W	M	T	S	D	V	O	I
B	R	C	P	B	M	G	K	E
C	G	S	T	E	N	N	H	A
D	R	E	R	D	O	L	U	R

A8, C5, C3, B1, D7, D4, B8, D8   C8, D6, C4, D1, A3
A1, C8, C3, B2, C7   A7, D7, C3

I n t r u d e r   a l e r t

w a t c h   o u t

CHAPTER 10

"There's a van in front of Oliver's house," said Jazz as the threesome drove into the Samuelson carport.

"Look," Heather whispered, her eyes wide with shock as a man carrying a lamp entered the van. "They're taking Oliver's furniture away."

Jazz said, "You help Aunt Myrtle into the house and I'll visit the eager heirs." He unbuckled his seatbelt and left the car, quickly approaching the van.

"I want to watch," Myrtle said unbuckling her seatbelt.

"Into the house with you, Auntie. Jazz will handle things."

"You folks need any help?"

Vern Higgins and a night stand were headed toward the truck. "Thanks for the offer," Vern said, admiring the athletic figure of the man offering assistance. He was a dyed-in-the-wool sucker for dark blue eyes, and at the moment found himself staring into eyes bluer and darker than Chris's. "We're doing just fine. Are you a neighbor?" He'd just chased one curious old lady away and wasn't interested in any more nosey questions, not even from a handsome man.

"Actually I'm not. I'm a Madison County Deputy Sheriff." Jazz whipped out his badge and waved it under Vern's nose. "I'd like to know who gave you permission to run off with Oliver's property."

At that moment Olivia walked from the house carrying a French eight-day porcelain-panel mantle clock. She stopped when she saw Jazz.

"Olivia," he greeted. "Nice seeing you again."

"Jazz," she whispered. She looked like a deer caught in a car's headlights.

"Aren't you a little premature claiming things for yourself when you have cousins who will want their share?"

"I...I," she stammered.

"Maybe you should move things in the other direction for the time being so no one will accuse you of stealing. Does that make sense?"

"It's all supposed to be mine," Olivia said, pouting. She headed back to the house with the ornate clock. "Uncle Oliver promised."

"What about you, buddy?" Jazz addressed Vern. "Do you need additional convincing?"

"Although that sounds like a whole heck of a lot of fun, I'd say that unless you have a writ of some kind to serve on me and my wife, then you have no business interfering with our activities."

"Wife? When did that take place, and where?"

"It's none of your damn business. Get out of here before I file a complaint with . . ."

A horn's blast drown out the rest of Vern's comments.

"What's going on?" shouted the irate driver of a sedan blocking the van's departure. "Those things you're loading in that truck are mine. Take them back in my house this instant."

With shocked expressions Jazz and Vern looked from the insistent woman back at each other. "Sharon," they mouthed in unison.

The unloading of the rental van took place amid explosive directions from Sharon Bigelow. Following that, she ordered everyone, including Jazz, into the house.

"Now," she grumped, standing with arms crossed while the others sat in chairs. "Let's find out exactly who tried to steal my inheritance. You first." She pointed at Olivia.

Olivia stared at her dark-haired cousin in the loose-fitting dress that covered an ample frame. "I'm Olivia Lloyd as you darn well know, Sharon. All of Uncle Oliver's things were supposed to be mine. He told me I'd be rich, and now I won't be. If he hadn't screwed up his will I'd have gotten everything."

"Except for ten percent for two of his friends," Jazz chided. "Isn't that what you mean, Olivia?"

"Put a lid on it, Buster. You're next." Sharon's finger pointed accusingly at Jazz.

"I'm Jazz Finchum, Sharon." He met the stern look of the woman with enormous blue eyes, and smiled. "I'm a deputy sheriff with Madison County and . . ."

"So! My thieving cousin has law enforcement helping her steal things. I suppose your job was to drive the truck to some secondhand fence."

"No, Sharon. That's not true. I was . . ."

Again Sharon interrupted. "It's Mrs. Bigelow, to you, Buster." The finger turned to point accusingly at Vern. "Your turn."

"I'm Vern Higgins, he said, twitching as he spoke. "I'm Olivia's fiancé and we're . . ."

Sharon interrupted again. "That's enough. No more talking. Now then, how many of you are currently living in this house? Let's see hands."

Meekly Vern and Olivia eased their hands over their heads.

"I see." Sharon turned her frosty gaze back to Jazz. "Then I'll want information on how I can reach you, after which you are excused."

Jazz handed Sharon a business card, then hurried from the premises.

"We're ready for you now," Sharon said into the phone after she'd called Attorney Hamilton. The cowed Olivia and Vern were at opposite ends of the living room as Sharon directed them.

"Sharon, you listen to me," yelled Olivia as her cousin hung up the phone.

"Did I ask you to speak, Olivia?"

Olivia shook her head, glaring at her cousin.

"No, I didn't think so. I understand you two have been selling Uncle Oliver's antiques and pocketing the cash. Am I right, Olivia? Yes or no?"

"We needed money for the funeral and...."

"Then you'll have contacted the hospital and had his body sent to a mortuary. Right?"

Again Olivia shook her head.

Sharon added sarcastically, "I didn't think so." The doorbell sounded. "You may answer the door, Olivia."

The man standing on the Lloyd porch wore a three-piece business suit that had wilted in the heat of the day. "I'm Chance Hamilton," he said. "Sharon Bigelow asked me to stop by."

"Come in, Mr. Hamilton," Sharon called, her hand extended to shake his. "Got your camera?"

"Indeed I do, Mrs. Bigelow."

"Well, start taking pictures. We want every little thing to show up in our inventory."

Vern jumped to his feet, "Now just one minute."

"Did anyone ask you to speak, Vernon? Or are you eager to tell this lawyer how you were loading a truck with Uncle's things when I arrived? Maybe you can't wait to confess to felony charges?"

Vern resumed his seat, his face flushed.

"That's better. Now let's all wait quietly while Mr. Hamilton goes about his business."

"I tell you that woman is either a school teacher or a prison matron." Jazz was still chuckling as he reported on Sharon Bigelow's appearance on the scene. "That woman could probably handle a yard full of unruly prisoners, although I suspect she teaches junior high students. I thought she'd send me to the principal's office." Jazz settled on one of the two sofas in the Samuelson living room and wiped his brow. "It's a little hot in here, don't you think?"

"A little," agreed Heather. "I need to call the repairman back. His cooling system stopped functioning again. It's too bad you didn't stick around to watch Sharon deal with her thieving cousin and the lying fiancé."

"Are you kidding? I'd been dismissed. If I hadn't left, I'd have been sent to detention." He chortled again, waving at Sally as she came into the house.

"Am I interrupting a meeting of some kind?" she asked.

"Olivia's cousin Sharon just arrived," explained Heather. "Jazz was telling us how that went."

"Move over, Heather." Sally collapsed beside her sister and fanned herself. "That cooling system needs fixing again, doesn't it?"

Heather nodded. "With Sharon in residence and the housecleaning at Oliver's stopped, we can finally get back to settling in here. I'm calling that repairman again. I want his cooling system fixed once and for all."

"We're not finished at Oliver's," Myrtle murmured. "After all, as his fiancée I have an interest in what actually killed him, and I did promise to look after Olivia and take Max for walks." She twisted Oliver's ring around her finger as she spoke.

"You're right, Myrtle. I didn't mean to be insensitive."

"How did the appointment with Dr. Blair go this morning?" asked Sally.

"Here's your chance, Aunt Myrtle," Heather said. "Tell Sally about your medications."

Myrtle looked at her niece, and seeing her curious expression said, "I didn't want to worry anyone by reporting on something that happened two years ago. I was only hospitalized a short time." She glanced down at Oliver's ring again. It seemed to have shrunk. "Anyway, the blood clot didn't cause any real problems, but it meant they put me on a small dosage of a blood thinning medicine. Its function is to keep the clot from becoming larger while preventing new ones from forming."

"I suspect you've had to make other changes," Sally said.

"A few, but they're only minor adjustments to my life. I use an electric shaver instead of a razor blade, and I avoid aspirin, vitamins, alcohol and foods high in vitamin K."

"But something's upset Myrtle's meds recently," Heather interrupted. "That's why she's bruising so easily. When she went swimming that first day, she didn't have any bruises. Since then she's been hiding most of them under long sleeves and turtlenecks." Heather glanced back at her aunt. "Do you think we've fed you something that wasn't good for you? Maybe that's what's contributing to your sleepless nights."

"If you and Sally would stop roaming around the house I could sleep soundly. Mostly it's that quiet hammering you often do. You should wait until daylight to hang pictures." Myrtle missed the questioning looks the sisters exchanged. "As far as food goes, I haven't knowingly eaten anything that would add to the blood thinning ability of my medicine."

"I'm intrigued," Sally offered, "with your use of the word *knowingly.*"

"Leave it to a cop to pick up on that," teased Jazz. "You might as well tell us all your suspicions, Auntie."

"What suspicions?" Heather's eyes opened in surprise. "Are you still holding out on us, Aunt Myrtle?"

"Jazz is teasing. It's like you said earlier, Heather. I'm curious about Oliver dying due to excessive bleeding. When I consider my clotting problems and Olivia's, it makes me curious."

Sally looked from her aunt to her sister.

"Myrtle's talking about a nosebleed Olivia had when we told her of Oliver's death," Heather explained. "She could hardly get it stopped."

"In retrospect," Myrtle continued, "the only foods I've had that I haven't seen being prepared were a couple of lattes, and a mocha or two from that little restaurant on Fillmore Avenue. Of course I've eaten a few cookies and some coconut cake supplied by the Bender sisters. There was also a cup of peppermint tea Oliver gave me when I first visited him."

"Does that mean the tea was prepared out of your sight?" Sally asked.

"It means that the cup of tea Oliver gave me had been given to him to drink, but he passed it on to me since he hadn't tasted it yet."

"Wait a minute. What this is coming down to is that Olivia may have put something in Oliver's tea and you got hold of it." Heather's eyebrows arched in surprise.

Myrtle nodded. "Now that you mention it, she had a fit because Oliver gave me his tea. She said she'd dissolved vitamins in it."

"Oliver told us at dinner the other night, that Olivia was feeding him high-powered vitamins," Sally said. "What if she's been giving him something that wasn't really a vitamin?"

"But Olivia had bleeding problems, too," Heather reminded them. "She wouldn't put something in the food that would cause her problems."

"Maybe she didn't think it would affect her," Jazz suggested.

"I suspect, if the dosage of an anticoagulant was high enough," offered Myrtle, "say five to ten times higher than what I normally take, it might not take long to cause bleeding even in someone who isn't already taking a similar medication."

"But since you are, it reacted faster on you?" Heather asked.

"Right!"

Heather said, "I think we should call Dr. Blair again. We need to tell him one of Oliver's heirs was feeding him something that may have been harmful."

A LOOK AHEAD

Below is a crazy quilt of words, each of which can be found in an irregular configuration. Move from letter to letter vertically or horizontally; not diagonally. Each letter is used only once. Clues to murders yet to happen are included, along with a word in the chart that isn't listed below. Can you find it?

poison

A	C	C	R	I	T	M	U	R	O	I
E	D	I	E	E	D	R	E	D	P	S
N	S	N	H	A	D	Q	U	E	S	O
T	T	I	A	N	T	I	E	T	A	N
S	U	F	F	D	E	S	P	E	R	J
M	A	R	E	O	N	M	E	A	L	E
A	I	R	D	R	A	E	M	I	T	W
G	T	U	N	E	H	M	Y	R	T	E
E	R	P	O	L	S	K	C	O	L	L
F	O	E	C	I	H	E	M	L	E	S

accidents, antiques, dead, desperate, fortune, hemlock, inherit, jewels, marriage, mealtime, murder, Myrtle, police, Sharon, stuffed

CHAPTER 11

"Now here's the way we're going to do things," said Sharon Bigelow, as she scrambled eggs in an iron skillet. Slices of toast popped from the toaster, ready for butter and jam. "Tonight I'll fix dinner and you two will clean up. Breakfast and lunch are yours to fix, after which I'll do the cleaning. We'll keep to that schedule until everything is worked out and the estate is settled."

"But you're a teacher," Olivia said, pouting. "Don't you have to get back to the classroom?"

Sharon looked at her cousin and rolled her eyes. "Not in the summer, Olivia. Only kids like you, with learning difficulties, attend summer school. Now get out of my way so I can serve dinner. While we're at it, no more eating food, then putting the empty dishes back in the refrigerator. Put them in the dishwasher. Do we understand each other?"

Vern and Olivia frowned as they exchanged looks that said, *Not me. Was it you?*

"Well, do we understand each other or should I go ahead with charges against you two?" Sharon gave a final stir of the omelet as she issued her threat.

For a while Vern and Olivia continued exchanging puzzled looks, then shrugged. After that the evening meal proceeded quietly. The only sounds were forks scraping against bone china.

"This reminds me," Sharon exclaimed. "Tomorrow I'll buy plastic plates. These dishes are too valuable to eat from on a regular basis. Vern, your special job will be to take the garbage out each evening. Got that?"

Vern responded with a grumpy sound.

"I'll take that as a *yes* and count on you doing that little job for the ladies of the house. Now then, I have a few questions for you two, and I advise you to come up with the right answers."

"What questions?" Olivia asked. "You took the bedroom at the head of the stairs, and have the only private bathroom. What else needs to be decided?"

"We have to decide when you're going to bring back the furniture and pictures you took out of this house before I stopped you. Any suggestions?"

"What are you talking about? We emptied the truck." Vern paused, staring at Sharon.

"A little birdie told me a certain antique dealer has been selling Oliver's things on consignment. I suggest you get that stopped immediately, and return those things to the house."

Olivia hung her head while Vern huffed wordlessly.

"If I have to repeat myself I'll be making a trip to the courthouse tomorrow."

"Don't bother," Vern said, pushing his plate away. "We'll take care of it in the morning."

"That's a good plan, Vernon. Now you two clean up your plates and I'll reward you with a little surprise for dessert."

"I'm going to reward that cousin of yours with a little surprise," Vern said when he and Olivia retired to the master bedroom they'd shared since Oliver's death.

"What are you talking about?"

"I'm talking about getting rid of her," he hissed. "One less cousin takes your inheritance back up to fifty percent."

"Are you talking about killing Sharon?" Olivia asked. "I won't be party to a murder, Vern." She ran her fingers through her hair, patting it out of her eyes and pushing it to the side of her face.

"I'm not talking about a murder. I'm talking about an accident. One she might have while we aren't around."

"That still sounds like you're planning to murder her." A shiver shook Olivia's body.

"Jeez! Your cousin's right. You do have difficulty learning."

"You make it sound like I don't have good sense. If that's the case, why do you want to marry me?"

"Ah, Sweetheart," he crooned, backing down immediately as the vision of escaping dollars loomed darkly in his future. "Don't take what I said wrong. We're good for each other, don't you think?"

"Oh yes," Olivia agreed, a happy smile lighting her face. Vern was the first man to pay serious attention to her, and he was drop dead handsome.

"Your cousin Sharon isn't really so bad." Although he'd softened his verbal evaluation of Sharon, the look in his eyes remained calculating. "In fact I'll always be grateful to her for sending me out back with the garbage. Your uncle has an interesting plant in his garden."

"Uncle Oliver liked growing things, but as he got older it was harder for him. That's why I've been coming out here every summer, to help plant things for him. What did you find that's so interesting?"

"He has a sort of 'wild parsley' that was introduced to this country from Europe. It doesn't grow just anywhere. Your uncle's plant has obviously been in his garden at least a couple of years. I'll pick some in the morning and when we make Sharon's breakfast, we'll be able to add something fresh to her plate. Better yet, we'll leave the *parsley* in the refrigerator for her to use when we aren't around." Vern, the pharmacist, smirked like a mischievous child. *Wild parsley?* He laughed. The plant he'd discovered was poison hemlock.

While poison hemlock could be mistaken for parsley, it did not have the same effect on the body that parsley had. Vern's smirk grew as he thought fondly of Socrates and the hemlock cocktail that ended his life. Maybe he would experiment with a little hemlock tea-for-two after he became Olivia's husband. With Sharon and Olivia both gone, inheriting Oliver's assets could rest heavily on his capable shoulders, allowing him and Chris to be comfortably set for life.

Olivia raised her head when she heard Vern's quiet snickering. There were times she felt almost afraid of him.

But how could a bride-to-be have doubts about the man she'd soon be promising to love, honor and obey?

That was it. Her twinges of uncertainty had to do with the idea of getting married. Her uncertainty had nothing at all to do with doubts regarding the groom.

"Gee whiz, Mom," moaned Binky's son as he stared across the Bender dinner table where plates of cookies, brownies, one pie and two cakes waited. "Can't you branch out? Maybe cook vegetables or meat once in a while?"

"You watch your language, young man, or I'll send you back to that academy." Binky Bender stirred the pan of fudge she'd been nursing. She was bound to discover Tommy's favorite dessert before long. Then he'd be happy and everything would be like old times.

"You listen to your mom, Tommy," added Baby. "Binkey's been bent over a hot stove for days, getting all these treats ready for you. Show her you appreciate her efforts."

"I do appreciate all your baking, Mom, but while I was gone, I learned to like meat and vegetables. You know, fruits and things that don't have sugar added to them."

"No sugar? Are you fooling me? Are you saying you don't eat sliced tomatoes with sugar on them any more?" Binky glanced across the room at the bowl she needed for the fudge. "Grab that dish for me, Baby. I don't have enough hands."

"Glad to, Binky." Baby pushed the dish closer to the stove. "You git your spoon ready, Tommy. We'll be eating this here fudge before you know it."

"Just what I'd hoped to have for dinner," Tommy mumbled. "Fudge and cookies. At this rate I'll be eating all my meals out."

"If you're want'n some fruit," Binky said, trying to soothe him, "have some'a that nice strawberry rhubarb pie sitting next to that chocolate cake with raspberry filling."

The next morning Vern and Olivia wasted no time leaving the housing area in his new Lexis.

86

"I had to get out of there before I strangled your cousin," Vern complained, flooring the gas pedal and daring any cop to stop him. He'd harvested Oliver's supply of hemlock and added a sprig to Sharon's breakfast plate. But according to her the eggs had cooked too long, the hash hadn't cooked long enough, the toast was barely more than warmed bread, and the frozen butter was about as easy to spread as a block of day-old concrete. When she returned the tray of food untouched and complained that the coffee was weak, that had been the last straw for Vern. He grabbed Olivia's hand and rushed to his car.

"I told you nothing would please her," Olivia said. "She's always been bossy. Things have to go her way or the highway, so to speak. She can also be downright mean. I try not to go against her."

Vern drew a deep breath. "I could use a couple of those vitamins you brought for your uncle. Do you have any left?" The question was meant to check on loose ends that had been out of Vern's control.

"Of course not. You told me to make sure Uncle Oliver took them all prior to his surgery. I gave him the last four when he went to the hospital. He planned to take two the evening before surgery and the others the next morning."

Olivia ducked her head. This didn't seem like the best time to confess she'd taken some of the vitamins meant for her uncle. With Vern upset over Sharon, there was no point in adding to his distress. Or anger. Olivia had never been around angry people and they frightened her.

"I think we should stop at the hospital and claim your uncle's body. You don't want them doing an autopsy."

"An autopsy? It was a natural death. Why would they do an autopsy?"

"Hospitals have teaching labs," he improvised, groping for an explanation Olivia might believe.

"That's terrible." Olivia shivered. "Let's order his body sent to a mortuary immediately."

"Good idea," Vern agreed.

"Breakfast first, hospital second."

Sharon Bigelow was on the phone talking to her sister. "You were right about Olivia trying to steal things, but I stopped her."

"That's good. As long as we're getting this unexpected windfall from Uncle Oliver, we want to make sure it's divided equally. Have you met the Samuelsons yet?"

"I've been too busy. One thing Heather didn't mention is Olivia's fiancé. He seems to be in the driver's seat. I suspect Olivia is clay in his grasping hands."

"If you need me to join you, just holler. I can hire a babysitter and...."

"I'm doing fine. I've got Olivia trembling in her boots, and this effeminate Vern character thrown totally off balance. If I need anyone to back me I'll call Richard. One usually absentee husband ought to trump one grasping fiancé, don't you think?"

"I suspect if you alone have Olivia ready to pee her pants, inviting Richard to lend a hand will send her into cardiac arrest." Marilyn chuckled. Cousin Olivia had not made friends among her family members. Having a dead father and a mother who deserted her mattered only to her Uncle Oliver.

"Uncle Oliver always said my marriage to Richard was like the mating of two Sherman tanks," Sharon added.

Marilyn laughed. "Where's the absentee husband now? Back in Washington D.C. telling the President how to run the country?"

"He's in Washington all right, only it's Seattle this time. Some idiot is on trial for pocketing *samples* he took home from his job."

"I don't suppose he was a grocer?"

"He worked as a teller in a bank. It was money he took home. His defense is that embezzlement is a crime that involves breaking a relationship of trust. But, since he had a criminal record to begin with, the bank was at fault for putting their trust in him and giving him a job that tempted him. It's one of those nutty defenses that twists the law but hasn't been tried before so there's no clear precedent. Richard can hardly wait to see what the prosecution's response will be."

###

"Yes!" crowed Dr. Blair, as he read Oliver's autopsy results. "We found it."

Detective Sally Samuelson had followed through on a hunch and called for autopsy findings.

Dr. Blair continued, "Once we knew what to look for it was easy. There were traces of anticoagulants in Oliver's stomach and it turns out that the custodial staff found a pill under his bed. Oliver or his fiancée must have dropped it."

"My Aunt Myrtle would not have fed Oliver any anticoagulants, so forget that. She didn't do it."

"You can bet I didn't prescribe them. When I tested Oliver's clotting time Friday it registered as it should have. That means a blood thinner was introduced to his system after Friday."

"His niece arrived Sunday, and at dinner Monday he told us she was giving him vitamin pills. Is there any chance that could be what you found?"

"Believe me; what we found is not vitamin residue."

"Thanks for the information, Dr. Blair. I think someone in our department needs to have a little chat with Oliver's niece. We need to find out what kind of *vitamins* she fed her favorite, rich, unmarried uncle."

"See if she mentions numbers on them; the higher the number the more potent the dosage. A pill like the one we found under Oliver's bed is the strongest blood thinner that exists."

WATCH OUT, LEWISBURG
HERE COMES RICHARD

Find the little word that fits within the bigger word.
Use each little word only once.

Hard, Lion, Lone, Pare, Ring, Tops, Vast, Vest, Vice

A P _ _ _ _ N T	A U _ _ _ _ Y	D E _ _ _ _ S
I N _ _ _ _ I G A T E	M I L _ _ _ _ S	S P _ _ _ _ S
D E _ _ _ _ A T I O N	R I C _ _ _ _ S	C Y C _ _ _ _ S

CHAPTER 12

"I only gave Uncle Oliver some vitamins." Olivia had been at the police station talking with Detective Sally Samuelson for more than an hour.

"I'd like to see some of those vitamins." Sally sat facing Olivia with only a few feet between them. Invading a suspect's personal space was an interrogation technique that usually got quick results.

"I don't have any more. They're gone. They were to speed up my uncle's recovery, so he took them all before his surgery." Olivia squirmed in her chair.

"Describe them."

"They were ordinary. White! Like aspirin!"

"And like aspirin, did they have a brand name stamped on them?" Sally asked the question sarcastically.

"A brand name?" Olivia looked puzzled. "No, not a name." She suddenly smiled. "They had numbers."

"What numbers?" Sally asked the question as if only mildly curious.

"Tens! They were all tens. I remember Uncle Oliver asking if he should eat numbers one through nine first."

"Where did you get these *vitamins*?" A surge of excitement pulsed through the detective. She knew now that Oliver had been receiving an anticoagulant of the highest dosage. Pills of that kind, taken for three or four days prior to surgery, explained why he died in recovery. Had Olivia planned his death so he couldn't change his will? Could she be that concerned about the amount of her inheritance?

"I got the vitamins at the pharmacy in Rhode Island," Olivia answered, ". . .at the place where I work."

"Did the pharmacist give them to you, or did you just grab some off the shelf?"

Olivia burst into tears. "Stop confusing me. You're making it sound like I fed Uncle Oliver something that killed him. I didn't. I only gave him vitamins to keep his energy level high so he'd heal quickly."

"These are straight forward questions, Olivia. They shouldn't confuse you. Did someone hand you those pills or did you grab them off the shelf yourself?"

"You don't understand." Tears rolled down Olivia's face. "I took some of the vitamins because I was coming down with a cold. Uncle Oliver didn't even get all of them because I swallowed some."

Sally moved closer, leaving only inches between them. "Once more, Olivia. How did those pills come into your possession?"

"I don't remember. I just don't remember. I was working half-days and packing for this trip. I booked my flight and took finals. I studied late every night. Learning has never been easy for me. I had to take sleeping pills just to get a little rest." Another burst of tears flowed down her cheeks and a drop of blood leaked from her nose. Olivia grabbed a handful of tissues. "I don't remember how I got those vitamins."

"Heather," called Aunt Myrtle as she looked out the living room windows. "Come quick."

Heather hurried in from the kitchen. "What's the matter?"

"That beau of Olivia's just drove in. Alone. You said you wanted to meet him. I thought this might be your chance."

"Perfect." Heather dashed out the door as Vern was crawling into the back of a truck. "Hi there," she called. "I'm your neighbor, Heather Samuelson."

Vern paused, his hands on the table he'd retrieved from Vivian Dexter. He turned toward Heather, but remained silent.

"I wanted you and Olivia to know how sorry your neighbors are about Oliver's death. If there's any way we can help . . ."

"Grab the other side of this table," he said, gesturing with his hands.

Without a word, Heather supported one side of the table as Vern eased it from the truck. They carried it up the front steps.

"I didn't get your name," Heather said as Vern opened the unlocked door and backed into the house. Heather was right behind with her end of the table. "My God," she gasped, as the room behind Vern came into view. She dropped her end of the table and pushed past Vern. "Call nine-one-one," she yelled, hurrying to the foot of the stairs where a body lay. The woman's twisted neck made it clear she was beyond help.

Following her morning at the police station, Olivia returned home, expecting to find Vern still retrieving Oliver's antiques from various locations. Instead, there was an ambulance just pulling away from the house, and a police car still at her front door. An officer in the car was writing in a notebook as he talked on a cell phone.

Olivia parked in guest parking and slowly approached the house, noting that both Vern's car and the truck he used were in the carport. Who had needed the ambulance?

She paused. Had Vern followed through with his threat? Had he strangled Sharon?

And at the Bender house Baby was saying, "Look at that, Binky. An ambulance is just leaving Oliver's."

Binky had been at the stove whipping up a butterscotch pudding for lunch, but she ran to the window for a quick peek, then turned to her son. "Did you see the ambulance?" she asked, eager to include him in the neighborhood's unusual burst of activity.

"Darn right, I'm sheeing that am-bue-lanze," Tommy responded, slurring his words nicely. He hiccupped. "People falling down sh-tairs need their am-bue-lanzes."

Vern poured himself a measure of Scotch just as Olivia stepped into the room.

"Vern, what happened?" She waited for an answer. "Are you all right?" Her expression was grave.

Vern gulped the liquor and refilled his glass, not yet focusing on the woman standing beside him.

"Talk to me. What happened? Where's Sharon?"

At last he spoke. "When I came back with the last load, your neighbor and I found her at the bottom of the stairs. Her neck was twisted at a disgusting angle." He shivered. "Your neighbor, Heather Samuelson, told me to call the cops, so I did." He paused. "They just left. We're assuming Sharon tripped and fell since no one else was in the house. She had a small rug twisted around her feet. It looked like she must have been hurrying and got tangled in it. I think she rode it down the stairs like a toboggan." He gulped down the second measure of scotch as if it were mother's milk. "Her head," he shuddered and started again. "Her head looked like it had been put on backwards."

"My God," Olivia sighed, moistening her lips. Slowly she sank into a chair and rested her elbows on the table.

Frowning, Vern noticed for the first time that he had an empty glass in his hand, one he'd gotten from the cupboard. A second glass, showing it had been used, sat on the table. Come to think of it, when he entered the kitchen the Scotch had been on the table, too. Cousin Sharon must have had a little liquid libation for breakfast once she'd rejected what he and Olivia fixed for her. He poured his third shot. Perhaps that was why she fell.

He paused. The cops said that his call for an ambulance was the second one they'd received, though the first caller hadn't given an address. Maybe Cousin Sharon had entertained a red hot lover. But if she did, there should have been two empty glasses on the table. Vern shook his head, trying to clear his mind.

"Promise me you didn't cause Sharon's death," Olivia whispered. "Please. Promise me." Tears were streaming down her face.

"I wasn't even here. That woman at the antique shop will remember me." He emptied the shot glass a third time and thumped it on the table. "She'll remember when I was there 'cause she didn't want me taking the table.

"One of the things I learned," Vern continued, "was that the picture we gave her on consignment had already been sold. She didn't want to look up who bought it, but after I made a promise or two that she didn't want me to keep, she checked her records."

"Why do we care who bought Uncle Oliver's picture?"

"We needed to know because, as it turns out, it was your neighbor."

"What neighbor? I doubt anyone living around here would remember seeing it except maybe . . ." She stopped in mid-sentence. "You mean that aunt of the Samuelson's bought it?"

"Bingo!"

"She'd remember it all right," Olivia shrugged, "but what difference does that make?"

"She bought it the first day it was in the shop; only minutes after informing you of your uncle's death. That means she knows we didn't wait until after he died to begin selling things."

"I knew we should have waited. I shouldn't have listened to you. Uncle Oliver would have missed that picture, too. His surgery wouldn't have confused him enough to make him forget exactly what he had in the house."

"We'll never know now, will we?"

"The ambulance is gone, but there's still a police car at the Lloyds'." Myrtle gave the report as she nibbled on a cookie from the recent delivery made by one of the Bender twins. "Olivia's home now. I wonder how she feels about her cousin's death?"

"I think I'll give Sharon's sister a call," Heather replied, picking up her phone to call Marilyn Jefferson. "Marilyn," she continued when the woman identified herself. "I'm calling to tell you that your sister has had an accident."

"Is she hurt? Why isn't she calling me herself?"

"She fell down a flight of stairs and they've taken her to the hospital."

"How bad was her fall?"

"It's bad enough that you should call the police to get a report."

"How did she happen to fall? Do you think Olivia had something to do with it?"

"I don't think anyone knows exactly what happened."

"I'll bet Olivia pushed her."

"I suppose if your cousin is greedy enough and the amount of her inheritance is large enough, she might resort to desperate measures. Who knows? I haven't seen the police report, but if I can help, let me know."

"Call the attorney for me, will you? Let him know. I'll check with the police and then I'll notify Sharon's husband. I have a feeling Olivia will be meeting Richard Bigelow very soon now and it serves her right. I wouldn't want to be in her shoes when he gets to town."

Richard Bigelow, a born competitor, relished combative encounters. After three years as a Green Beret, he became a police officer, destined it seemed, to forever be assigned to districts that experienced the highest crime rates. Considering the mortality rate of cops assigned to those areas he immediately enrolled in night school where he graduated from the law program faster than anyone had previously managed. Because he had a keen sense of when to attack and when to defend in messy cases, his success rate as a defense attorney was very nearly one hundred per cent. His cases included everything from drunken driving to sex crimes, and from homicides to embezzlements. As defense attorneys went, none was better than Richard Bigelow.

Crossing Richard unnecessarily was a mistake, and taking something away from him resembled stepping into the lion's cage.

Unfortunately for residents of Lewisburg, Richard's beloved wife had been taken from him under what seemed suspicious circumstances. At the moment his suitcase contained one change of clothes, and a few bottles, vials, and appliances used by crime scene investigators.

Unfortunately for Lewisburg, he was prepared to make an assault on the community.

###

DINNER'S READY

The Samuelson family is ready for dinner.
Unfortunately, they're having a difficult time agreeing on the seating arrangement. Please help them get seated.

Heather gets to sit in seat number 5.

Sally refuses to sit in seat number 1, but wants to sit next to Myrtle.

Rachel wants to sit between Tom and Heather.

Tim will sit in a chair on the other side of Heather.

| 1 | 2 | 3 | 4 | 5 | 6 |

CHAPTER 13

"Is it true Richard Bigelow is coming to Lewisburg?" asked Jazz when he stopped to take Heather out to dinner that evening.

Heather nodded. "He'll be here in the morning. Do you know him?"

Jazz smiled. "By reputation. You do, too. Remember that child molestation case in Vancouver a couple years ago? The suspect admitted his guilt prior to receiving his Miranda rights and his defense attorney claimed racial discrimination."

Heather nodded. "I remember. Who wouldn't? His case was temporarily tossed out of court, and there were enough lynch mobs up and down the western United States that the guilty man had to be put in Witness Protection."

"That's the one. Bigelow was the defense attorney."

Heather laughed. "In that case, I think Olivia and Vern are about to be reined in. What's your guess?"

"My guess is that if those two are the least bit intelligent, they'll hightail it out of town and wait for their share of the loot to show up in the U.S. Mail."

###

"He's gone," Myrtle yelled, rushing from the Samuelson house as Jazz and Heather returned from dinner.

"Who's gone?" Heather hurried to her aunt's side. "Take it easy, Aunt Myrt. Who's gone?"

"Max! Oliver's golden retriever! He's gone. I went over to take him for a walk, but those idiots dropped him off at the dog pound. Sally checked and he's not there anymore." Tears filled Myrtle's eyes.

"Do you mean he's been put to sleep?" Heather threw her arms around her distraught aunt.

"I mean they don't have him. They don't know where he is. Their records don't show he's been put down, and they also don't show he's been given away." Myrtle hiccupped and pulled a tissue from her pocket. "He should be there, only he isn't." Tears streamed down her checks.

Heather glanced at her watch. "The Humane Society is closed for the night, but I'll look into it in the morning. Don't worry, Aunt Myrt. We'll find him."

Jazz gave both Heather and Myrtle brief kisses and left after Heather promised to call him as soon as she learned anything about the missing pet.

"I'm sorry I spoiled the best part of your date," Myrtle apologized, "but this situation is becoming too much for me. My heart is just breaking with the deaths and skullduggery that's going on. And I hate to say it, but someone's been into my jewelry box."

"Are you sure?" Heather's eyes opened wide. "When did that happen?"

"I'm not sure when, but I'm an orderly person and someone has stirred up my things in a way I never would."

Heather studied her aunt's serious face. "It certainly wasn't Sally or me, and I can't imagine the twins doing something like that. Is anything missing?"

"A dinner ring is gone, but it's just a paste, so it isn't terribly valuable. It's the idea of someone going through my things that upsets me."

"We'll get answers," Heather assured her. "Don't get worked up. It isn't good for you."

"You're too late. I've got a headache." Myrtle massaged her forehead.

Heather reached out to take her aunt's arm. "Let's get you in bed. You've had a stressful day."

She went up the stairs with Myrtle, and soon had her tucked in bed. As Heather started to turn off the lamp on her desk, she noticed items that had belonged to her mother scattered across it. The carton that had held them was now empty.

"I hope I didn't mess up your project," Myrtle said. "You'd left all those things on my bed so I moved them to your desk, but I kept them in the same order."

"You didn't take them out of the box?"

"No. They were on my bed when I needed to lie down."

"You did just fine." A thoughtful look clouded Heather's face. The items had been salvaged from Mattie's desk after her death, and no one touched them except Heather. "I'll take care of these," she said, as she repacked the box. She tucked it under one arm, and headed for the kitchen telephone.

"Rachel," Heather said, once her sister answered, "we've got a mystery, and I need your help solving it."

"You've got it."

"Aunt Myrtle thinks someone has been going through her things and a ring is missing. Have you given our house key to the twins yet?"

"They haven't been swimming since you suggested that, so they haven't needed the key. But you can't think my boys would go through someone's personal belongings."

"If they did, Rachel, it would be the first time." Heather waved at Sally as her sister entered the house and locked the door behind her. "I'm just trying to figure out what's going on."

"The boys are asleep, but I'll check with them in the morning," Rachel responded.

"Any chance you could come over for an hour tonight?"

"If it's important I'll ask Jason to watch things."

"It's important."

"Okay. I'll see you in a few minutes."

Heather hung up the phone and followed Sally into the kitchen. "It looks like we have a problem, only I'm not sure what it is."

"Keep talking," Sally said, opening the refrigerator door. "I need my dinner; it's been a hard day."

"Aunt Myrtle told me someone has gone through her things."

"You've got to be kidding." Sally looked at her sister's serious expression.

"I wish I were," Heather said.

Sally turned back to the refrigerator and continued searching. "Anything else?"

"Whoever did it took Aunt Myrtle's dinner ring."

"Damn," exclaimed Sally, pulling an empty bowl from behind a row of condiments. "Someone put this empty bowl in the refrigerator, after they ate the salad I saved in it for my dinner tonight."

"Jazz took me out for dinner and Aunt Myrtle had a sandwich. We knew that salad was yours. We didn't eat it."

"I think our aunt is getting absentminded," Sally whispered. "I think she ate my salad and didn't bring the ring with her." She slammed the refrigerator door and grabbed a jar of peanut butter from the pantry.

"You may be right," Heather agreed reluctantly. "None of this started until after Myrtle arrived, but I called Rachel. She'll talk to her boys in the morning to make sure they didn't carry their search for loot and secret passages too far." Heather began searching through the box she'd carried downstairs.

"What are you doing with that collection of Mom's things?" Sally found a spoon and began eating peanut butter straight from the jar.

"Myrtle said these were spread across her bed, but I didn't put them there. Is there any chance you...?" Heather looked up, and seeing Sally's expression, pointed to a box on the counter. "At least put crackers under your peanut butter."

"I didn't touch those things. I've got too much going on in my life to spend time with them. That's your job." Sally helped herself to the crackers.

Heather put the box of keepsakes on the floor beside her, but continued holding what the sisters were calling the *puzzle letter*. "Well, it appears that someone was messing with them."

"Have you made sense out of Mom's letter yet? And what about her puzzle?" Sally was referring to a jigsaw map of the United States Mattie's attorney gave Heather.

"I started working on the puzzle yesterday. Wait until you see it. All the pieces are blank. Any identifying information has been torn off, so there's no state name or highway to guide me. There are just blank pieces of cardboard that should form the United States once I fit everything together."

"I'm learning more about Mom's personality since she died than I discovered while she was alive." Sally laughed, and at that moment the doorbell rang.

"That'll be Rachel." Heather headed toward the front door. "Hi, Rachel. Come in. I want to run some ideas past you and Sally."

The women settled in the living room and Heather began. "I'll review what we know about Mom's items first," she said. "There's a collection of birthday cards that were mailed to her, one each year, after Dad died."

"I remember," Sally said. "The handwriting on them and on that unidentified flower arrangement at Mom's memorial service all looked like Dad wrote them." She went back to munching crackers with peanut butter.

"Except for Dad being dead, he'd be the answer to some of the questions we have," Rachel added.

Heather nodded. "Besides the cards, there was that strange scrapbook in Mom's desk."

"Remind me what's in the scrapbook," Rachel said.

"I'll get to that later. I want to talk about her letter first, and the part of it that suggests she invented fairy tales for the boys."

"Only that didn't happen," Rachel said. "Mom didn't make up stories for Tim and Tom."

Heather nodded. "Now for some new ideas." She watched her sisters' faces. "I've gone over the fairytale section of Mom's letter and I think her references to Prince Charming and Cinderella are really references to Dad and herself."

"How did you come to that conclusion?" Sally put her spoon down.

"The letter says that Prince Charming was ruling his *divisional* kingdom. That didn't make sense to me at first, but now I think it's referring to Dad's accounting firm. I think Mom chose the word *divisional* only to catch our attention so we'd consider the possibility of an accounting firm."

"If that's true, then there was a problem of some kind," Sally added.

"Right. The Prince was *lending his skills,* which is what accountants do. Then he discovered that the person who hired him, Mom's *Big Bad Wolf,* was somehow hurting others." Heather frowned.

"Keep going. I think you might be on the right track." Sally's eyes sparkled with excitement and Rachel staggered to her feet and began pacing.

"The Prince went to the *Game Warden*, a type of law enforcement officer," Heather continued, "and reported the crime. But, in order to get Big Bad caged, the Prince had to *tell the whole world what Big Bad had done.* I think there must have been a trial and Dad was a witness. Do either of you remember him being involved in a special trial of some kind about nine years ago?"

Sally spoke first. "Dad always represented his firm in court cases and there were several of those. If Mom mentioned one nine years ago I wouldn't have given it much thought unless she made it sound special. I was getting ready to quit law school and go to the police academy so was pretty self-absorbed."

"I remember various trials Dad took part in, but nothing that was out of the ordinary," Rachel said. "Jason and I were halfway across the continent with sick twins nine years ago."

Heather nodded. "And I moved in with you to help out and get another degree. None of us even visited Lewisburg for a couple of years."

"What I remember about what happened nine years ago was Mom's fall, and Dad's death."

"I think that's covered in the puzzle letter." Heather paused for a moment then continued. "I think that when Big Bad was finally caged, he hired an assassin. That's the only thing that makes sense to Mom's reference that Big Bad used his *wonderful gifts for his friends if they'd do away with Prince Charming.* I think the hit man couldn't find Prince Charming, so he attacked Cinderella, knowing the Prince would come out of hiding to be with her."

"My God," gasped Rachel. "Mom always said her fall wasn't an accident. She insisted someone tried to kill her and we all laughed. We thought she was making an excuse to cover up her clumsiness."

Heather nodded. "Next point. Her letter says the Prince did a *Humpty Dumpty.*"

"Took a fall," supplied Sally. Her face turned pale.

"That's what happened," Rachel whispered. "Dad fell to his death on Mt. Hood."

"Right," continued Heather. "When Prince Charming fell it satisfied Big Bad so he left *Cindy and the babies* alone."

"When you read it that way," said Sally, "it sounds like it wasn't just Mom who was in danger, but we girls were, too. My God. Think of what Mom went through alone, with none of us here to lean on or give moral support."

Tears filled Heather's eyes.

"You've got it all figured out, haven't you?" Rachel asked.

"Not all of it. But if we go on the assumption that everything in the puzzle letter is factual in one way or another, then I don't understand the reference to the King's Men *putting Humpty Dumpty together again.*"

"You're right. Dad's dead, so he can't be revived." Rachel calmly shredded a tissue.

"I need to study Mom's scrapbook," Heather continued. "It contains information about a trial that took place prior to Dad's death, and there are some obituaries Mom collected."

Sally stared at her sister. "Do you think the man who was on trial is Mom's Big Bad Wolf?"

Heather studied Sally's pale face, then Rachel's nervous hands. "Joel Bishop was the defendant in the trial that's the subject of Mom's scrapbook. He's also a multimillionaire. He would certainly have *wonderful gifts for his friends.* In addition to that, after he was sentenced, he left the court room screaming that he'd see to it that they were all dead. I'm beginning to think he put out a contract on anyone connected with his trial."

"My God." Sally leaped to her feet. "His trial judge drowned earlier this week. What if it wasn't an accident?" She knotted her hands into fists. "What if Mom's letter isn't just a story? What if there's a hit man who is still killing people?" Sally reached for her coat. "I've got to check on how Bishop's appeals have…."

"No! Stop! Mom clearly said you were to *quietly do nothing.* We don't know why she said that or why she wanted us to keep the contents of her letter to ourselves, but for some reason she didn't want you going through department channels to investigate any of this. We've got to be patient."

###

The next morning Heather temporarily set aside her work on a website for Coffman Jewelers and arrived at the Humane Society just as their doors opened.

"I'm here to ask about a golden retriever that was dropped off by mistake last week. His name is Max."

The attendant at the desk looked up. She had hair piled high on her head, and wore eyeglasses with lenses that distorted her eyes. She smiled in response to Heather's comment and adjusted her desk lamp, then began checking documents recording the flow of pets in and out of the facility.

"Here it is," she reported, her finger tracing the correct entry. "Max is still here."

"Could I see him to make sure?"

The attendant nodded. "I'll get him." She left the reception area, but returned a moment later. "That's strange. He isn't in his cage. Let me see if I've missed something. Perhaps someone already claimed him."

She checked the records again, then opened another drawer and withdrew a second set of documents. Heather impatiently shifted her weight from foot to foot.

At last the attendant shook her head. "That dog should still be here. Let me look again."

"Could I come with you?" asked Heather. "I'd be able to recognize him if he's in the wrong cage."

"Come along. I'm sorry this is taking so long."

The two women entered the caged area and were greeted by dozens of barking dogs, but none was a golden retriever named Max.

"Were you on duty when Max was admitted?" Heather asked.

"No, Arlyn admitted him."

"Could I talk to Arlyn, please?"

"He has the weekend off and left early today. He'll be back on Monday."

"Could I call him at home? It's important."

The attendant shook her head. "I'm sorry, but we don't give out that kind of information. You'll have to wait until Monday."

"You're sure Max hasn't been put down?"

"I'm sure."

"Okay," Heather said, moving toward the doorway. "Thanks for your help. I'll be back on Monday."

Two more days of not knowing where Oliver's golden retriever was? Would the absent Arlyn remember the friendly pet and be able to tell her what he'd done with it?

On her way back home Heather stopped at Coffman Jewelers to pick up new details Abe Coffman wanted on his website. He was getting ready to sell one of the largest groupings of diamonds recovered from a robbery that took place three decades earlier at Detroit's International Jewelry Fair. Abe insisted the jewels were jinxed and for that reason he wanted to get rid of them.

Heather was anxious to get his website up and running. Finishing the Coffman account meant a large commission and hopefully, fewer calls from the pushy owner of the shop.

Early that same morning Rachel had a serious talk with her boys.

"Honest, Mom," exclaimed Tim. "Tom and I haven't been in Aunt Heather's house except when you were with us."

"And we weren't upstairs, even then," finished Tom.

"I believe you, but we've got a puzzle that I need help solving."

"Coool," responded the twins in a single drawn out breath.

"Is it like Aunt Heather's puzzles?" Tom added.

"This one is different," Rachel continued. "One of Aunt Myrtle's rings is missing from a jewelry box she kept in her upstairs bedroom. Other things in her room look like someone searched through them. We know Heather and Sally didn't do that. Can you solve this mystery for me?"

The boys looked at each other and nodded.

"It's the ghosts doing that stuff," Tom reported.

"What if I don't believe in ghosts?" his mother asked.

"We heard them, Mom. Both of us. That day we went swimming and wanted to use the *facilities*."

"No one answered when we knocked," Tim added, "but we could hear doors inside opening and closing."

"He's right," Tom added. "And the drapes moved like someone was taking a look at us after we rang the doorbell. We told Aunt Heather about it, but she didn't take us seriously."

Rachel puzzled over what the twins were suggesting. Was it possible someone other than her sisters had keys to their house? She reached for her phone and tapped the button for Heather's speed dial. "I think Aunt Heather will take you seriously now," she said.

###

STAIR STEPS
Fill in the blanks below.

Arrange the list of words so that the last letter of one word is the first letter of the next one.
If you have them in the correct order, they will fit in the grid in stair-step fashion - beginning on the first space and ending on the last one.

Big Bad, herb, neglect,
search, threat, Tommy, Vern, yes

CHAPTER 14

The yellow Hummer parking in front of the Lloyd residence that same morning looked as formidable as its driver. Richard Bigelow puffed on a cigar as he studied the residence where his wife had died. Then he slowly made his way to the Lloyd's front door and began pounding on it.

"Yes," greeted the out-of-breath Olivia, after running from the kitchen to see who was making so much noise. Standing on the porch was a well-dressed stranger polluting the air with cigar smoke. He had black curly hair and eyebrows that joined just above his nose. "I suppose you're with the Police Department and you want to do more investigating," she said, "but you can't bring that cigar into this house."

"Lady," Richard challenged, sending a cloud of smoke her way, "when I get through investigating you'll wish I had been part of your rinky-dink police department. I'm Richard Bigelow. Who are you?"

"I'm Olivia Lloyd," she responded, coughing. "Did you say 'Bigelow'? Were you related to Sharon?"

"I'm her husband."

"I didn't know she was still married. I thought her husband died."

"Miss Lloyd, you and I are not going to stand out here in this heat any longer. I want to come in and see where my wife is supposed to have tripped and fallen. I intend to pick up her belongings, and then stay in her room at least for the weekend."

Richard pushed past Olivia, but immediately extinguished his cigar.

"What's all that noise down there?" The question came from the top of the stairs where Vern stood wearing only a wet bath towel.

"Who the devil is that?" Richard thundered.

"That's my fiancé, Vern Higgins," explained Olivia. "It's okay," she called to Vern. "This is Sharon's husband."

"I thought you said he was dead." Vern headed back to their room muttering, "I suppose that means Olivia's inheritance is back to being only a third."

Richard was staring at the retreating figure. "That man is dripping water all over what is probably the crime scene!"

"It's not a crime scene," Olivia said. "It's more of an *accident scene.* No one knows exactly what happened because Sharon was alone when she fell. Vern got back after running errands and found her over there." Olivia indicated a chalked outline at the bottom of the stairs. "I was at the police station."

"I see." With an anguished look Richard studied the markings that depicted his wife's body. In a quiet voice he said, "Show me to Sharon's room, and then get the hell out of my way."

Olivia hung back, pointing up the stairs with a trembling hand. "Sharon's room is the first one to the left."

Richard loped up the stairs, turned left, and entered the bedroom. When the door slammed behind him, Olivia dashed up to confer with Vern.

"Did he say what his intentions are?" Vern asked.

"He said he'll stay the weekend and do some investigating."

"What's he going to investigate? The medical examiner already looked at everything and he's satisfied her death was an accident."

"I suppose he'll check the same things and then go home. At least I hope that's what he'll do. He makes me nervous." Olivia shivered and crossed her arms over her chest.

"That's why you've got me here, to protect you. Come over here and give your sweet-smelling Vernon a nice big juicy kiss."

As the morning progressed, Vern and Olivia became aware of Richard on his hands and knees at the top of the stairs. He examined the highly polished hardwood floor and the rumpled area rug that had been outside of Sharon's bedroom door. Following that, he donned unusual glasses and sprayed each stair with a liquid that he then highlighted with a special ultra violet light. Cotton-tipped swabs were occasionally dabbed against some invisible mark. With slow deliberation Richard descended the eleven steps to the first floor.

"Why would anyone have a throw rug on a highly polished hardwood floor at the top of the stairs? Especially a rug without non-skid backing?"

"It was s-something Olivia's uncle p-put there," stammered Vern. "It never s-seemed safe to us, but that room was normally empty. We didn't get around to removing it after Oliver died. Now we can't. Not until the police give us the okay. They think Sharon must have rushed from her room, got tangled in the rug, and took a header."

Richard looked suspiciously at Vern. "I understand you were running errands when that happened."

Vern nodded. "I was in an antique store at the approximate time of her death."

"Busy selling more things from the estate?"

Vern shook his head. "Sharon told us to return everything, and that's what I was doing, reclaiming items we'd turned over to an antique dealer."

"Are you hungry, Richard?" Olivia interrupted. She carried a dish in her hands. "It's almost lunch time and I just fixed this chicken salad. We can set another place, if you'd like to join us."

"No thanks."

"The salad is very tasty," Olivia continued. "I added fresh parsley from Uncle Oliver's vegetable garden. Vern picked it for me. He said it's a rare variety introduced to this country from Europe. He's a pharmacist so he knows about things like that. It's quite good and has an almost peppery taste that burns in the mouth. It goes nicely with the bland chicken." She headed back to the kitchen, with Vern following close behind.

"I thought we were going to save that parsley for a special occasion. You didn't eat it all, did you?"

"I only had a wee taste. There was so much of it I shared some with those nice old ladies who bring us cookies. Sit down and let's have lunch."

"Hold off a minute," Vern said, turning to Richard. "Is there anything else you need?"

"I want to talk to the Samuelsons," he responded. "Which residence is theirs?"

Vern pointed out the proper residence and Richard headed out the door. Vern turned back to Olivia. "Why don't you fill the water glasses while I get salad plates?" He took the salad from her and set it on the table, examining it carefully to see how much of the herb he'd called *parsley* she'd added.

"Ohhh!" The moan escaped Olivia just as the water pitcher slipped from her hands and crashed to the floor.

"Are you okay?" Vern asked, his suspicions about the poison hemlock confirmed.

"I suddenly feel shaky," Olivia answered. "Sort of like I've come unglued somewhere." She laughed. "It's probably a reaction to Richard Bigelow, but I think I'll skip lunch and take a nap."

"Why don't I heat a can of soup for us," Vern asked, putting the chicken salad back in the refrigerator. "That should perk you up. We want you well enough to get married on Monday. Let's save the salad for our first meal together after we're Mr. and Mrs. Vernon Higgins?"

"Oh good! That'll be perfect."

"You can have it all, if you want, on Monday."

"You're so good to me, Vern."

"I'm just that kind of generous fellow," he replied.

"I'm Richard Bigelow," Richard said when Heather answered her doorbell.

"Please come in," she invited. "I'm Heather Samuelson. We are very sorry about your wife's death."

"Thank you," he said, entering the house. "I understand from Sharon's sister, that you've been helping us. Could you please bring me up-to-date on what's been going on around here?"

"I'd be glad to tell you what I know," Heather replied indicating a sofa where Richard might comfortably sit. She took a seat across from him.

"Not good enough," Richard announced sharply, leaning forward. "I want to know what your gut instincts are and whether you have any suspicions about what's been happening."

"Of course! That's a different matter entirely and telling that story will take longer." Heather smiled. "I'd like to have my Aunt Myrtle join us since she has some of the details. Would you like some coffee? It's fresh."

Richard's stomach growled. "Please. I'd love some."

"I could fix you a little breakfast or lunch, if you like."

"That would be very kind of you. Perhaps a piece of toast? The truth is, I was driving half the night and didn't stop for breakfast."

Heather nodded and called up the stairs for her aunt, then headed for the kitchen.

Richard nodded at Myrtle as she joined him, and soon was devouring the light breakfast Heather fixed.

"My sister Sally and I moved into this house seven days ago," Heather began, sitting across the table from her guest.

"I'm only visiting," Myrtle interrupted. "From Boston."

Heather continued, "We wanted to get acquainted with our neighbors, so we had Oliver and Olivia here for dinner Monday."

"Earlier in the afternoon," Myrtle said, "after meeting Oliver at the pool, he gave me some papers to take to his attorney. He wanted to spend Tuesday at the beach before going to the hospital to have new batteries installed in his pace maker. The papers contained changes he wanted to make to his will. He planned to sign the new one when he got out of the hospital."

Richard nodded and mopped his brow. "Does it seem a bit hot in here to you ladies?"

"We're having problems with our cooling system," Heather responded. "A repairman is scheduled. He's been here every other day because his air conditioner isn't the least bit reliable."

Richard shrugged out of his jacket. "I hope removing my jacket won't offend you ladies."

"Make yourself comfortable, please," Heather said, nodding to Myrtle to continue the story.

"The morning I should have taken Oliver's papers to his attorney, I didn't feel well," she said, "so Heather delivered them. Oliver and Olivia were still at the beach."

Heather said, "I took the papers to Chance Hamilton and he told me that because Oliver had written his changes on the original will . . ."

"He invalidated it. So that's why he died intestate!" Richard's voice rose in pitch when he realized what Heather was saying.

"Oliver didn't know about the problem with his will," Myrtle continued, "because after he returned from the beach, he went right to the hospital to be admitted. I told him when I visited him that night. That's when we...," she looked at the ring on her finger. "...we got engaged."

At that moment the telephone rang and Heather got up to answer it

"Wait a minute!" Richard said, turning to Myrtle. "You'd only met the man the day before, and you got engaged to him the following night?" Richard's eyes opened wide, his eyebrows arching in surprise.

"You had to know Oliver to understand," Myrtle said.

Richard shook his head. "Go on."

"The next morning, after he died, I promised his doctor I'd contact the relatives, but I still didn't feel well." She nodded to Heather as she returned from answering the telephone.

"That was Rachel, my married sister," she explained to Richard. "She thinks we need to change the locks on our doors."

"Why would she suggest that?" asked Myrtle.

"She thinks someone other than those of us living here has keys to the house. She thinks that's why your ring is missing and why you've been hearing noises at night." Heather looked at Richard's puzzled expression. "I'm sorry for the interruption. Now then, getting back to what you want to know. Because Aunt Myrtle wasn't up to it, I called Oliver's relatives to notify them of his death."

"How did you know who to call?"

"Olivia told us about Sharon and Marilyn, and gave us Oliver's address book. We found the sisters listed."

"Were there other relatives?"

The two women looked at each other. "We relied on what Olivia told us," replied Myrtle, "and she said she just had two cousins."

"Wait," Heather interrupted. "There may be more. Olivia mentioned two aunts everyone has lost contact with."

"You're right," Myrtle agreed. "We didn't look through the address book to see if Oliver had their names listed."

"Could I see the book, please?" Richard asked.

Heather opened a desk drawer and removed a book she handed to Richard.

He paged through it, then asked, "Do you have any objection to my taking this with me? I'd like to start the search for Oliver's missing sisters."

"It's yours," Heather said, nodding.

"Go on with your story."

"That's about it," Myrtle replied.

"I don't think so," Richard charged. "You were going to tell me any gut instincts or suspicions. All I've heard so far are facts."

"Well, there are some additional things that seem to have been taking place," Heather admitted hesitantly.

"Let's hear it," Richard said.

Heather smiled at her aunt. "On Monday afternoon, after Aunt Myrtle and Oliver met, she went to his house for tea. That's when he asked her to take the papers to his attorney. But after an hour at Oliver's, she came home too dizzy to walk without assistance. It turns out she's taking an anticoagulant. When we took her to see the doctor about her dizzy spells and some terrible bruises she developed, he said she'd eaten something that increased her medication's blood thinning capabilities."

"And that's why I was getting dizzy and bruising," Myrtle added.

Heather continued, "When we told Olivia about her uncle's death, she started crying and got such a bad nosebleed that…."

"Wait," Richard burst out. "I understand Oliver died because he 'bled out.' Now you're saying," he pointed at Myrtle, "that you got hold of something that increased your medication's blood thinning ability? And Olivia developed a bleeding problem, too? Wow! One thing I don't believe in is coincidence. Anything else?"

"When Oliver came to dinner Monday, he told us he was taking high powered vitamins Olivia brought from Rhode Island. She works part time in a drugstore."

"Have they done an autopsy on Mr. Lloyd?"

Heather nodded. "Yesterday. After everyone got suspicious about the 'vitamin pills' they did the autopsy and rushed the lab tests. It turns out that Oliver had anticoagulant residue in his stomach and a pill on the floor under his bed. Olivia said she fed him vitamins with the number ten on them, but that describes anticoagulants of the highest potency. Not vitamins."

"Hot damn!" Richard exploded, slapping his hand against his knee.

Heather smiled and continued. "Olivia had a visitor the morning her uncle died, one who owns an antique store in town."

"We went to the Treasure Trove that same afternoon," Myrtle put in. "We wanted to see what was going on. It turns out Olivia consigned some of Oliver's things to the shop for sale even before she knew he'd died. I bought the picture that once hung over his fireplace."

"May I see it?"

"My sister Rachel has it," Heather said.

"Okay, so after Myrtle bought the picture, is that when you," he nodded at Heather, "called Marilyn and suggested she and Sharon hire Chance Hamilton to get the sale of antiques stopped?"

The women nodded.

"What can you tell me about this fiancé of Olivia's?"

"Not much," replied Heather. "When we told Olivia of her uncle's death, we think he was upstairs, but he didn't come down while we were there. When he drove in yesterday I hurried over and introduced myself. It was while I helped carry a table into the house that we found Sharon."

"I have one more question. Were either of you ever on the second floor of that house?"

"I was," Myrtle offered. "After dinner Monday Oliver took me there to see more of his paintings and some of his wonderful furniture."

"Tell me about the second floor, Myrtle," Richard coaxed. "What did you see there?"

"Well," she said, hesitating. "There's a mirror on the wall just at the head of the stairs. And a mid-18th century Louis XV carved console table with a marble top just under the mirror. On the walls are...."

"Skip the pictures," Richard interrupted. "Anything else in that hallway?"

"At the end of the hall, under a window..."

"I'm sorry to keep interrupting, but I have so little time before I have to head home for a trial. Anything on the floors? Rugs of any kind?"

"None that I remember. The house is mostly hardwood floors, except for a gorgeous Oriental carpet in the dining room. Is that what you mean?"

"I'm more interested in whether there were any smaller rugs in that upstairs hallway."

"None," Myrtle assured him. "Oliver didn't have things that weren't antiques. Except," she hesitated.

"Go on, except what?"

"He did have a little dime-store rug by the back door so he could wipe his shoes after gardening."

"Was it green?"

Myrtle nodded. "Sort of a sea mist shade of green. I told him he should have gotten a brown rug so mud wouldn't show, but he explained that green rugs didn't show grass stains."

"Thank you, ladies. You have helped me a great deal. Is there anything more you want to add?"

Heather said, "If you get in a bind with your trial and still have things to do in Lewisburg, I'd be glad to help out."

"I appreciate that and may very well call on you." He got to his feet and reached for his jacket.

"Would you like to have dinner with us tonight?" Heather asked.

"Thank you. I'd like that very much. I'd be afraid to eat anything Olivia and her friend fixed. I'd be afraid they'd poison it."

As soon as Richard left, Heather called a locksmith She considered herself a light sleeper so it didn't seem possible anyone could come into the house and not be heard. And because she operated her business from the house, it was seldom empty.

How could a prowler, even if he had keys, find a convenient time to enter the house?

###

STORY STEW

(For the experienced detective only.)
Re-arrange the letters to form words
with a common theme

ACIOORSTU	ACCEHINRY	CGINNNU
CDEEFILTU	ADEFLNRTUU	BEHILORR
ACIILMOUS	CDELNORSU	AIILLNOUSV

_ _ _ _ _ _ _ _   _ _ _ _ _ _ _ _   _ _ _ _ _ _ _

_ _ _ _ _ _ _ _   _ _ _ _ _ _ _ _ _   _ _ _ _ _ _ _

_ _ _ _ _ _ _ _   _ _ _ _ _ _ _ _ _   _ _ _ _ _ _ _ _

CHAPTER 15

Olivia wasn't tempted to eat the soup Vern fixed. All of her strength was being used to control the sweats and trembling that shook her body from time to time.

"You need to get your mind off whatever is making you ill," Vern coaxed softly. "For instance, you told me you were at the police station when Sharon died, and I believe you. Why do you keep asking if I killed her?" He stood beside Olivia's bed, fascinated by the pulse throbbing at her throat.

"I just . . . I just want to hear you say it." She burst into tears. "I was with Sally Samuelson all morning, so I didn't push Sharon down the stairs."

"Nobody pushed her," Vern said. "What did the cop ask about?"

"Uncle Oliver's vitamins."

"Good grief," Vern replied. "Why did you tell her about those pills?"

"I didn't. Uncle Oliver mentioned them the night we had dinner at the Samuelson's."

Vern moved away from the bed and began pacing. If the cop was asking Olivia about the pills, that probably meant the autopsy showed undigested fragments in his stomach. It made sticking around to collect the inheritance more dangerous than he liked to play the game. "What else did the cop want to know?"

"She asked if I had any left, and where I got them."

"And what did you tell her, Babe?"

"The truth. They were all gone and I got them in Rhode Island."

"And that's it?"

"I didn't know what brand they were. She asked if I got them off the shelf or if someone gave them to me. But I couldn't remember. Did you give them to me, Vern?"

"Of course not, Sweetheart. Try the soup again, and then get some rest. I've got to think about what to do next."

"About what?"

He paused, "About our wedding on Monday, of course." If no one knew where the pills originated, then Olivia would be the only one connected to them.

That sounded like the first break he'd had in this tangled mess.

When Richard Bigelow met with the Madison County Medical Examiner, it was to ask where his wife's body had been sent, and then to arrange with the funeral parlor for its release. "I'd also like to know what you discovered at the accident scene," Richard said, noting the youthful age of the county's doctor.

"I assure you," said the medical examiner, "that every square inch of that area was photographed and measured. I am well aware that the scene of a death often supplies investigators with the best information. In your wife's case, it wasn't possible to determine whether she fell or was pushed, but with a rug tangled around her feet, it looks more like an accident than a homicide. However, because I couldn't make a positive determination, I advised the detectives to do more in-depth checking than usual."

Richard raised his voice, "And that's supposed to reassure me? What steps has anyone taken with the homicide you *can* be positive about? With anticoagulants in Mr. Lloyd's stomach and his niece admitting she fed them to him, has she even been interrogated?"

"The lead detective interviewed her yesterday. If you stop at headquarters and ask, they might arrange for you to meet with Sally Samuelson."

"Samuelson? I'm having dinner with the Samuelsons tonight."

"You'll have a chance to talk with Sally then."

"The niece isn't being held, is she?"

"The department didn't feel anything would be gained by holding her. She's waiting for the payoff from her uncle's estate, and until she gets her hands on the money, she won't go anywhere that they can't find her. What we don't know is how she got hold of a controlled medication that requires a prescription."

"I'll tell you how she did it," Richard said, his voice gaining volume. "She works in a drugstore in Rhode Island, that's how. And if that's not enough, it turns out that her fiancé is a pharmacist."

"Is he? I don't believe Miss Lloyd mentioned that to anyone."

Richard shoved his chair back abruptly and headed for the door. "I suspect no one thought to ask. Isn't that what you mean? Did you think a guilty person would volunteer that kind of information?" He stalked out of the room mumbling, "I hate rinky-dink towns with their rinky-dink facilities."

###

Richard pulled out his cell phone and invited Chance Hamilton to lunch. "It was good of you to join me on a Saturday," Richard said once they were seated at one of the country club's window tables. "Especially on such short notice."

"Your reputation precedes you," Chance replied. "I would cancel an appointment with the Pope himself for the chance to say I'd had lunch and a martini with the famous Richard Bigelow."

Richard smiled. "Were you tempted to use the word *infamous*?"

"I wouldn't dare," Chance laughed. "Now then! How can I help?"

"I'm sure you know by now that Oliver's death was not due to natural causes."

"So I've been told."

"I suspect my wife's death was also not an accident, but I can't prove it yet. Once I do, someone's going to be damned sorry." Richard turned his head to glance out the window, but not before tears filled his eyes.

At that moment a waiter stopped to take their orders, giving Richard a chance to regain his composure. When the waiter left, Chance said, "I'd like to offer my condolences on your recent loss."

"Thank you," Richard murmured, turning back to Chance. "What can you tell me about Oliver's will?"

"Come on, do you really believe the reason for two possible murders might be Oliver's assets?"

"That's what I want you to tell me. Did the old boy have enough that it might tempt someone to knock him off and kill my wife in an attempt to cut down on the number of heirs?"

"The will doesn't list the sources of Oliver's wealth. It only awards percentages of the whole amount, but his reputation has always been that he was well-fixed."

"I see! Any idea who did his taxes?"

"None, though I suspect he did them himself. He was good with numbers."

"How about an investment counselor? Did he have one?"

"If he did, I have a friend who'll know. Here's his name." Chance scratched a name on his paper napkin and handed it to Richard. "I've begun the procedure to appoint myself as personal representative so I can look for Oliver's assets and close the estate, unless you'd like the court to appoint you?"

"Thanks, but I'm busy with other matters."

"When your life settles down we'd like you to consider addressing our local Bar Association. Do you think that's possible?"

"Anything's possible, but on this trip I have just today and tomorrow to take care of personal matters. Monday I'm due back in court in Seattle."

"Another interesting case?" Chance asked as the waiter delivered two martinis.

"I only take interesting cases," Richard said, "and this one's ready for closing arguments."

"I need to go to Oliver's house and collect papers and bank statements. Those might tell us if he had assets he didn't need to list on his taxes."

"Don't put it off," Richard responded. "I'd advise you to take every scrap of paper you can lay your hands on. I don't trust Olivia or her pretty boyfriend."

"I'll head over there as soon as we finish lunch," Chance said, ready to look for some of the answers.

"I always appreciate a man who isn't afraid to do a little hard work on weekends," Richard said.

###

For Richard, the hours following lunch included a phone call to the investment councilor whose name Chance supplied. As far as the councilor knew, Oliver's assets were in the middle six figure range.

"Not exactly a fortune," Richard mumbled to himself as he broke the connection, but perhaps to a couple like Olivia and Vern, that's exactly what it was.

A cell phone rang, startling its owner. *"Hello, who's calling?"*

"Good God! Who else has this number? I thought this was our private line."

"Sorry, Chris. My mind was elsewhere."

"How are things going? Any money yet?"

"A few hundred. That's all."

"How long before you can wrap this up? I miss you."

"You need to be patient, my love."

"Can't you give me some idea how much longer you'll be? Maybe I should fly out there so we can have a little time together."

"No! Don't do that. The next phase should be over soon. I'll call you when that happens. After that, we only have to wait for the money to show up."

"Okay, but don't do anything rash to gum it up!"

Richard had gone through Oliver's meager address book more than once before he realized that one or two of the people listed in it lived in town. He grabbed the map of Lewisburg, and looked up the streets he needed. A moment later, he was on his way to a residence at the south end of Lewisburg.

Because it was Saturday, Jerry Delahugh had the day off from his part time job as a gas station attendant. He was mowing his front lawn when a yellow Hummer stopped at the curb. Jerry looked up. Moving toward him was a powerfully built man.

"Can I help you?" Jerry asked, cutting the power to his lawn mower.

"My name is Richard Bigelow," Richard announced, extending a hand to be shaken. "I understand you were acquainted with Oliver Lloyd."

"Since high school," Jerry said, frowning. "His passing came as a shock. Tragic! I saw the death notice in the paper. No obituary yet, but one of them national press groups picked up the story and . . ."

"I'm sorry to interrupt, but my schedule is crowded. I'd like to ask you a few questions about him, if that's all right."

"What kinda questions?"

"For instance, were you related to him in any way?"

"Why're you asking about Ollie? You a cop or something?"

"Not a cop, but an officer of the court. An attorney. I'm trying to locate his heirs."

"Ollie had a will. His heirs are going to be listed there. I'm s'posed to be one of 'em. Gotta paper that says so. You wanna see it?"

"Later. What can you tell me about his brothers and sisters?"

Jerry studied the man asking questions. "You care to set a spell while I talk about Ollie? Maybe share a cup of iced tea since it's such a hot day?"

"Why not?" Richard replied, following the bent figure into his Cape Cod bungalow. When iced tea was poured, Richard asked, "Were you close to Oliver?"

"Might as well have been brothers," Jerry replied sipping his beverage through lips hiding teeth with gaping holes between them. "We were as good as brothers, him and me and Linny. We always looked out for each other like we'd been born to the same mom and pop. We growed up together and were best buddies all through school, at least as far as Linny and I got. Ollie had more schooling and it did good by him."

"You knew his family then?"

"Sure did."

"Are his parents living?"

"Are you kidding me? No. Of course not. They didn't have kids until late in life. They died when we was all still in high school."

"Tell me about Oliver's siblings?"

"His what?"

"His brothers and sisters. Tell me about them."

"Well, there was Milton. He was oldest, but he's dead now, too. Then the girls, Isabel and Evelyn. Edward came next, and then Ollie."

"Did any of them marry?"

"Milton did. He had three kids, but one of them died. I think it was the boy, not the girls. Of course Ollie didn't marry. No one knows for sure what happened to his sisters. Seems like they runned off right after their folks died. Left with high school sweethearts. Edward married eventually and had that girl he named after Ollie. Called her Olivia. After Eddie died his wife ran away with the guy that was hawking coffins. It was a sad thing, but Ollie stepped in and helped Olivia. She's visiting now. Only got to see him a few days 'fore he died. Poor girl must be all broke up."

"Do you have any idea what the names of the boys might have been—the ones who ran away with Isabel and Evelyn?"

"Can't tell you, but Linny might know. He stayed in school a year longer than me. He lives the next street over. Right behind me. You can cut through my back yard if you want."

The meeting with Linny Jennings was similar to the one with Jerry Delahugh, except for Linny's dog interrupting every exchange. Richard obliged by petting and admiring the pet, then scratching behind its ears. Finally Linny gave up and locked the dog in another room.

"I'm sorry Maximilian is such a bother," he said. "Not really much of a watchdog. Too friendly for his own good."

"I'm wondering," Richard began, "if you'd take over a responsibility for Oliver's family?"

"Be glad to. What can I help with?"

"Olivia seems to be dragging her feet about composing an obituary or even organizing a memorial service. Since you knew Oliver so well, I wondered if you'd do those things?"

"I'd be proud to do that for my old friend. Now, getting back to what you want to know about Ollie's sisters . . ."

The extra year in school had acquainted Arlyn 'Linny' Jennings with the boys the Lloyd girls had been dating. With their names tucked in his pocket, Richard hurried off to have dinner with the Samuelson clan.

###

THE SEARCH CONTINUES

Find a word that joins with the words connected by a blank line.
For instance: BLOOD_____GLASS needs STAINED
to form <u>blood stained</u> and <u>stained glass</u>.

BLUISH_____GROCER
BONE_____LINER
DINNER_____TONE
FATHER_____LESS
HATCH_____UP
HEAD_____SAW
HIDE_____LAW
STOCK_____PLACE
THROW_____BEATER

BACK, BAND, GREEN, HEAD,
MARKET, OUT, RING, RUG, TIME

CHAPTER 16

"I can't tell you what pleasant company you've all been," Richard said as dessert was being served. During the meal he'd been aware of Deputy Finchum's interest in Heather Samuelson. Young love reminded him of the deep feelings that burst into bloom the moment he and Sharon were introduced. Remembering that, he could better understand Myrtle becoming engaged to Oliver after knowing him only a few hours. "I have a favor to ask of you, Heather."

Heather set her glass back on the table. "I'm ready and willing," she said. "And I have a question I'd like you to answer."

"Fair enough. Today I located Oliver's two best friends, and one of them, Arlyn Jennings, knew the names of the boys Oliver's sisters ran away with."

"Arlyn Jennings?" repeated Heather. "That's the Humane Society attendant I hope to meet with on Monday."

"I don't understand."

"Olivia and her boyfriend gave Oliver's dog to the Humane Society. I'm waiting for Arlyn Jennings to return to work so he can tell me what he did with Max."

"Max?" Richard queried. "As in Maximilian?"

Myrtle looked up. "I suppose it could be Maximilian, but I only ever heard Oliver call him *Max.*"

"A golden retriever? About this high?" Richard measured a distance just over two feet from the floor.

"That describes Max all right."

Richard laughed. "Offhand I'd guess Oliver's friend recognized the dog and took him home rather than caging him."

"Thank goodness," cheered Myrtle.

Richard continued, "Mr. Jennings may have been so upset when he recognized Max, that he forgot to fill out the proper forms."

"Finding Oliver's dog is one problem solved," Heather said, smiling. "Now then, what can I help you with?"

Richard continued. "Now that we have the names of the young men Oliver's sisters were dating, I'd like you to see what you can find out about them."

"I'd be glad to do that," Heather responded.

"I have a question," Sally interrupted, addressing Richard. "I know you examined the accident scene. You probably even brought your own luminal kit." Richard nodded. It hadn't been easy, but he'd managed to get hold of blood-detecting spray sold only to law enforcement agencies. "Did you find anything our investigators missed?"

"Not a thing, although I still think Sharon's death wasn't an accident." Richard met Sally's questioning gaze with his own fierce stare. "It isn't that I think someone pushed her down those stairs, but I suspect that slippery little throw rug was put outside her door after she retired for the night." His voice broke. "What happened would have been inevitable. Sharon was always in a hurry.

"Chance said she had him take rolls of film cataloging Oliver's antiques. When those are developed, he'll send copies to me. I expect them to show that the day before Sharon's death, the little rug she tripped over was not on the second floor. My wife was tremendously upset with her cousin's dishonesty so it wouldn't take much to get her running from one room to another."

He paused and nodded at Heather. "Olivia and Vern will probably hold off stealing more treasures. However, another visit to that antique dealer might be a good idea."

"I agree, Richard. And you've just reminded me of something else." Heather nodded at Rachel. "We have a surprise for you."

Rachel went into the living room and retrieved a package she held up for Richard to see.

"Oliver's painting," he gasped. "No wonder you bought it, Myrtle. It's magnificent. I can't imagine ever growing tired of looking at it. You know, don't you, that you'll have to give it back?"

"I thought from the beginning I might have to," Myrtle said. "That's why I was careful to use a credit card. But when the heirs get ready to dispose of things, I'd like to buy it again, please."

"I'll keep that in mind." Richard pushed back his chair and stood. "Please excuse me for leaving now, but I was up late last night."

"We understand," Sally said. "You aren't sleeping at Oliver's, are you?"

"I wouldn't be, except that I wanted to spend tonight in the room that was Sharon's."

"I hope you won't underestimate Olivia and Vern."

"I'm a light sleeper, but you can bet my door will be locked with furniture piled against it. I have some personal things to take care of tomorrow, but let me know as soon as any of you get new information. I'll leave cell phone numbers that will reach me any time."

"Wait," Heather said. "I need an answer to my question."

Richard paused, giving her his full attention. "And it is?"

"If I wanted a list of people who took part in a trial or who served on a particular jury, where would I go?"

"Well, a lawyer might be able to subpoena a list of jurors and witnesses, assuming you went the legal route for that information."

"And if I didn't do it legally?"

"Then I suggest you bribe or threaten a court clerk."

As soon as the library opened Sunday, Heather began searching microfiche copies of back issues of the *Clarion,* looking for births or deaths of people with the names Richard had given her. She'd already checked on the internet, but with hundreds of hits for Dougie Fisher and none for Clint Warberg, tracing the Lewisburg runaways that way hadn't worked.

From the phone book she created a list of people named Fisher still living in Lewisburg. As soon as church services ended, she intended to call them. With luck, one of the Fisher families still in Lewisburg, might be related to the missing Dougie.

At the Lloyd residence that Sunday morning, Olivia seemed no better than the day before. Whatever problem her body was battling had not gained on her, but it also had not given up. She was refusing to eat or to see a doctor, even though her current problems included abdominal pain, and vision difficulties. When she complained of being cold, Vern pulled blankets from a hall closet and piled them on her.

Richard offered his help that morning as he packed his wife's belongings in the Hummer, but Olivia declined. He left then, looking for a quiet place where he could compose his wife's obituary and make a few phone calls to prepare a resting place for her close to home. In only a few hours, he needed to head back to Seattle.

Vern continued feeding Olivia aspirin and chicken soup, but nothing he did seemed to help. He knew he had to protect her. She needed to be well enough to attend their wedding on Monday.

"Vern, honey," she mumbled, "I'm warmer now, but I think I'd feel better if I had some ice cream. Do we have any?"

"I'll check," he said, heading downstairs to look in the freezer. On his return he said, "Looks like we're out."

"Could you get me some, please?"

"Sure, Sweetheart. I'll go to the store right now. Will you be all right if I leave you alone for a while?"

Olivia smiled. "What have you done to your face? It looks fuzzy this morning. Didn't you shave?"

It was while Vern searched among ice cream flavors at the grocery store that Binky's son Tommy arrived at the Lloyd's front door and found it unlocked.

"Anyone home?" he asked, pushing the door open.

Tommy was reasonably sure everyone had gone, although he hadn't actually seen how many were in the car that had just left. He didn't expect today's visit to be anything like the last one at this house, when he'd thought he was alone and a stranger started yelling at him. That woman had been so upset she took a header down the stairs. What a corker that had been, seeing her with her neck twisted as if looking behind her. He knew the house contained small antiques that he could pawn, and today, with no dead woman on the stairs, he'd be able to collect them.

But then, remembering what good scotch he'd discovered the day of the accident, and the fine toasted cheese sandwich he'd fixed a couple of days before that, he let his appetite take him to the kitchen.

"Is this the Fisher residence?" Heather asked after dialing the first name on her list.

"Who's calling?" shouted a man.

"I'm trying to locate Dougie Fisher," Heather said, moving the cell phone closer to her mouth. "Dougie went to Lewisburg High School about thirty years ago. Are you related to him?"

"Don't want any," Abe Fisher shouted back. "Never read that kind of thing." He hung up.

Puzzled, but not discouraged, Heather dialed the George Fishers, where she had no better luck getting information. After talking to the Harlan Fishers, two James Fishers, a Rachel Fisher and one Thomas Fisher, she hit pay dirt.

"Yep! I knew Dougie," replied Warren Fisher. "He was my mom's brother."

"Where does he live?" Heather asked, trying to curb her excitement. "Do you remember his wife's name?"

"He was married to Aunt Isabel, but she's gone now. They both are. They lived in Denver. Why are you asking?"

"Isabel's family has been searching for her and Evelyn, and any of their children. Did Isabel and Dougie have children?"

"Just my cousin Brian. Would you like his phone number?"

###

IDENTIFY THE HEIRS

Start with letter O: O

Move one space north.   __

Move two spaces north & two spaces west.   __

Move two spaces east.   __

Move one space west.   __

Move three spaces west & three south.   __

Move three spaces north.   M

Move two spaces east and two spaces south.   __

Move one space east.   __

Move two spaces north and two spaces west   __

Move one space west and one space south.   __

Move four spaces east.   __

Move two spaces south and one space west.   __

Move one space west.   R

Move two spaces west and one space north   __

Move one space east.   __

Move one space north.   __

Move one space east.   __

Move one space east.   __

Move two spaces west and two spaces south.   __

Move four spaces north.   B

Move one space west.   __

Move four spaces east.   __

Move 2 spaces west.   __

Move 1 space east.   __

R	B	A	N	I
M	I	I	I	V
L	H	A	R	Y
I	C	A	R	L
A	D	R	N	O

CHAPTER 17

Olivia noticed a blurry figure in the shadows of her bedroom doorway. "Vern, Honey? What are you holding? Have you brought an entire gallon of ice cream upstairs?"

At that moment a clock chimed.

"Oh! It's a clock you're holding, isn't it? What did you do with the ice cream?"

The figure in the doorway gasped and nearly dropped the antique he'd just removed from one of the bedrooms. Once again Tommy wasn't alone in this house.

He backed out of Olivia's doorway and headed for the stairs. At the top he skidded to a stop, and dashed into the bedroom where he'd found the clock. He returned it to the dresser, then rushed down the stairs and out the front door. He was in such a hurry to get away that he didn't stop for the rest of the tasty chicken salad he'd planned to polish off.

###

"Fisher residence," came the cheerful response once Heather curbed her excitement long enough to place a call to Denver. "This is Brian speaking."

"Mr. Fisher, my name is Heather Samuelson. I've called you because Oliver Lloyd's family in Lewisburg, Oregon, asked me to search for information concerning Isabel Lloyd Fisher and her sister Evelyn. Their brother Oliver died Wednesday and the family wanted them to know."

"Isabel was my mom, but she's been dead for two years. I didn't know she had a brother."

"He was a few years younger than your mom. Do you have any brothers or sisters?"

"No, there's just me."

"The family will be delighted to have found you. Did you know your Aunt Evelyn?"

"I think that was the name of Mom's sister, but she died before I was born."

"Do you know if she married or had children?"

"I have no idea."

"How about her last name. Could it have been Warberg?"

"I don't think so. I think it was Lloyd."

"Do you know where she died? Which state?"

"I'm sorry, but I don't."

"Thanks for being patient with me. I have only one or two more questions. First of all, the family has always wondered why your mother didn't stay in touch after high school."

"That's easy. She and my dad left Oregon as soon as he graduated. I think Mom was already pregnant, but not married. She didn't want her family to know. The world was a different place thirty years ago."

"Yes it was. You have two cousins in Oregon. I could give you their phone numbers, if you'd like to have them."

"Probably not. We've gotten along all these years without knowing each other. But since you're checking on the family, are you interested in knowing about my Aunt Margret? I think her last name was Lloyd. That's the only family mom kept in touch with."

Heather grabbed her note pad. "What can you tell me about Margret?" It was a name Heather hadn't heard before.

"I think the reason mom stayed in touch with Maggie was because they both felt they'd disgraced their families. When Margret's husband died, she abandoned her only child to run away with the guy who was selling burial plots."

"Was Margret's child a girl?" Heather asked. "Could her name have been Olivia?"

"I don't think I ever heard."

"What happened to Margret?"

"She and the salesman stayed together for a while, but he finally left her. She was sick a lot after that and died in that flu epidemic we had a few years ago."

"Brian," Heather said. "You've been very helpful. If you have a pen handy, I'll give you the phone number for Chance Hamilton. He's the lawyer handling Oliver's estate."

"Does that mean there might be an inheritance?"

"Mr. Hamilton will answer that question for you," Heather said.

It would be Chance's job to let Brian know of his good fortune, and, to notify the rest of the Lloyd family of a further decrease in theirs.

"Aunt Myrtle, why are you sitting there?" Heather had returned from the library to find her aunt huddled in their carport. "It's hot out here. Why aren't you in the house?"

"You got a bomb threat," whispered Myrtle.

"A bomb threat?"

"The man on the phone told me to get out of the house because there was a bomb in it. I didn't even call 9-1-1; I just dropped the phone and ran out here."

"Where's Sally? Any bomb threats we get are probably related to something she's working on."

"After lunch she went back to work, so she wasn't here when the call came in. I didn't try to reach her and I didn't know where you were. I just hung up and left the house. The phone's been ringing a lot," she added, "but I've been afraid to answer it." They could hear the muffled sound of the ringing phone.

"Stay here," Heather said, rushing inside. She grabbed the receiver in time to hear someone hang up. However, messages on the answering machine were all of a male warning that the place was set to blow up and occupants should get out of the house as soon as possible. Heather immediately dialed Sally's work extension.

"Mom-m-m," moaned Tommy, stumbling against the kitchen doorway. He slowly sank to the floor.

"Tommy!" Binky screamed. "What's the matter?" She rushed to her son, still holding the ladle she'd used to stir cake batter. It dripped on Tommy's shirt as she knelt beside him.

"Mom-m-m," he moaned again.

"Tommy, speak up. What's wrong?"

He felt too weak to answer. Worse yet, there was something wrong with his eyes because he couldn't see clearly any more. Muscles throughout his body twitched like little volcanic eruptions and his heart raced uncontrollably. Drawing a deep breath was no longer possible.

"Tommy Fuely," Binky shouted. "Stop scaring me. You tell me what's wrong with you."

He wanted to answer, but it took more energy than he had. He wished now he'd told her about being in state prison and not an academy. He should also have explained where she could find a fortune in stolen jewelry, but now that the locks next door had been changed, his key no longer opened the door. His mom knew how to cook but she probably had no idea how to pick a lock.

He moaned.

Binky got to her feet and rushed from her house yelling, "Help! Help!" She spotted Myrtle in the Samuelson carport. "Help me. Tommy's on the floor and I can't get him up."

Myrtle responded by running to the Samuelson's front door and yelling hysterically for Heather who was still on the telephone.

"I'll call you back on my cell phone, Sally. We've got another emergency of some kind." Heather grabbed her cell phone and hurried outside to see what new problems had developed in what the realtor had called an "extremely quiet neighborhood."

Binky was standing beside Myrtle jabbering senselessly, but it was easy to understand her desperation. When she turned to run home, Heather followed, already dialing Sally's number. Inside the Bender house Tommy lay on the floor, his eyes closed; his body thrashing.

Binky dropped to her son's side and patted his arm. "Do something! Make him stop that shaking."

Heather took one look at the convulsing man and said, "Put a pillow under his head, Binky." To Sally she said, "Send an ambulance. It's Tommy Bender. I don't know what his initial symptoms were, but right now he's having convulsions and he's unresponsive."

"Not Bender," Binky corrected, "Fuely. Tommy's last name is Fuely."

By the time the ambulance arrived, Tommy's heart rate had slowed, but he was still unresponsive. The medical technicians hooked him to oxygen and a saline solution, then rushed off with him.

"I want to go, too," cried Binky, turning toward Heather, "but Baby's got the car. You've got to take me."

"Get rid of that gooey spoon first," Heather said, backing away from the distraught woman, "then we'll go."

As a bomb squad checked the Samuelson residence and the townhouses on either side, neighbors began congregating at a distance, interested in the activity. Like Myrtle, the Corbins had been escorted from their house to wait in the shade of a carport across the street.

The only quiet activity taking place in the community was happening a short distance from the danger of exploding bombs, as Olivia slowly but happily consumed chocolate ice cream.

At the hospital Heather continued supporting an hysterical Binky, leaving Sally to deal with bomb threats and their aunt. Recorded messages on the Samuelson's answering machine were now in the possession of the lead investigator who agreed with Sally that it sounded like kids playing a prank. Experience had taught the investigators that when pranksters made such calls, they often lived close enough to watch the activity their calls created. In a community of few children, suspicion pretty much rested on the Corbin brothers.

"Nothing shows up," the lead investigator reported when various searches failed to discover any explosives. "You're clear; but we put in a phone trap-and-trace line in case you get more calls."

"Thanks," Sally responded. "Good job."

"I almost forgot. Here's a tool belt we found on the floor by your furnace."

"How are Binky and her son doing," Myrtle asked when Heather returned from the hospital.

"The doctor gave her a strong sedative and Baby's with her now," Heather responded. "Tommy's in a coma."

"Has he had seizures before?" Sally asked.

"Not that anyone seems to know about," Heather answered. "It's unclear what caused this attack. The lab's checking for some kind of toxic exposure. All the doctor can do at the moment is treat Tommy's symptoms. His heart keeps stopping so his prognosis isn't encouraging."

"While I was on the line with you," Sally said, "did I hear Binky tell you that Tommy's last name isn't Bender?"

"Caught that, did you," laughed Heather. "I guess we should have listened more closely when the Bender twins said they'd been a decade walking in our door without knocking. With Binky's son living next to them, it's no wonder they felt at home here. By the way, there was a key to our townhouse in Tommy's pocket."

"If he was coming in here that might explain the food we've been missing." Sally was recalling Tom *Foolery's* modus operandi.

"Rachel's boys might be right about his loot still being here," Myrtle offered. "Why else would Tommy keep a key?"

"That might also explain the hammer and chisel the furnace repairman found and the tool belt the bomb squad picked up today," Heather added. "It might even explain why the furnace's cooling system works for a while, then stops."

Sally said, "As much as I hate the idea, perhaps we should do a bit of late spring house cleaning."

"It's too hot and our cooling system is on the fritz again." Heather looked from Sally's expectant face to Myrtle's. "What you're both suggesting is that we go on a treasure hunt. Surely you don't expect us to find something that trained officers have searched for and not found?"

"If the tools belonged to Tommy, and he was searching for something in our house," Sally studied her sister's demeanor, "then we need to figure out what he was looking for."

"And you'll help? This isn't just some harebrained scheme to get me cleaning this place all over again?" Heather focused a suspicious look at her sister.

"Need I remind you of the reward money being offered?"

Heather sighed, starting up the stairs. "Okay. Tomorrow I start the search." She headed for her office, ready to catch up on work, foremost of which was the discovery of where her mother had made a September reservation that hadn't been cancelled yet.

"Try eating a little more broth, Olivia dear. You need to be strong enough to go to the courthouse with me when it opens at noon. This is our wedding day."

It was Monday and Vern was alarmed at Olivia's dwindling health. He knew he couldn't waste time because she was going downhill more quickly than he'd expected. She could skip her uncle's memorial service, but she needed to be strong enough to take part in their marriage ceremony. He spooned chicken soup into lips barely open, and reminded her of the chicken salad she could eat after they were married. As soon as she rested, he'd help her get dressed and they'd head for the courthouse.

At Oliver's memorial service that Monday morning Heather Samuelson took note of those attending. She and the other Samuelsons were there, along with attorney Chance Hamilton, Oliver's two best friends, members of his cribbage club, and every antique dealer within a five hundred mile radius. Antique dealers had read the United Press story of Oliver's demise. Because heirs often didn't recognize the value of a deceased relative's assets, hopefuls in the antique furniture business had shown up eager to depart with treasures Oliver's heirs let slip through their fingers.

What Heather found surprising was that none of Oliver's relatives were at the service. No one expected Richard Bigelow, and Marilyn had called to say one of her children had chicken pox and she couldn't find a babysitter, but Olivia should have been there.

As the service ended and people began leaving, Myrtle approached a sad-eyed man who had been one of Oliver's best friends. "Mr. Jennings?" she inquired.

Arlyn turned and extended his hand toward the woman he suspected of being the one Oliver had been engaged to. The prankster had called Arlyn and Jerry as soon as Myrtle left his hospital room, bragging about having more vigor and vitality than anyone guessed. His friends had responded by teasing their buddy about his conquest of a lovely damsel.

"I'm Myrtle Wilson, a neighbor of Oliver's," Myrtle continued. "I understand you have Max. I want to thank you for not putting him in a cage at the Humane Society."

"Couldn't leave him in a cage," Arlyn answered, still clinging to Myrtle's right hand. "Ollie counted on Jerry and me to help with things he couldn't manage alone. Saving Max from the gas chamber is what he'd expect. Have you met Jerry yet?"

She shook her head. "He's talking to some of the others."

Arlyn beckoned to his friend.

"I promised Oliver," Myrtle continued, "that I'd take Max for walks and I was very upset when I discovered he'd been given away." With her left hand she gently tried to remove Arlyn's fingers from around her right hand.

"I don't wonder you were upset. If you'd still like to take Max for walks, stop in any time. I'm sure he could use more exercise than I'm able to give him."

"Who's this charmer ya'll got in your clutches," Jerry Delahugh asked as he approached his longtime friend.

"This is Myrtle Wilson, Jerry. She's that neighbor of Oliver's you and I have been wondering about."

"Yore right, ole buddy. But she's more'n just a neighbor." Jerry laughed, reaching out to claim Myrtle's left hand. His fingers massaged her ring finger. "She's the one, all right. This here's Ollie's ring she's wearin'."

The two men grinned like conspirators, displaying rings that matched the one Myrtle wore.

"You see," Myrtle began.

"No need to explain, you cute thing," Arlyn said. "Ollie called us right after you left the hospital that night. He was so pumped with you accepting his ring that they probably had to club him with a baseball bat to get him to sleep."

"Linny and me, we'd like to have coffee with you before you head back to Boston," Jerry added politely. "We got us something to worry over and thought you might help us figure it out, you being Ollie's intended."

###

When the courthouse opened at noon, Olivia and Vern were at the head of the line, ready to take their vows. Olivia felt better. After all, she was marrying the handsomest man she'd ever met. She was so busy thinking about life with Vern Higgins that when the judge asked if she'd take Vern as her husband, she didn't hear the question.

"Olivia, Dear?" Vern was perspiring as he whispered her name and nudged her. "The judge asked you a question." Twice he had dropped the onyx friendship ring he was getting ready to slip on Olivia's left hand at the proper time.

"I'm sorry," Olivia whispered, coyly. "Could the judge ask me again?"

###

Chance Hamilton successfully reached Brian Fisher Monday afternoon. "You'll need to keep in touch," Chance said. "Once bills are paid and antiques are disposed of, we'll be settling the estate."

"This is really exciting," Brian said. "Should I consider coming out there?"

"It wouldn't hurt," Chance agreed. "At least you'd get to meet your cousins." Following that phone call he contacted Marilyn and Olivia to report that their bachelor cousin, Brian Fisher of Denver, Colorado, had been found and would be joining them the next day.

The news of another heir hit the new bridegroom hard. "Damn," mumbled Vern. With four people dividing Oliver's assets that meant shares would amount to only twenty-five percent. Unless Oliver's fortune equaled the gold at Fort Knox, it wouldn't begin to pave the way to a better life for him and Chris.

How the heck could he get the numbers to move in the opposite direction?

Vern sat at the table with his bride, reassessing the matter. She was propped up in a kitchen chair eating what remained of the chicken salad she'd prepared two days earlier.

As Olivia munched on the salad, Vern struggled with the problem of too many heirs. It was fortunate Sharon was out of the picture, but her husband had been thrust into it, and he was no one's fool. Richard Bigelow knew only too well that he'd be inheriting his wife's estate, so getting rid of him not only wouldn't be easy, it would probably be impossible.

Then there was that sister of Sharon's with her pack of kids. If anything happened to Marilyn, her kids would get her share. Disposing of an entire family seemed like more trouble than Vern wanted to go to, no matter how much their demise might contribute to his needs.

With Marilyn and Richard in on the jackpot winnings permanently, that only left the newcomer in Denver to consider. If Brian Fisher was single, perhaps when he made his trip to Oregon, it would be the last traveling he ever did. Thirty-three percent was certainly better than a measly twenty-five percent, especially if Olivia's share didn't have to be shared with her.

Vern glanced at his new wife as she finished the salad that had been laced with the fresh *parsley* she'd liked so well. As he watched her, he made plans for greeting his new cousin-by-marriage.

Of course there was one more, small matter not to be overlooked, but once he sent the remaining poison hemlock down the garbage disposal, that wouldn't be around to draw anyone's curiosity.

Heather was at her computer when the doorbell rang. Before she could get out of her chair, it rang again, more insistently.

"I saw you come home," Helen Corbin explained apologetically once Heather came to the front door. "I need to talk to you."

Heather nodded. "Come in," she invited.

"I'm sorry about being so slow welcoming you to the neighborhood," Mrs. Corbin said, settling into the rocking chair near the fireplace. "And you've been very tolerant of Johnny and Joey. I just hope they haven't done something wrong." She bowed her head. "It's just that I found them playing pirates again."

"Does that mean they've been digging in the backyard?"

"Mostly it means they were burying treasure they found. I want to make sure one of those treasures doesn't belong to you." She handed Heather what appeared to be a very expensive diamond ring.

"It isn't mine," exclaimed Heather excitedly, "but it might be the one my aunt is missing. She's resting upstairs. Let me get her." Heather handed the ring back to Helen Corbin and dashed up the stairs to wake Myrtle.

"I'm sorry to bother you, Aunt Myrtle," Heather murmured softly, "but you're needed downstairs. One of our neighbors has found a ring and it might be the one you lost."

"I did not lose it, Heather," Myrtle chided, now fully awake. "How many times do I have to tell you? I hadn't even removed it from my jewelry box because I was saving it for a special occasion." Myrtle got out of bed and headed down the stairs.

The ring quickly exchanged hands.

"This ring *is* mine," Myrtle exclaimed. "Where did you get it?"

"My sons had it. They said they found it in that grassy stretch outside our back doors."

"That doesn't make sense," Myrtle replied. "I've been here eight days and hadn't worn it yet."

"But my boys have never been inside this house," Helen assured her. "I believe them when they say they found the ring in the yard. Of course that means it got out of your house without my boys being involved."

Tommy Fuely! The name leaped to Heather's mind. Perhaps he hadn't just entered their house looking for a treasure he'd left in it years ago. Perhaps he was up to his old tricks of stealing things.

"He died!"

The sad bulletin was delivered by Baby Bender just as Helen Corbin was leaving the Samuelson's. Great tears streamed down Baby's face. Helen, Myrtle and Heather surrounded the distraught woman.

"I'm so sorry, Baby," said Heather.

"Sorry," Helen Corbin added, escaping to her home.

"Sorry," murmured Myrtle, struggling to slip the newly found ring on her finger. It seemed to have shrunk in size during its absence.

"Come in and talk with us, Baby," Heather invited.

"Can't," Baby wept. "I gotta take care of Binky. She's in a bad way. She's sayin' there's no point even talkin' about ghosts if Tommy ain't gonna be living in this house no more."

Heather stared at her neighbor. Had the Bender sisters started the rumor of ghosts, hoping the house wouldn't sell so Tommy could own it again? "Does anyone know what happened to Tommy, or what caused his death?"

"Not yet. They said something about a *taxi-colony* report they're waitin' on. That's all we know."

"Toxicology," murmured Heather. "If we can help in any way, please let us know."

Baby nodded, and returned home.

"Aunt Myrtle," Heather said, noting the expensive sports car once more in the Lloyd carport, "I'm going to find out why Olivia missed the memorial service this morning."

"You go ahead, Heather. I'm headed for another little lay-down. You girls have too much going on around here. Ladies my age like things calmer and quieter."

"Believe me, Aunt Myrtle," Heather responded, "we youngsters like things calmer and quieter, too."

"Yeah, what do you want?" Vern asked, greeting Heather at the Lloyd's front door.

"I stopped by to see how Olivia is doing since she missed her uncle's memorial service this morning."

"Heather?" The weak voice belonged to a very pale, obviously ill Olivia. She shuffled from the kitchen toward the sound of voices at the front door. "Is that you, Heather?" She could no longer recognize either the woman at the door, or the man who opened it.

"Olivia," Heather responded in alarm. "You're ill. No wonder you weren't at the memorial service."

"I got married, Heather." Olivia heaved a sigh and reached for the support of Vern's arm. "This's…my…husband." Her slow speech was a testimony to the effort each word took. "Vern, Honey," Olivia moaned. "I doan feel sooo gooood." Her voice faded to a whisper as she collapsed to the floor.

"Call 9-1-1," shouted Heather, trying to support Olivia's head as she began convulsing. When Vern didn't move she shouted at him again. "Call 9-1-1. Now!"

This time Vern rushed to the telephone. He dialed the appropriate number and delivered the emergency message. "They said they'd have an ambulance here right away," he assured Heather. "What's the matter with Olivia?"

"I have no idea, but these are the same symptoms that Binky's son had yesterday."

"I don't know any Binky," Vern responded.

"She's one of the cookie ladies," Heather explained.

"Her son collapsed? With convulsions?"

The ambulance arrived, and Heather was spared further conversation with Vern.

"Another one?" the medical technician asked in surprise, having been to Taborhill the day before. Again a saline drip was started, oxygen was supplied, and with their patient unresponsive, the emergency crew rushed off.

"What should I do?" Vern asked.

"Maybe you should consider driving to the hospital to see how your wife is doing," Heather responded.

"I-I," he stammered, displaying trembling hands that would have made driving unsafe.

"Okay, come with me," Heather sighed. "I'll drive."

###

ASK THE RIGHT QUESTIONS

	1	2	3	4	5	6	7	8
A	Y	L	T	S	D	V	O	I
B	R	C	P	B	M	G	K	E
C	G	W	T	E	N	N	H	A
D	R	E	R	D	O	L	U	R

C3, C7, B8   B7, A8, D6, A2, C4, D8

B1, D2, A6, B8, C8, D6, A4   B2, A2, D7, C4, A4

T__ _____ _____ _____

CHAPTER 18

"What's taking that doctor so long?" asked Vern. "I want to know how Olivia's doing." He'd been pacing the hospital waiting room for the last hour.

"Where are you from, Vern?" asked Heather, "before Rhode Island, I mean."

"Kansas," he blurted out. "I went to college at the University of Kansas. In Lawrence. Where's that damn doctor? Why isn't he letting us know how Olivia's doing? Do you think she regained consciousness? Do you think she's able to talk?"

"The doctor is probably so busy trying to save her life that he doesn't have time to chat with us. Tell me more about your background. It will keep your mind off how sick Olivia is."

Vern threw himself into a chair and studied Heather's face for a moment. "I loved pharmacy, right from the beginning. For a while I thought about pharmacognosy—the study of medicinal plants, but at that time herbal medicine wasn't popular. I got good grades, but . . . but . . . . It's not working. Where's that doctor? I'm going to be sick."

"The men's room is to your left," said Heather, pointing.

Vern rushed down the hall and disappeared through the appropriate door.

While he was gone, Heather put in a call to Sally.

"What's going on at Taborhill?" Sally asked. "Tom Fuely died this morning, and now you're telling me Olivia's in the hospital with the same symptoms?"

"As nearly as I could tell the symptoms were the same. She greeted me, but her speech was extremely slow. When she walked toward me it looked like she was having trouble, either with her balance or with her vision. Maybe both. She announced she'd gotten married to that guy she's been hiding, then collapsed. I'm at the hospital with him now. He was too shaken to drive.

"After Olivia collapsed, she went into convulsions. See if you can get the lab to rush their results on Tom Fuely. With two of our neighbors collapsing with identical symptoms, we need to find out if there's something in the neighborhood we've all been exposed to."

"I'll tell them to put a rush on it," Sally replied. "Until then, let's put anything that comes from the Bender house off to one side in case we need to run tests on it later. Those baked goods are probably the only link between the Benders and the Lloyds."

"Good thinking. Consider the food taken care of. I'll call Aunt Myrtle and warn her."

An hour later, Heather drove Vern back to the Lloyd residence to get his car, then she hurried home to make sure the Bender treats would not be eaten. That done, she called Chance Hamilton to report on Olivia's health.

"Thanks for the information," Chance replied. "By the way, I sent a set of the pictures I took at Oliver's to Richard Bigelow this morning. Special delivery. My guess is that when he sees them he'll return to Lewisburg."

"Could I have a set? It would help me identify any of Oliver's antiques still in Vivian Dexter's Treasure Trove. I'm going to check her shop again tomorrow."

"Good idea. Stop by the office. I had some extras made in case they were needed."

When Richard Bigelow returned to his office, his secretary handed him Heather's phone messages and Chance Hamilton's pictures cataloging the antiques in Oliver's house when Sharon arrived.

Richard closed his office door and settled wearily in the leather chair behind his art deco desk. Sharon's funeral was set for the next day and saying a final farewell to the woman he'd loved for a decade saddened him.

He sighed and pulled the Hamilton photos from their envelope, studying each one carefully. It was obvious Oliver Lloyd had collected antique furniture and art worth a fortune, but not enough to give him the reputation of being well-heeled. Richard stopped sorting through the pictures. What else could a collector of things from the past find to invest in? There were several interesting options, but pursuing them would have to wait for another day.

And then he noticed the picture of Oliver's upstairs hallway.

The slippery rug that caused Sharon's death had not been upstairs when the pictures were taken. Vern Higgins had lied. The rug had shown up later, perhaps after Sharon went to bed. Pinning the blame on the guilty party would be difficult, and if Olivia died, her new husband would certainly lay the matter entirely at her feet.

Someone at Oliver's wanted money badly enough to have fed him blood thinners prior to his surgery, and to arrange for Sharon to have a deadly accident. Richard rested his elbows on his desk. Would he be a target as the killer worked at eliminating heirs? As soon as Sharon's funeral was over, he'd take a little time off. He'd see if he could help the Lewisburg prosecutors deal with their serial killer before there were more victims.

Richard reached for his phone and dialed. "Chance!" he greeted, when the other attorney responded. "Thanks for the pictures. They arrived this morning."

"My pleasure. You must have noticed that upstairs hallway, just as I did."

"I saw it," Richard answered. "The rug Sharon tripped over wasn't there when she arrived."

"Something bad is going on in that house, Richard. First with those anticoagulant pills they fed Oliver, and then with the rug outside Sharon's bedroom door."

"I hope you got all of the important papers out of there."

"As many as I could find. Olivia married her boyfriend this morning, and, if you've heard from Heather recently, you'll know that the new husband hasn't wasted any time. Olivia is in critical condition."

"Vern's not willing to share Olivia's inheritance even with Olivia, is he? That leaves only Marilyn, me, and the nephew in Denver between him and the whole pot."

"My God! Brian's on his way to Lewisburg and he plans to stay in that house."

"Single man, isn't he? That makes him more vulnerable."

"True."

"Keep him out of there, Chance, or we'll have another dead body on our hands."

"I'll see if I can get him stopped."

"How are you doing in there?" asked Aunt Myrtle, crouching beside the low doorway leading to the furnace. A light bulb with a thin pull chain glowed dimly in the attic opening.

"I haven't found anything yet, Aunt Myrtle," Heather responded. She crawled from behind the furnace to the doorway. Ducking through it, she joined her aunt in the hallway, and stood slowly. "That's better." She heaved a sigh and flexed her back muscles. "It's hot under there and I didn't find even a hint of where Tommy Fuely hid his loot."

"Let's get you downstairs where it's cooler."

"Good idea." Heather turned off the light in the furnace area and closed the door.

"Don't give up," Myrtle said as she and Heather walked down the stairs. "Tommy's stolen jewels have to be somewhere close to the new furnace."

"Do you want to crawl around and help me look?" Heather laughed at the image of her aging auntie on hands and knees bumping face first into cobwebs.

"If you want help," Myrtle said, "get Rachel's boys. They should be able to explore tighter spaces than you can squeeze into."

"Good idea," Heather responded. "But after I rest a while, I'll have another cobwebby look by myself."

###

It was almost dinnertime. Heather had stopped crawling among the cobwebs, and had taken a refreshing bath. She was now preparing dinner.

"Heather?" Sally's shout came from their front doorway.

"Coming." Heather ran to her sister's aid. "What is it?"

"My inspection team and I have to enter the Bender house next door. I'd like you to run interference. You take care of the occupants while we search for the cause of Tommy's death."

"Do you know what caused it?" Heather dried her hands on her apron as she slipped out of it.

"Conium maculatum," Sally said. "Poison hemlock."

"Like Socrates was forced to drink?" Heather followed Sally to the Bender's front door.

Sally nodded at her teammates as one of the investigators rang the Bender's doorbell. "Apparently not a liquid concoction this time," she replied. "Tommy apparently ate part of the plant. It really doesn't matter whether it was the leaves, roots, or stems. Or even the seeds. Any part of that plant is poisonous."

"Yes?" Baby had opened the Bender's front door. "Yes?" she repeated.

"Baby, we're sorry to trouble you, but we need to look around inside your house." Sally handed her a copy of a search warrant.

"What's this paper? And why're you wantin' to come in?"

"That paper is a search warrant. It gives us permission to look around inside. We think we know what made Tommy sick. We just want to make sure there's not more of it around. We don't want you and Binky getting sick."

"I came with them to see how Binky's doing," interrupted Heather, stepping forward. "Why don't the two of us talk to her? We'll stay out of the way and let Sally's helpers do what they need to do."

"George," Sally said, nodding at the tall officer. "You take the exterior. Abel and I will take care of things inside." She nodded to Abel Fryer and he disappeared into the Bender's kitchen. Sally turned to Baby, "Could you please show me Tommy's room?"

"Binky's in there and she won't come out."

"Let's talk to her." Heather put her arm around Baby as they started up the stairs.

"Binky," Baby whispered as they stepped into the first bedroom. "These folks think they know what killed Tommy. They're wantin' to see if it's something that'll make you and me sick."

Heather leaned over Binky, now curled in a fetal position. She patted the older woman gently. "You've had a hard couple of days. Why don't you sit up and eat some soup?"

"No," howled Binky, fresh tears running down her face. "My only son is gone forever. He's not coming back this time. What will I do without him?"

"Like I said," Baby put in, "you can share my Jimmie Joe. He'll be here soon."

"Detective," it was Abel in the doorway behind them. "This was in their refrigerator." He held a damp paper towel that had been wrapped around leafy green sprigs.

Sally examined it and nodded. "Ladies?" She turned toward the bed where the sisters were comforting each other. "Can either of you tell me where this came from?" She held the carefully preserved poison hemlock sprigs where the sisters could see them.

Baby leaned over to examine the contents of the paper towel. "Oh, that's the stuff Oliver's niece gave us. Binky's been cookin' desserts so we didn't need no parsley."

"Would Tommy have eaten some of this if he found it in your refrigerator?" Sally asked. "You know, just nibbled at it or made a sandwich and added some to the sandwich?"

"I doubt it. Mostly, he was eating his meals out and just coming home for desserts."

"If Olivia gave the hemlock to the Benders, there has to be some of it growing at Oliver's," Heather said. "It couldn't have been transported from Rhode Island and arrived in such good condition."

Sally nodded and dialed the hospital. "Doctor Evans," she said when the resident finally came to the phone. "We think Olivia Lloyd ate poison hemlock."

"That news comes too late, Detective Samuelson. She died a few minutes ago. The medical examiner is getting ready for an autopsy and the usual toxicology screens. Olivia's death and that of her neighbor, Tommy Fuely, have the staff on full alert."

"Will Olivia's husband give permission for an autopsy?"

"We may not need his permission."

Sally broke the connection and thanked the Bender sisters. Since George Hilbert hadn't located hemlock growing in the garden outside of the Bender home, Sally quickly moved the inspection team across the street to the Lloyd residence so they could examine the grounds around Oliver's house. In his backyard they found a fairly-well stripped plant that they photographed, pulled and then bagged.

"I thought you'd be interested in knowing that Olivia died this afternoon," Heather said when she called Richard Bigelow. "She'd been eating poison hemlock."

"Where would she get that? I didn't think it grew in this country."

"I went on-line to learn about it. It's a weed introduced to North America from Europe and it's poisonous to people and animals. One of the few places it grows is in the Pacific Northwest. Oliver had one of those weeds in his garden."

"Does it resemble parsley in any way?"

"The leaves do."

"My God," Richard gasped. "I was there when Olivia told me Vern picked a rare kind of parsley for her from her uncle's garden. The fact that it was uncommon was why she was anxious to taste it. She'd had a small sample and thought its peppery flavor would go nicely with the bland chicken salad she'd prepared. She offered me that salad for my lunch."

"If Vern knew it was introduced to this country from Europe, then he had to know what it was."

"I agree. That bastard intended even then to kill Olivia. As soon as I can clear my calendar, I'm coming back to Lewisburg. I want that jerk's hide nailed to a wall."

"Let us know when you get to town. You're invited for breakfast, lunch, dinner and any other meals. We will not be fixing salads."

###

WATCH OUT, VERN

R + 2 =	D − 3 =	A + 2 =	D − 3 =	W + 2 =
D + 4 =	X − 6 =	K + 4 =	H − 2 =	R − 3 =
A + 4 =	A + 4 =	K + 2 =	R + 2 =	Q + 4 =
W + 2 =		K − 2 =	A + 4 =	
		K + 3 =	T − 2 =	
		D + 3 =		

T _ _ _   _ _ _   _ _ _ _ _ _   _ _ _ _ _   _ _ _

CHAPTER 19

"Do you know anything about Vern's background?" Heather asked her sister that evening.

Sally nodded. "We got some of the information at the marriage license bureau, and we're in touch with people in Rhode Island who are very good at tracking disreputable individuals. Knowing where Vern worked as a pharmacist gives us a head start on learning about him."

"At the hospital I tried to keep his mind off of Olivia. He told me he'd grown up in Kansas and attended the university in Lawrence."

"Nice going, Sis! That will help."

"Are you girls suggesting the man Olivia married deliberately poisoned her?" Myrtle asked.

"It looks that way, Aunt Myrtle," Heather replied.

"But Tommy died of the same thing. Did that man poison him, too?"

"We think Tommy was breaking into houses," Sally responded, "probably stealing things he could pawn, and eating whatever he found in their refrigerators. His mom only fixes desserts."

Heather added, "Richard Bigelow told me Olivia made a chicken salad while he was there. She told him it contained a rare kind of parsley Vern picked for her. It was probably poison hemlock he picked, and not parsley. We're assuming Tommy broke into the Lloyd house and ate some of Olivia's salad. If he did, that's where he got the poison."

"And when Olivia ate it, then she died, too?" Myrtle's eyes filled with tears.

"We can be sure her polite husband declined the salad because he knew what it contained," Heather said. "He let her eat it, probably not knowing Tommy had been in their house and had eaten some."

"Olivia didn't know it was poisonous, did she?" Myrtle continued.

Heather shook her head. "I don't think she'd have shared it if she'd known. And she certainly wouldn't have eaten any herself. I think she gave some to the Bender sisters as a special treat, to thank them for the cookies and cakes they were bringing over. It's a good thing none of their cookie recipes called for parsley, or there's no telling how many people those sisters could have done away with."

"The scientists from the U.S. Department of Agriculture are going to check our area for more hemlock," Sally volunteered. "That plant needs to be destroyed. There's no telling how many years it's been growing in Oliver's yard, or how many seeds it's scattered."

The ringing telephone interrupted their conversation.

"I tried to reach Brian Fisher before he left Denver," Chance said to Heather. "I wanted to warn him about staying at Oliver's."

"Thank goodness," Heather said.

"You don't understand! He's already on his way. I left a message on his answering machine, but since I didn't reach him in person, I'm hoping you'll keep an eye out for his arrival. Talk him into staying elsewhere. I don't think it's safe for him to be alone with Mr. Higgins."

Because the plane from Denver to Portland had been overbooked, Brian politely gave up his seat and took a later flight. Then, instead of renting a car and driving straight to Lewisburg, he reconsidered. He was not about to pass up the chance to see the Pacific Ocean. With a bit of sightseeing in mind he arrived in Portland on the later flight, picked up his rental car, and drove to a motel to settle down for the night.

Earlier in the evening when the first plane from Denver was landing, Portland's airport paging system repeatedly asked Brian Fisher to pick up a white phone. Had he arrived on the early flight and been able to do so, he could have avoided renting a car. His cousin-by-marriage was waiting to drive him to Lewisburg via a nice little riverside dumping ground that Vern found before he discovered Oliver's garden with its poisonous plant.

###

The Samuelson phone rang shortly after two o'clock in the morning.

"Yes," murmured Heather, coming out of a deep sleep. She'd been dreaming of cool breezes and sandy beaches in a Hawaii she'd only heard of but never visited. "Yes," she repeated.

"You gotta bomb in your house," whispered a voice. "You better get outta there while you can." The line went dead.

"Perfect," Heather said, now wide awake and ready to solve at least one of the puzzles she was working on. She rushed into Sally's bedroom. "Wake up, Sally. We just got another bomb threat. Call your department. I'll make coffee."

Sally was awake instantly. "Nice going," she said, dialing the station. "It's Samuelson. We need an emergency trace. We just got another bomb threat. Track it and get back to me."

"Do you have to go to work this early?" asked sleepy-eyed Aunt Myrtle from Sally's doorway. She was yawning and trying to clear sleep from her eyes.

"I'm waiting for a call. We just got another bomb threat."

Myrtle became wide awake immediately.

"It's okay, Auntie. We are not going to leave the house. I think I know who's been making these calls, but I want to have the trace verify my hunch."

Myrtle sat on the edge of Sally's bed. "Are the calls related to some case you're working on?"

Sally laughed. "No! I think they're related to a couple of boys who aren't going to reach their teenage years if they don't stop screwing around, trying to scare folks."

"Tim and Tom wouldn't do that," Myrtle said. "You can't think that they would."

"I wasn't thinking of the twins. Try Johnny and Joey."

"Oh, no. That poor widowed Mrs. Corbin. She already has her hands full."

"If her boys don't get a firm hand applied, there's no telling where they'll take their spurts of creative energy."

"Coffee's ready," Heather called from the bottom of the stairs.

"You aren't going to wake the Corbin's this early in the morning, are you?" Myrtle asked. She zipped her robe and headed for the stairs.

"You mean wake their mom, don't you? Those boys are already wide awake." Sally padded to her closet for a robe.

"Why do you suppose they're making those calls?" Myrtle asked.

"When you can't sleep, it can be lots more fun watching cops outside your window than seeing them on television."

"Talk about a reality show," Heather mumbled, pouring coffee into three cups.

"Exactly," Sally replied, settling down to wait for the next phone call. "Do we have any cookies? Some from the grocery store?"

"Mrs. Corbin?" The investigator who knocked on Helen Corbin's door at eight o'clock that same morning flashed his badge at Helen. "I'm George Hilbert, from the Lewisburg Police Department."

"Yes?" Helen replied, giving a couple of futile swipes to her tangled hair. She pulled her bathrobe more tightly around her.

"I'm sorry to bother you so early, but I'd like to come in and chat with you and your sons."

"What's this about?" Helen asked, standing her ground.

"It's about the bomb threats your neighbors have been getting."

"Oh! Come right in," she invited. "I've been worried about those threats. If my neighbors have a bomb in their house, my sons and I are in danger. Please, have a seat." She gestured toward her sparsely furnished living room. "I've just made a pot of coffee. Would you like a cup?"

"I would very much like some coffee, if you don't mind." George took a seat and waited while the attractive woman filled two cups and handed him one.

"Cream? Sugar?"

"Black, please."

"I'm sorry that I'm not dressed properly," Helen apologized, "We were sleeping late. All our bedrooms are on the second floor where it's extremely hot. We don't have air conditioning so these terrible July temperatures make sleep difficult."

"I'd like to have your boys join us, if you wouldn't mind."

"They're still sleeping."

"I think they'll want to hear what I have to say as much, maybe more, than you do. Please?" he asked.

Helen nodded and left the room, returning in a few minutes with two sleepy sons in pajama shorts. Her hair had been tamed slightly and a little lipstick applied.

"Hello, boys," George greeted, standing to shake hands with them. "I'm Lieutenant Hilbert and I'm with the Lewisburg Police Department. Which of you is Joey and which is Johnny?"

The boys identified themselves and waited quietly.

"Did you know that one of the ladies living next door to you is a police officer?"

"So?" Johnny responded.

"So, when a police officer gets threatened, her buddies take it seriously. You see, we do what we can to protect each other. After all, a police officer's job is to catch bad guys. If an officer is having her sleep interrupted by people telling her there's a bomb in her house when there isn't one, she won't be able to do her job the way she should. Do you follow me so far?"

"Sorta," Joey responded. "Are you saying she shouldn't be getting calls at night?"

"Not when there really isn't an emergency. Not when the callers are having trouble sleeping because their bedroom is too hot and they don't know what else to do."

"Wait just one minute," Helen interrupted. "Are you suggesting my boys made those calls to Sally and Heather?"

"What do you think, boys? Am I suggesting you made those calls?" George waited for the boys to answer.

"So, how are you going to protect your police buddies against calls like that?" asked Johnny, ignoring the previous question.

"For starters we're going to hook up a trace line to her phone. That means that every phone call she gets from then on can be traced back to the telephone where the call was made."

"Can you do that?" Joey asked.

"We can and we did. We can even tell when a caller hangs up without the call having been answered." He studied the boys as they digested his information.

"Now then, this morning at ten minutes after two, our police officer next door got one of those threatening calls that interrupted her sleep and worried her for a while. Of course there wasn't really any bomb in her house."

"Cut to the chase, officer," interrupted Helen. "Let's hear the phone number where that call originated."

Lieutenant Hilbert focused a sad look at Helen Corbin and recited her phone number.

Helen paled, and looked at her sons. "Boys?" she asked.

"I told him we shouldn't do that anymore," Joey said. "We couldn't sleep, Mom. It's boring when we can't sleep and you won't let us watch late night television."

Helen Corbin buried her face in her hands. Silent tears slid down her cheeks. "I'm so embarrassed," she murmured. "I thought I was raising such good boys and now I find that..."

"Mrs. Corbin," George said sympathetically. "Don't be too hard on yourself or the boys. Just get an air conditioner installed so everyone can sleep through the night. July's hot weather will end soon."

"That's a very good idea, Lieutenant," she agreed, drying her eyes. "But my boys owe you and all the others some apologies."

"I'm sorry," Johnny said. "I won't do that anymore."

"I'm sorry, too," Joey added. "Mom, does this mean we'll be grounded until time to collect our social security?"

"I'm thinking of grounding you even longer than that," Helen assured the guilty parties.

CHAPTER 20

"There's a police car at the Corbins," Heather said, entering the house with the morning newspaper tucked under one arm. "I hope they aren't having problems."

"I think Helen will be able to handle things just fine," responded Sally. "Except, perhaps for the bill she'll receive for the bomb squad. I don't think she has a lot of extra cash."

"Do you think her boys will do any more phoning in the middle of the night?"

Sally smiled. "I'm sure the lecture Lieutenant Hilbert is delivering will straighten out their active imaginations."

"When I finish breakfast," Heather continued, "I'm going to stop at Mr. Hamilton's office and pick up a set of the pictures he took at Oliver's. Then I'm going to pay a visit to the Treasure Trove. If Tommy Fuely was eating at Oliver's, then the chance of him stealing things from there must be pretty good. The pictures will help me identify any questionable antiques in Dexter's shop."

"Give me a jingle if you find anything. I'll get a warrant and join you as fast as I can."

After Heather studied the pictures the attorney took, she drove to the Treasure Trove, ready to scout out any items belonging to Oliver As she entered the shop, Vivian Dexter jumped to her feet.

"May I help you?"

"Thanks," Heather replied, "but I think I'll just look around."

"Do I know you?" Vivian asked. "I usually don't forget a face."

"I accompanied my aunt when she bought an oil painting from you. She's very pleased with it." Heather turned her back on the proprietor, ready to survey the shop's contents.

Along with miscellaneous kitchen bric-a-brac there were antique lamps, spittoons, a collection of teddy bears, and a small grouping of clocks. A mantle clock caught Heather's attention and she opened her purse.

"Where did I put it?" she mumbled, sorting through pictures. Finally she found the one displaying the mantle at Oliver's. On it was the mate to the clock now sitting on the Treasure Trove's table. "This is remarkable," Heather said, picking up the clock. "Tell me about this lovely piece."

"You have a fine eye," Vivian complimented her, looking over the top of her reading glasses. "That clock is the best of those in that collection. It only came in a week ago. It's a French eight-day porcelain-panel mantle clock from the early nineteen hundreds."

"My aunt gave some of her antique furniture to me and my sister. We expect to furnish our house with matching bits of history. This might fit in perfectly." Heather turned the clock around to study its back

"You couldn't do better," Vivian said, "and it still works."

"I need to look around a bit more," Heather said, stalling for time. "Maybe the thing to do is call my sister. If she agrees that this is something we want, we'll take it with us today."

"You can use my phone," Vivian offered.

"No thanks." Heather whipped out her cell phone to punch in a programmed number.

"Detective Samuelson," Sally announced, answering her phone.

"Hi, Sally," Heather said, smiling at Vivian Dexter. "I'm at the Treasure Trove. I think I've found exactly the right clock to sit among our antiques."

"Are you saying you found something of Oliver's at the Treasure Trove?"

"It's true."

"And you have a picture of his clock so a comparison can be made?"

"That's right."

"I'll get a warrant and join you. Stall!" Sally broke the connection.

"That's what I'm doing," Heather told the dead receiver, as she continued holding it against her ear. "I'll hang on to it so no one else can come in and buy it." She paused for a while. "Okay, but don't take too long." She nodded, finally hanging up. "She's on her way. One of the advantages of a small town like ours is that everything in it is only five or ten minutes away from everything else. I'll look around while I'm waiting."

"It was good of you to join us, Myrtle," Jerry Delahugh said, pulling out a chair for Myrtle. "I hope you don't mind an early lunch."

"It isn't every day two handsome men invite me to dine with them." Myrtle smiled, nodding at the men who had been Oliver's best friends.

"It's no wonder Oliver was excited about hooking up with you," laughed Arlyn Jennings. "If you'll stick around, Jerry and I will try filling Ollie's shoes." He gave Myrtle a hopeful look.

"Actually, when I get back to the house today I plan to make arrangements for my flight home."

"We better git us on with it then," Jerry said, pulling a paper from his breast pocket.

Arlyn pulled a similar paper from one of his pockets.

Myrtle watched, fascinated. Carefully the men unfolded their documents.

"These are copies of papers Ollie gave us," Arlyn explained. "He said they would make sure we got a little something after he died."

"Linny and I ain't greedy," Jerry added. "But we could both use a little more cash than what Social Security gives us each month."

"I understand," Myrtle assured them, looking at the typed, signed and notarized documents. "I just don't know what you expect me to do with these."

"If'n what we hear is right," Jerry continued, "something happened, so that Ollie's will isn't any good."

"That's what they tell me," Myrtle replied. "But these should probably go to the attorney handling the estate."

"We called him, but he said they weren't any good. He said if we got anything at all it was up to the heirs to give it to us out of their shares."

Jerry spoke up. "We was hoping you'd take these copies to that Olivia and . . ."

Myrtle said, "I'm sorry to give you bad news, but Olivia died yesterday."

"Seems like lots of people in your area are dying," Arlyn said.

"The girls think there's a serial murderer on the loose. At the moment he's after Oliver's heirs."

"Is there one of those heirs still alive who might be willing to honor Ollie's wishes?" Arlyn asked.

Myrtle smiled. "I'll bet the attorney whose wife fell will help. He likes taking on tough cases and the girls tell me he's coming back to town."

"We knowed you'd have answers," Jerry crowed contentedly.

"Hold on to your documents until Richard shows up," Myrtle replied. "Now then, I have a favor to ask of you."

"What's that?"

"I want to give you Oliver's ring. I only knew him one day and his ring will mean more to you than it does to me."

Arlyn and Jerry looked at each other and nodded. Each held up his left hand to show off matching rings. "We all three bought matching rings. Why don't you keep Ollie's, or give it to someone in his family?"

Myrtle pulled on the ring. "I'll see which of the others might like to have it," she said, twisting it back and forth. "I shouldn't have eaten all those cookies and things," she whispered as she pulled. "Now I'm paying for it. I'll probably have to go to a jeweler and have the ring cut off."

"Why don't you wait until morning?" Arlyn suggested. "You'll have better luck then."

"There's my sister," Heather announced as a police car pulled up in front of the Treasure Trove.

"Your sister's a cop?"

"She is."

"Hello, Heather," Sally said as she and a uniformed officer entered the shop. "What is the item you want to show me?"

"This wonderful mantle clock," Heather responded. "See! It's just like the one in this picture."

Sally took the picture from Heather and held it beside the clock. She and the officer at her side compared the two clocks.

"Do you want to tell us about this piece, Vivian?" Sally asked.

"It's a French eight-day porcelain . . . ," Vivian Dexter began.

"Cut the crap," Sally interrupted, taking a step closer to the woman she knew accepted stolen items. "You know the drill. Let's hear how you got the clock."

"I'm selling it on consignment."

"Care to tell us who you're selling it for?"

"I'll have to check my records. Gimme a minute."

"Take your time."

Vivian flipped through pages in a notebook. Finally she stopped and shook her head. "I remember now. I got it from a short, skinny guy. Said he needed the money to buy food for his widowed mother. He seemed like a nice enough young man, helping out his mom."

Heather interrupted, "Mrs. Dexter just told me that she never forgets a face."

"Did she?" laughed Sally. "What about that, Vivian. Did the man who left the clock look familiar?"

"I don't always remember every face, especially those that haven't been around for a couple of years. I just tell customers that I never forget. It helps business."

Sally turned to the officer beside her. "Aren't you amazed, Lieutenant Hilbert, that Ms. Dexter can't remember faces she hasn't seen in a couple of years. When was it that Tom Fuely was arrested for bringing stolen goods to Vivian?"

"I'd say it was right at two years ago," laughed George Hilbert. "The judge gave him a long sentence, but Tommy was released after a year and a month due to over-crowding in the prison."

"Fences should probably expect long sentences too, don't you think," Sally added. "And with the new prison being built, they might get to stay for their full term. Why don't you lock up and come with us, Vivian? We've got a few questions to ask, after we remind you that you have the right to remain silent. Anything you say can and will be used against you in a court of law. You also have the right . . ."

"Cut the crap," Vivian interrupted, thrusting her hands behind her to accept handcuffs. "I've got that whole damn song and dance memorized."

WHAT TIME IS IT?

	1	2	3	4	5	6	7	8
A	W	M	T	S	D	V	O	I
B	R	C	P	B	M	G	K	E
C	H	S	T	E	N	N	F	A
D	R	E	R	F	O	L	J	R

A3,A8,B5,D2, A3,D5   D4,A8,C6,A5
A3,C1,D2   D7,C4,A1,D2,D6,C2

<u>T</u>_ _ _   _ _   _ _ _ _   _ _ _   _ _ _ _ _ _

CHAPTER 21

"I could use your help, Heather." Myrtle was at the kitchen sink, running cold water on her swollen ring finger. "I want to take Oliver's ring off, but it's stuck."

Heather went to her aunt's side and looked at the problem. "Your finger's swollen. Give it a rest. Try again after the swelling goes down, or first thing in the morning."

"Oh bother. That's what Arlyn told me to do. I wanted to make sure I could get this off before I arrange a flight home."

"Obviously you are destined to stay with us another day or two."

Myrtle dried her hands "What are you up to this afternoon?"

"I'm going to crawl around the furnace, looking for hidey holes."

"You should let Rachel's boys do that. They can get into tighter spaces."

"Tommy Fuely was about my size. If he could get into small places, then I should be able to."

"I beg your pardon," Myrtle laughed. "That man was hardly more than a scarecrow. You, my dear, are nicely rounded."

"Is that a reminder of too many cookies, cakes and pieces of fudge?"

Myrtle nodded. "That's why I can't get this darned ring off."

"I'll call Rachel to see if her boys are free to search. I'll at least let them destroy cobwebs for me." Heather picked up her cell phone, just as the doorbell rang.

"I'll get it," volunteered Myrtle, hurrying out of the room.

Heather nodded, waiting to see who was at the door.

Standing patiently on the Samuelson's front porch were the Corbin brothers.

"We came to apologize for scaring you," said Johnny. "Our mom said we had to."

"We were just having fun," Joey added, "but Mom explained that you guys weren't having fun, so we shouldn't be selfish and do all the enjoying."

"Your mom was right about that. Thank you for apologizing."

"We're supposed to ask if we can help you do something," Johnny said.

"If you let us help you, Mom will subtract one whole year off the time we're being grounded." This was Joey's contribution.

"An entire year? How long is she planning to ground you boys?"

"About a hundred years," Joey complained.

"Wait," declared Myrtle. "I've got an idea. Come in and let's see if we can't find something for you to help with. Heather," she shouted. "Hold on."

Heather walked into the living room. "What's up?"

"Let Tim and Tom off the hook," Myrtle suggested. "These contrite young men have come to apologize. Their mom has grounded them for a hundred years." Myrtle paused to look at the boys. They nodded in agreement.

"A whole century?" Heather asked.

"If we can help you do something . . ."

"Yeh! Anything," Joey interrupted. He sounded desperate.

". . .Mom will subtract an entire year off the grounding for each thing we do to help. She told us if we didn't do good deeds we'd be old and gray by the time we worked off penalties for making *bonus* phone calls."

"Bonus? Do you mean bogus?" Heather asked, smiling as the boys shrugged. "Do we need to check with your mom to see if the thing you're going to help with is something she's willing to have you do?"

"Naw! She told us we could do anything that wasn't dangerous to us or to someone else."

"Okay, boys. Follow me." Heather led them upstairs to the half door that led to the newly installed furnace. She explained that it was a treasure hunt she was sending them on, but nothing about the furnace or its wiring needed to be touched.

"What about nails?"

"Avoid them unless you want a tetanus shot."

After arming them with flashlights and turning on the one weak bulb that was meant to give the furnace repairmen enough light to make repairs, she watched the boys squiggle through the low doorway.

Sleeping late was a real treat for Brian Fisher. His public relations job for an advertising firm in Denver kept him at his desk both early and late. But this morning he took his time. He showered and shaved, then leisurely dressed. After he checked out of the motel he stopped at a coffee shop. He often skipped breakfast, but never his morning coffee.

"Which way to the ocean?" he asked the clerk, filling an extra-large coffee cup for him.

"Like they say, *go west, young man, go west*'" The clerk smiled and added, "Do you want the north beaches or the south?"

"I want to end up wherever I can get out on the sand and dip my toes in the water."

"You can do that at Lincoln City or points south. Right now you're on highway I-205 south. Stay with it until it joins I-5 still headed south. When you get to Salem head west. You want highway 22. That'll take you right to the ocean with lots of beaches to walk on and some popular lookout points. There are also some nice beachside motels, if you want to stay a while."

"205 to I-5 to 22 West? Right?"

"You've got it." The sales clerk smiled as a five dollar tip changed hands.

As Brian drove away, he found a radio station playing country western. Content to have his coffee and the music he liked best, he headed south.

"How's it going? You ready to come home?"

"Yes and no," Vern answered. "I drove to the Portland Airport last night and I'm really tired. I miss you. I'm thinking that things here are getting too dicey. I'm considering coming home to wait for whatever dollars show up in the mail."

"Any chance staying there could add to the amount?"

"If I'd found the new heir who was supposed to arrive on the plane from Denver last night, we might have had a chance. So far no luck with that."

"The bride's gone?"

"She did it to herself. The problem is that somehow the stuff she ate seems to have been eaten by a neighbor. He croaked, too. That's what makes me think I should head east."

"Can you be connected to the ugly stuff?"

"I don't think so. A few missing pills from a Rhode Island pharmacy won't point to me, and Olivia was the one handing those blood thinners to her uncle. She put poison in her own salad, and no one pushed the fat broad down the stairs. I should be clear of it all. The problem is there're too many dead people showing up."

"Don't chicken out. If there's a chance to increase the take, we won't have to go through another long separation."

"I won't chicken out. You took care of Pamela in Kansas, and I'm going to take care of inheritance problems in Oregon."

###

"What's going on upstairs?" asked Sally when she arrived home for lunch. "It sounds like we have mice."

"Johnny and Joey are helping search for Tom Fuely's loot," Myrtle reported from the rocking chair where she'd been reading. "Heather thinks it has to be somewhere close to the furnace."

"I hope she's right, but why Johnny and Joey instead of Rachel's boys?"

"When they finish, I'll let them tell you in person. It's part of what they have to do as penance for making those phone calls."

"Maybe I'll see how the search is coming along," Sally said, heading up the stairs. She found Heather on the floor beside the open doorway to the furnace.

"Hi, Sally. We're searching," Heather explained, looking up from the task of filing her fingernails. "Oops! You've come home for lunch and I don't have it ready."

"Don't rush. I've got a little time."

"No problem. Boys?" Heather called to the two investigators dislocating cobwebs. "It's lunch time. I'm going downstairs to fix Sally's lunch. Turn out the light and close the door when you want to stop. You can leave your flashlights next to the door."

"Okay," responded a small voice.

"Any luck?" Sally asked as the sisters headed for the kitchen.

"None. The boys found a small amount of loose insulation, but that seems to be all. How was your session with Vivian Dexter?"

"Boring. Nothing we didn't already know. She accepts whatever merchandise walks in her door and refuses to check lists of stolen items police departments send out."

"But she knew who Tommy Fuely was, and she knew he'd been sent to prison for stealing things in the past." Heather washed her hands. "Sandwiches or soup?"

"A sandwich, please." Sally turned as her aunt entered the kitchen. "I was just telling Heather what we learned after talking with that antique dealer."

"Good, then I haven't missed anything important." Myrtle took a seat at the kitchen table.

"To answer your question, Heather," Sally continued. "Dexter knew who Tommy was, she just didn't care."

"Can I fix anything for you, Aunt Myrtle?" Heather asked.

"Just a glass of milk, please." Myrtle gave her swollen finger a sad smile.

"Heather," called Johnny Corbin. He and his brother were descending the stairs. "We're going home for lunch, but we broke the chain that turns on the light."

"Yeh," Joey added. "I tried to pull it like you did, but the light didn't turn on and the chain broke."

"We left it with the flashlights by the door. Do you want us to come back after lunch?"

"I think it will be too hot up there after lunch," Heather answered. "Let's try again tomorrow morning."

"Hi Sally," Johnny said. "Joey and me apologize for phoning about bombs. We didn't mean to make you so sleepy you couldn't catch bad guys."

"Mr. Hilbert explained it," Joey added. "We won't call any more. Besides, our mom is buying an air conditioner so we can sleep nights."

Sally nodded at the boys. "Maybe one day soon we can get together and I'll take you on a tour of the Police Station. Would you like that?"

"Sweeet!" said Joey.

"Boy, would we," agreed Johnny. "We'll ask Mom if it's okay with her."

"It's a date then," Sally said. "As soon as your mom agrees."

Myrtle escorted the boys to the front door. "Nice boys," she said when she returned to the kitchen. "I have a feeling they're going to turn out all right after all. What other news do you have for us, Sally?"

"We have Vernon Xavier Higgins' history. He's a former resident of Lawrence, Kansas, and a mediocre pharmacy student." Sally sat down at the table as Heather put a roast beef sandwich in front of her.

"He has a checkered past! Right?" Heather asked.

"Very checkered. Between his junior and senior years at the university, he married another pharmacy student. They took out huge insurance policies on each other, meant to pay off student loans in the event either one of them died."

"You're going to tell us his wife died, aren't you?" Heather said.

Sally nodded. "And Vern collected a couple hundred thousand to help ease any debts he had."

"How did she die?"

"While Vern was in class one day someone broke into their house and raped, then strangled, Pamela."

"Not Vern, though?"

"He was cleared. His alibi checked out and the DNA results weren't his."

"Then how's his past checkered?"

"People die when Vernon is around. Kansas police couldn't pin anything on him regarding Pamela's death, but if there's money involved that might go to Vernon, the money holders live short lives. His grandmother got all the money in the family after his parents died in a questionable accident. Vern was an only child, so when his grandmother fell down her cellar stairs, he collected quite a nice bundle."

"Olivia didn't stand a chance after he came into her life, did she?" Myrtle said.

Sally nodded. "He probably knew she was set to inherit the estate of a wealthy antique dealer. We think he gave her those so-called vitamins she fed her uncle."

"Since the poison hemlock came from Oliver's garden," Myrtle added, "I suppose there's no way to prove Vern really knew what it was."

"Wait! There is," exclaimed Heather excitedly. "At the hospital he told me he considered taking up the study of medicinal plants. Pharmacognosy, he called it. I'd never heard the word before so it stuck with me."

Sally rose from the table. "I guess we'd better check his class schedules to see exactly how many poisonous plant identification skills he has."

"Before you get started on that I have a new subject to introduce," Heather said. "Does it occur to you that Brian Fisher should have shown up by now? He was due on the Denver to Portland flight late yesterday afternoon. Is there some way we can check on whether he arrived?"

Sally looked thoughtful. "I'll see if there are any strings we can pull at the station. Vern was gone several hours yesterday afternoon and evening. He might have driven to Portland and met Brian's flight."

"I hope that's not what happened," added Heather. "If he met Brian's plane, I'd guess there's already one less heir to the Lloyd fortune."

"Do we know yet how big that fortune is?" asked Myrtle.

"The attorney thinks he has it all, but he's puzzled because it was his impression the estate should be worth several million dollars and not an amount under one million."

"We should see about getting into that place. I'll bet Aunt Myrtle could recognize any antiques with secret compartments or drawers. Couldn't you, Aunt Myrtle?"

The doorbell rang and Sally answered it.

"Mom said to give you this," said the Corbin brothers, handing Sally a written permission slip for a tour of the Police Station any time it suited Sally.

"How about going now?" she asked. "Tell your mom we'll be gone about an hour. Do you want to join us, Heather?"

"No thanks. I'll fix the chain on the light upstairs, and do a little more searching before it gets too hot."

"Okay, Sis. We'll see you later. Come on, boys. Let's check with your mom and then take a ride downtown."

While Myrtle went to her bedroom to rest, Heather went to the half door that led to the furnace. Beside it lay the flashlights the boys had been using, along with the broken chain.

Crouching before the doorway, Heather prepared to reattach the chain to the light fixture, but what she found was that the pull chain to the only light in the furnace area was still in place. Puzzled, she pulled on it and the light turned on.

Heather sat down to examine the chain the boys had pulled loose. It looked ordinary even though it was difficult to make sure in the dim light inside the short doorway. She moved to the bathroom where the light was better, and carefully examined the tarnished strand. It hadn't been made from coarse, durable material normally used for pull chains. Instead, it was a fine, more relaxed mesh. If it had been highly polished, it would have felt like a piece of jewelry.

Heather gasped. A moment later she rushed down the stairs to her cleaning supplies and pulled out a jar of polish that she rubbed on the chain. After giving it a bath, she scrubbed on the chain with a soft cloth. It began to sparkle.

Could it have come from the Fuely stash?

She hurried upstairs, ready to see if she could detect where the boys had found it. If they thought it was for another light, it had to have come from the ceiling. The ceiling, however, contained insulation that had been thoroughly searched by investigators. Heather sighed. She'd have to wait until the boys returned from their Police Department tour.

Time inched by.

The hour tour of the police station had already taken almost three hours, and Heather could hardly concentrate on what to fix for dinner. When she finally heard a key in the door, she rushed to greet her sister.

"Where are the boys?" she asked.

"With their mom," Sally replied. "She met us downtown. She's taking them to dinner and then to a show.

"She can't do that. I need them back here."

"What's got you so antsy?" Sally asked, following her sister into the house.

"Look at the chain they thought they pulled from a light fixture. I polished it. It's not a pull chain. It's a piece of jewelry. It has to be from Tommy's stash."

Sally examined the gold chain, and understood immediately why her sister was so excited.

"Sorry, Sis," she sympathized. "It looks like we'll have to wait until tomorrow to send the boys back into the cobwebs. You realize, of course, that they may be entitled to the reward money."

"But they found it in *our* house." Heather studied the expression on Sally's face. She knew police were not entitled to rewards. "All of it?" she asked.

"Possibly."

Heather shrugged. "Let's collect Myrtle and go out for dinner. I'm too excited to do any cooking."

###

WHERE IS OLIVER'S MISSING FORTUNE?

To reveal the answer, blacken the squares with the letter O.
Leave those squares with the letter J as they are.

```
J J J J J J J J J J J J J J J J J J J J
J J J J J J J J J J J J J J J J J J J J
J J o J o J J o J J J J J o J J J J J J
J J o J o o J o J J J J o J o J J J J J
J J o J o J o o J J J o o o o o o J J J
J J o J o J J o J J o J J J J o J J J J
J J J J J J J J J J J J J J J J J J J J
J J J J J J J J J J J J J J J J J J J J
J J J J J J J J J J J J J J J J J J J J
J J J J J J J J J J J J J J J J J J J J
J o o o J J J J J J J J o o o J o o o o
J o J J J J J J J J J J o J J J o J J J
J J o J J J J J o J J J J o o J J o o J
J J J o J J J o J o J J J o J J J o J J
J J J o J J o o o o o J J o J J J o J J
J o o o J o J J J J J o J o J J J o o o
J J J J J J J J J J J J J J J J J J J J
J J J J J J J J J J J J J J J J J J J J
J J J J J J J J J J J J J J J J J J J J
J J J J J J J J J J J J J J J J J J J J
```

CHAPTER 22

For Heather, eager to uncover Tom Fuely's stash, Wednesday morning arrived slower than most mornings. For a while she paced the length of her living room, but as soon as it sounded like someone next door at the Corbin's was awake, she hurried over and rang their doorbell.

"Hi, Helen," Heather said, when the door opened. Sally and Myrtle hovered in the background.

"Yes?" Helen looked surprised at the early morning visit from three neighbors. She pushed uncombed hair off her forehead. "Do you want to come in?"

"No thanks. Are your boys awake?" Heather stepped to one side to look behind Helen for signs of her sons.

"They were up late last night and now that we have air conditioning, they're probably still asleep."

"But it's almost eight o'clock!"

Helen checked her watch. "What difference does that make?"

"I don't know if I can wait any longer," Heather said. "I need to talk with them. Look what they found." She dangled a chain in front of Helen.

"Nice necklace. Did they find it in the grass like the ring?"

"No! It came from my attic. Your boys found it when they were searching yesterday." Heather slipped the necklace back in her pocket.

"I didn't understand why you had them doing that."

"Don't you know the history of our house?"

Helen shook her head. "I guess not."

"Okay, here's the story. A jewel thief lived in our house a couple years ago. Lots of whatever he stole has never been recovered. There's a huge reward for finding it. This necklace may be part of what everyone is looking for. I need to have your boys show me where they got it."

"Talk about a treasure hunt," Helen laughed. "And a big reward? No wonder you can hardly stand still." She hadn't moved from the doorway.

"We called the attorney this morning," Heather continued, "on his private line. Because his office wasn't open yet."

Myrtle and Sally crowded closer. "Hurry up," coaxed Sally. "This is taking too long."

Heather nodded. "The attorney said we were each entitled to half the reward if we've found the missing jewels."

Helen looked puzzled. "Each who?"

"Each family. Mine. Yours. That's twenty-five thousand."

"Dollars?" Helen clutched the door with both hands.

Heather nodded. "Twenty-five thousand dollars *each*."

"Don't move," Helen said. She turned and race down the hall to the stairs, leaving her door standing open.

Within three minutes, two sleepy boys were standing before Heather. "Sorry to take so long," Johnny apologized. "We had to use the bathroom."

"Let's go to my house," Heather invited.

"In our pajamas?" Joey asked.

"Do what Heather says," Helen prompted, giving the boys a gentle push. "We'll explain later."

In the Samuelson living room the group paused briefly. "Did your mom tell you what I want you to do?" Heather asked.

The boys shook their heads.

"It's that chain you thought you broke. Can you show me where you found it?"

"I can," volunteered Joey. "I'm the one who broke it."

"We'll deal with that later," Heather said. "Let's go to the attic so you can show me."

The party of four eager adults exchanged smiles and little reassuring hugs as they climbed the stairs behind the boys.

"I don't know how I can thank you, Heather," Helen said. "You have no idea how much some extra money will help us."

Heather nodded, but kept hurrying.

Sally said, "I can hardly wait to show up at work." She smiled. ". . . with a fortune in stolen jewels."

"Okay, boys," Heather said when they reached the attic door. "You lead the way and I'll follow."

The Corbin boys picked up the flashlights they'd left beside the doorway and ducked to avoid hitting their heads as they entered the attic through the short opening. After picking up a screwdriver, gloves, and a pair of scissors, Heather crawled behind the pajama-clad figures to the back side of the furnace. The boys pointed to a section of insulation strapped to the ceiling.

"It's so dark back here," Johnny said. "We just wanted more light."

"But there's no light fixture up there," Heather said, focusing her flashlight on the seam where one length of insulation joined another. "Show me where the chain was."

"Right there." Joey pointed to an area beside a furnace duct where two sections of insulation joined. After the furnace repairman's last visit, the duct was now held firmly in place by two secure straps. "We pushed a piece of insulation back inside, and when we did that, the chain fell partway down. We thought it would turn on a light if we pulled it."

"You weren't supposed to touch the fiberglass," Heather said. "People need gloves and breathing masks when they work around it."

"We didn't touch it very long."

"If you'll hold this light for me," Heather said, "I'll try to do some surgery on the aluminum foil jacket that covers the insulation. There's already a small hole there."

Richard Bigelow returned to Lewisburg and immediately checked in with Chance Hamilton.

"Thanks for coming, Richard. There's a problem I'd like to discuss with you." Chance ushered Richard into his office and motioned to a chair. "I seem to have located all of Oliver's bank accounts, along with his stocks and bonds. My problem is that the estate total isn't near what I expected it to be."

Richard leaned back in the chair and folded his hands behind his head. "I've been giving some thought to where a collector of antiques might invest his cash. If he was interested in old stamps, coins, or old maps, do you have any idea where he'd purchase them?"

"Give me a minute," Chance said, his forehead knotting.

"I think Oliver found a way to put his money into something that wouldn't lose value, but that he could ignore and not report on his taxes."

"That brings us back to the small stuff, doesn't it?" Chance said.

"What were his hobbies? Did he collect stamps? Coins?"

Chance laughed. "Cribbage. His one passion and his only hobby was playing cribbage and attending cribbage tournaments. He was very good at the game."

"There's not much money in that," Richard said. "I think we need to attack the problem from another direction. Let's contact coin and stamp dealers to see if they know the name *Oliver Lloyd*."

Chance reached for his phone. "I'll call a couple of my clients. They'll know which dealers to contact."

"Hurry up, Heather," Myrtle called from the hallway where she and the others waited impatiently.

"I'm hurrying as fast as I can," Heather replied. "I've got a bigger hole in the aluminum foil barrier. As soon as I get my gloves on, I'll poke around in it. I think there's some kind of cloth inside. I'll see if I can pull it out, or poke a hole in it."

"Let's hope she doesn't go through the roof," Sally whispered.

"Wait," Heather called. "I did it. I tore it." There was a pause. "Look out!" she warned.

"What's happening," Sally yelled. "Do you need help?" She was on her hands and knees, ready to join the searchers. She heard Johnny say, "We're watching out."

"Heather, what's going on?" Myrtle was wringing her hands. "What's happening?"

Helen called out, "Are my boys in your way? Do what she says, boys."

Excited whispers could be heard, but none were loud enough to let the others know what was going on.

From the darkness they finally heard Heather say, "We're coming out." Scuffling sounds reached the eager threesome at the doorway.

"No luck, huh?" Sally asked.

Heather and the boys emerged from the crawlspace with wide grins.

"You *found* something," Myrtle said. "I can tell."

"Joey first," Heather prompted.

Slowly Joey uncurled his fist to display a ring that he handed to his mother. The diamond it held was the size of a small hazelnut.

"My God," Helen said. "Is it real?"

"Let me see." Sally held out her hand. "Wow!" She turned the ring every which way before passing it to Myrtle.

"Now, Johnny," Heather prompted. He uncurled his fist, displaying an emerald ring with a gem equal in size to that of the diamond.

"You did it," laughed Sally turning to hug Myrtle. "She found what the professionals couldn't find."

"Isn't there more?" asked Myrtle.

"This's it for now," Heather said. "The rings fell out after I poked a hole in a cloth that's probably wrapped around the jewels. We're going to need that furnace technician back. He'll have to undo the straps he put on the duct to keep it from coming loose."

"Can't we unhook the straps ourselves?" asked Sally.

"I don't think we're strong enough. That furnace repairman made sure he wouldn't have to come back to fix another drooping duct."

"I'm calling him right now," Sally said, punching numbers on her cell phone.

"H-holy c-cow!" Brian Fisher hopped up and down, flapping his arms to restore circulation. He, like others on the beach at Lincoln City, wore swimming trunks. But unlike the others he'd raced to the surf and thrown his body into the fifty degree water.

"What did you expect?" asked a young woman shuffling along in ankle-deep waves. She was wrapped in a brightly colored beach towel.

"W-warmth. Something c-closer to b-body t-temperature." Brian could hardly talk he was trembling so hard.

"Along the Oregon coast?" The woman laughed. "You're new to the area, aren't you? Where are you from?"

Brian was still dancing vigorously. "C-Colorado," he stuttered as another chill shook him.

"And you've never seen an ocean before, am I right?"

He nodded vigorously, several times. "C-Colorado doesn't have any."

"Borrow my beach towel." The young woman handed him the colorful expanse warmed by her body. Brian accepted it gratefully. "The best you can hope for in moderate ocean temperatures would be along the southern California coastline where it gets into the sixties."

"Talk about a public relations job," Brian laughed, beginning to warm up a little. "All those pictures of people surfing and swimming *while they're smiling.*" He paused, "That's false advertising!"

"It depends on where you are. Once you get about halfway between the equator and the North Pole headed north, you can kiss any hope of warm water good-bye."

"My dream has been shattered," Brian said.

"Care for a little coffee? It'll be hot."

"My name's Brian Fisher," he said, nodding, "and you're saving my life."

"I'm glad to be of service," his benefactor said. "I'm Kate Gifford. Is that a yes to hot coffee?"

"Please."

Together they walked to the base of a rocky cliff where Kate had spread a stadium blanket she'd weighed down with a picnic basket, shoes, and a bottle of suntan lotion. She motioned to Brian to be seated while she took a thermos from the basket and poured coffee into its cap. She handed it to Brian. "Try this," she said, "but be careful; it's still very hot."

Brian took the cap and gingerly tested the temperature. "Thanks. This will help. Does the wind always blow this hard along the coast?" He still clutched the beach towel with one hand.

"Usually. In Oregon at least."

"The sunshine was so brilliant and the water so inviting, I thought a swim would be fun."

"Didn't you notice that no one else was swimming?"

Brian shook his head. "I guess I didn't. I saw all the kites flying and just headed for the water."

Kate Gifford laughed. "Didn't you even come to the beach with a blanket or a towel?"

"I'm in that motel further along. They have warning signs about taking their linens to the beach, so I didn't bring any with me."

Kate laughed again.

"Have you lived in Oregon a long time?" Brian asked.

"Most of the last few years," she replied. "My dad was a military man so I got used to moving to lots of places. I liked Oregon best, so when it came time to leave the nest, this is where I settled."

"And you've never been sorry?"

"Never."

"Why?"

"I like green plants and temperatures that don't vary a whole lot. Add an ocean that changes colors hourly, and mountains that aren't far away . . ." She sighed. "I'm an artist. There are tons of things for me to sketch. Right now my easel is in a protected area above the cliff, south of Cape Foulweather." She motioned to a section of the beach where waves first crashed against the headlands, then rolled calmly onto the sandy beach.

"Any drawbacks?"

Kate laughed. "For lots of green plants it takes lots of rain."

"That's it?"

"Mostly. This is an earthquake zone and some sections of the beach now have tsunami warnings. But I still like it. What brought you to Oregon? The promise of warm water?" She smiled.

"I've just learned that I have cousins living here. Some I didn't know even existed. I came to Oregon to introduce myself. They were expecting me a couple of days ago, but I've been playing hooky and doing some sightseeing."

"Where are your cousins?"

"In Lewisburg."

"That's in the Willamette Valley," she said. "Have you seen that area yet?"

"No, I'm headed there later today."

"You'll like it. Lewisburg is a friendly place. In the spring their rhododendrons and azaleas are spectacular." She noticed him looking at his wrist. "No watch either, huh! Do you need to know the time?"

He nodded.

Kate checked her watch. "Ten o'clock."

"It looks like I should head back to my room. Check-out time is eleven." He handed her the beach towel along with the thermos cap. "Could I interest you in a bit of lunch later?"

"That's a tempting offer, but," she nodded at the picnic basket, "I packed lunch for one and I'll settle for that. I've been waiting for the sky to change so I can get back to painting."

Brian stood slowly, reaching down to shake hands. "Kate Gifford," he said, "it has been a pleasure meeting you, and I don't really want you to feel guilty."

Kate looked startled. "Why should I feel guilty?"

"Because you saved my life. You're responsible for it now, according to legend. But it's all right. I'll just wander back to my room, then go meet the family."

Kate laughed. "Thanks for showing up on my private section of beach. If you're ever back this way and need saving again, look me up."

"It's a deal," he said, waving as he started back to the motel.

He was thinking how a few casual words exchanged with another human being could bring such pleasure. Of course the fact that Kate had chocolate eyes, auburn hair and a smile that warmed him as no beach towel could, hadn't hurt.

As soon as he checked calls on his answering machine in Denver, he'd head for his Uncle Oliver's house in Lewisburg.

###

Desperate MEASURES

WHAT'S AHEAD?

A, A, D, E, E, H, H, N, O, R, T, T

Add one letter to each of the words below to form a new word. The addition may be at the beginning, end, or within the word. Place the added letter on the line below the boxes. The added letters, reading from left to right, will form one 7-letter word and one 5-letter word to tell you what's ahead.

lone	doe	fur	race	eat	thy	thee
alone						

___a_____

rink	her	bed	here	air

CHAPTER 23

The car that entered the Samuelson carport was a sleek black Mercedes-Benz SLK 350. The man exiting it fit the car exactly. He was well-groomed and wearing an Armani suit that must have been far too warm for the day's temperature. His dark glasses hid the personality behind them as he knocked on the Samuelson's door.

"Yes," Heather said.

"Heather Samuelson?" The man waited for Heather to nod. "I'm Daniel Elliot. I'd like to speak with you, if I may." He flashed a badge at Heather.

"Come in please." She stood back, motioning him to a chair.

"I understand you've recently requested the witness and jury lists from a trial that took place eight or nine years ago. May I ask why?"

Heather sat down across from the federal agent. "My mother died a few months ago. I discovered that she'd saved detailed newspaper articles regarding the Joel Bishop trial. I was trying to understand why they were important to her."

"And you thought the lists you requested would give you that answer?"

"I didn't have expectations one way or another. Why are you asking these questions?"

He ignored her. "I'm assuming you saw the story of Judge Hardwick's recent death."

Heather nodded. "I did. I understand he was the judge at the Bishop trial."

"The lists you've requested won't be released to you, Ms. Samuelson. Since Mr. Bishop threatened everyone involved in his trial, we're not releasing their names to anyone."

"Does that mean he's been able to make good on his threat to have people killed?"

Daniel Elliot stood. "Good day, Ms. Samuelson. Thank you for your time."

"Wait! I have a question." Heather got to her feet.

Her visitor paused.

"Did my father take part in that trial?"

Without answering, Daniel Elliot turned and walked out the door.

"Answer me," Heather shouted. "Did my father take part in that trial?"

"How much longer before you'll be auctioning off these antiques?" Vern asked, admiring the treasures surrounding him. It was his third call to Chance Hamilton in as many days, always with the same question.

The attorney sighed. "Let's see," he responded thoughtfully, as if looking up new information. "Nothing has changed since yesterday when you called, and Oliver has now been dead exactly one week, so not a lot of time has gone by. We haven't had the antiques appraised and all the bills aren't in." He paused. "Other than the fact that I'm still looking for assets, there needs to be a search made for other heirs."

"Other heirs? Who's left?"

"We have to make sure Elizabeth Lloyd didn't have any children who are entitled to a share of the estate."

"That could take weeks," Vern moaned.

"Actually it will more likely take months. Has your cousin, Brian Fisher, arrived?"

"I haven't seen him. Give me his phone number, and I'll call Denver to see if he's been delayed."

"I don't have the file with that information on my desk at the moment, Mr. Higgins," Chance said, then lied, "and I have a client waiting to see me."

"Fine, but first tell me where you've looked for assets. Banks? Investment companies? Brokerages?"

"Most of the places you've suggested have shown up on Oliver's tax returns."

"Maybe that means you've got everything. What makes you think there's still something you haven't found?"

"Rumors. He was rumored to be very wealthy and what I've found so far, doesn't meet the usual criteria for being *very wealthy.* On a hunch I'm consulting rare coin and stamp dealers. That sort of thing."

"But if he had money in those, he'd have to store them in a safety deposit box somewhere."

"That's true, but that box wouldn't necessarily be in Oregon."

"Well, do what you can. Don't forget, your fee is partially coming out of my inheritance, so you're working for me."

Chance Hamilton breathed a sigh when Vern hung up. He picked up the phone again and began dialing. If he learned that Oliver collected coins and stamps, he'd at least know what he was looking for. But it still came down to the fact that a collection of that kind needed a storage place. The best storage place would be in a bank's safety deposit boxes, none of which had been located. It was unlikely that Oliver, limited in the amount of travel he could manage on his own, would have gotten a safety deposit box in another state.

Was it possible he had a safe in his house? If so, getting Vern Higgins out of there was of the highest importance.

Unfortunately when Vern ended his conversation with Chance, the thought of a safe hidden within the walls of the Lloyd house hit him full force. Early on he'd wondered about wall safes and had encouraged Olivia to move pictures to different locations, strictly for the purpose of checking behind them. She'd saved him having to look behind pictures, but not from tearing the house apart as he searched other locations.

Tired of waiting for the furnace technician to show up so she could go to work with a million dollars' worth of jewels, Sally headed out the door. Lunch was over, the Corbins had gone home, and it was well past the time she should have shown up at work. As she left the house, a blue convertible with the top down pulled into the Samuelson carport. "May I help you?" she asked.

The driver of the car wore a loose fitting shirt and faded jeans. He was tall, blond, and wore horn-rimmed glasses. He didn't look any older than Sally's twenty-some years.

"Are you Heather Samuelson?" he asked. "Have I come to the right place?" He stretched his lean body as he got out of the car.

"My sister is inside. I'll get her. Who should I say is asking for her?"

"Brian Fisher."

Sally grabbed his hand and shook it. "Are we glad to see you! Come with me." She propelled him toward her front door. "Heather," she called stepping inside. "Someone to see you." She turned to Brian. "Have a seat." She couldn't seem to stop grinning. Her morning had included the possibility of finding jewels, but instead of jewels, she'd found the missing heir.

"I thought I'd stop here before I went to see the attorney who called me. Is that all right?"

"Then you haven't been to the Lloyd house and met Vern Higgins?"

"From the panicky phone message Mr. Hamilton left Monday afternoon when I was already en route, I thought that meeting any cousins should wait until I got the *all clear* signal."

"Hello," Heather said, descending the stairs, with her curious aunt a short distance behind.

Brian jumped to his feet. "Hello, Heather," he said. "I'm Brian Fisher."

"Thank goodness." Heather jumped down the last two stairs and hurried to his side. She grabbed his hand and shook it enthusiastically.

"Kate Gifford was right," Brian laughed. "Lewisburg is a friendly place."

"This is our Aunt Myrtle Wilson," Sally said. She understood her sister's enthusiasm and excitement.

"We were afraid you were dead," Heather said, releasing Brian's hand.

"Why would you think that?"

"You were supposed to arrive two days ago. We thought something," she paused, "something bad must have happened to keep you from showing up."

"I guess I should have called. I just didn't think about it after I landed. I've never been this far west and I wanted to do some sightseeing before I had to settle down to business."

"Where did you go?" Myrtle asked.

"Straight west. Did you know the ocean temperature this morning was only fifty degrees?" He shivered.

"That's average," Heather said. "As I remember, Mr. Hamilton called you Monday afternoon."

Brian nodded. "He told me that my cousin Olivia had just died, and he asked me to stay away from Uncle Oliver's house."

Heather nodded. "Three people in that house have died within the last week."

"Three?"

"Oliver died because someone fed him blood thinning medications just before he had surgery. Your cousin Sharon Bigelow fell down the stairs and broke her neck, and on Monday, afternoon immediately after her marriage, your cousin Olivia died."

"That's staggering!" Brian said. "Impressive, but staggering. Is anyone in that house still alive?"

"Olivia's new husband is there," Sally said. "They were married only hours before she died."

"More like minutes," Heather mumbled.

Brian looked at the sisters. "I'm beginning to get a picture of a man who is not very nice."

"You say that so gently and kindly," Heather laughed. "We've been talking about Vern Higgins with a lot of four-letter words tossed in."

"More visitors," called Myrtle from her position looking past the group and out the window. A yellow Hummer had just pulled into their carport. "It's Richard!"

"Richard?" Heather and Sally jumped to their feet, ready to greet him, and introduce him to his cousin-by-marriage.

"Nice meeting you," Richard said, shaking Brian's hand.

"It's good to see you again," Heather said.

"I stopped to see Chance Hamilton on my way through town. We did some brainstorming on where Oliver might have other assets. As I left, Chance got a call from Vern Higgins, asking how long before money would be handed out."

"But Oliver's only been dead a week," Myrtle said. "Does that man think there was cash waiting to be spread around the minute Oliver died?"

Richard smiled and explained to Brian, "Myrtle was engaged to Oliver so she has a special interest in what's going on."

"That reminds me, Richard," Myrtle pulled papers from the buffet drawer behind her. "I had lunch with Oliver's friends, the two who were supposed to be included in his new will. They asked me to give copies of some papers they have to whoever I thought would pay attention to them." She handed the papers to Richard.

"Do you know what these say?" he asked.

"I had to read them to know who would pay attention to them."

Richard scanned the first handwritten page, then the second one. "I'll have to check with Chance on Oregon law," he said. "These might meet requirements for holographic wills."

"What's a holographic will?" asked Myrtle.

"Some states allow you to handwrite your last will and testament. Generally state law is very particular with respect to that kind of will. These are signed by Oliver and notarized, and they seem clear about the portion each recipient is to receive. So, if the State of Oregon feels there's no ambiguity or unintended result, they'll quite probably allow these to stand as legitimate wills. I'll turn them over to Chance," he said.

Myrtle clapped her hands. "Thanks, Richard."

"Okay," he laughed. "Getting back to Mr. Higgins. Chance is concerned that Oliver may have a safe hidden in his house. He's afraid Vern will start searching for it."

"And if he finds it?" asked Brian.

"If he finds it and can get it open, I think both its contents and Vern Higgins will disappear."

"Could he do that?" asked Heather. "Could he just walk away from his life in Rhode Island in the blink of an eye?"

"I think he's already planned that," Sally said. "When we did a background check we learned his employer refused to give him this week off, so he quit."

Richard added, "He's probably arranged things so that he's free to disappear with a minute's notice. Chance invited me to stay at his house this trip, but I think I should stay at the Lloyd house to prevent Higgins from tearing it apart."

"If it's safe for you to be there," said Brian, "then I'll stay there too, if there's room." He looked questioningly at the others.

"Oliver's house has three bedrooms," Richard said. "If we're both there, that should keep Vern under control."

"Do not eat or drink anything he offers you," Heather warned as a jingling doorbell interrupted.

Waiting to be admitted to the Samuelson house was the technician from Heating System Specialists. Bud Reeder's expression didn't show eagerness or even willingness to be where he was. He'd done his usual excellent job of installing the Samuelson's furnace and if the ladies within would keep their hands off the equipment and limit themselves to simple adjustments of the thermostat, his boss wouldn't be threatening to fire him. "Be polite. Be polite," he kept reminding himself, as their door finally opened.

"Come in, Mr. Reeder," greeted Heather.

"My boss said your furnace needs more adjusting, so I'm here to fix it. Again," he added spitefully as he entered the house.

"Sit down, Mr. Reeder," Heather said. "We have some explaining to do."

"Here! Take this," Sally said, handing him a cup of coffee, as her sister continued.

"The jewel thief who used to own this house," Heather began, "was breaking into it, trying to get something he hid a couple of years ago. But he couldn't get what he wanted because your furnace was in the way."

"He's the one who's been unhooking the braces," added Sally.

Quietly Bud drank his coffee. "Okay," he said. "I'll hook it up again."

"No," laughed Heather. "You don't understand. We need you to *unhook* the braces. Once we get the insulation removed and retrieve what he hid, you can hook everything back up."

Shaking his head in disbelief, Bud handed his empty cup back to Sally.

"Here," said Heather, thrusting her fist toward him. "Hold out your hand."

When he did, she dropped two rings in his palm. He looked into the expectant faces surrounding him. "My boss won't believe this story, even with these props," he explained, handing the rings back.

Richard whipped out a business card that said: *Richard Bigelow, Attorney-at-Law.* He handed it to the puzzled technician. "I am who that card says. If these ladies say those rings are real, then they are. This one," he pointed to Sally, "is a cop. She doesn't tell lies. These other ladies don't lie either."

"Well thanks for that belated vote of confidence," huffed Aunt Myrt. "I'm going to bring the Corbins over so they can see the treasure before Sally takes it to the police station."

"Could I see the rings again," Bud asked. Heather handed them to him. For a long moment he studied them, then asked, "Are you sure they're real?"

Heather nodded, pulling Bud Reeder to his feet.

"We're going upstairs now, Mr. Reeder! Get moving. We've waited too long to see what Tommy Fuely stashed in our attic."

###

COFFEE BREAK!
SHARPEN YOUR WITS TIME!

Locate the following words in the maze to the right.

Creepy
Evidence
Explode
Fortune
Ghost
Haunting
Jewel
Perish
Poisoner
Quest
Secrets
Trap
Trial
Twist
Warning
Watch
Wedding

t	x	x	x	x	x	x	x	x	x	h	x	x	x	x
w	x	p	o	i	s	o	n	e	r	a	x	x	x	x
i	z	e	z	z	z	z	z	z	z	u	z	z	z	z
s	z	r	z	z	z	z	z	z	z	n	z	z	z	z
t	r	i	a	l	x	x	x	x	g	t	r	a	p	x
x	x	s	x	x	x	x	c	x	h	i	x	x	x	x
z	z	h	z	z	z	z	r	z	o	n	z	z	z	w
z	z	z	s	e	c	r	e	t	s	g	z	z	f	e
x	x	x	x	x	x	c	e	x	t	x	x	h	o	d
x	x	x	x	x	n	x	p	x	x	x	c	x	r	d
z	z	q	u	e	s	t	y	j	z	t	z	z	t	i
z	z	z	d	z	z	z	z	e	a	z	z	z	u	n
x	x	i	x	x	x	x	x	w	a	r	n	i	n	g
x	v	x	x	x	x	x	x	e	x	x	x	x	e	x
e	x	p	l	o	d	e	z	l	z	z	z	z	z	z

192

CHAPTER 24

"This is a fine time to be showing up, Detective Samuelson," snarled Lieutenant Dan Steele when Sally arrived at work that afternoon. A shopping bag dangled heavily from her left arm. "I was getting ready to send a search party looking for you. I hope you have a damn good excuse for not calling in."

"I think I have one," she said. "Maybe it's even a damn good, damn fine, damned original one. Want to see?"

She lifted the bag to the center of the lieutenant's desk.

He bolted as if a snake were about to slither from the bag.

"Ready?" Sally asked, slowly upending the bag to allow jewelry of all kinds to flood the desk.

"What's this?" Lt. Steele asked. "Did you rob a jewelry store?"

"It's the Tom Fuely loot that searchers couldn't find a couple years ago when Fuely was on trial. My sister and two boys found it and they want the reward."

He moved forward to examine the find. "Do they?"

"I expect you to guard these jewels until the insurance company collects them and pays the ransom."

"I don't know about a relative of a cop claiming a reward. You know police aren't entitled to rewards. Finding stuff like this is just part of our job."

"I know that and you know that, but I didn't find it. The boys who live next to us found a necklace because my sister had a hunch about where they should look. She went poking around and found something that convinced her we needed to have our furnace uninstalled so the jewels could be retrieved. Don't disappointment me, Steely," she teased, using the nickname he hated. "You know Heather and the boys are entitled to all that nice crisp green reward money."

"The insurance company will have to verify that everything's here."

Sally nodded.

"And you know that money isn't going to be delivered here next week."

Sally laughed. "I don't expect it to be delivered here at all. I want it delivered to the people who found all these pretties and who trusted me to deliver them to you."

"Do you think Uncle Oliver might have invested in expensive jewelry like the stuff that came out of the Samuelson attic?" Brian asked as he and Richard walked from the Samuelson residence to the Lloyd residence.

"He might have, but you and I aren't going to talk about things like that where Vern can hear. Remember, we mostly stay together. We don't eat a thing in this house, and if we don't see the water come out of the faucet, then we avoid drinking it. We'll use bottled water we carry with us at all times so Vern can't add something deadly when we're not watching."

"Okay."

"Quietly search your bedroom for any sign of a safe. We'll do the rest of the house when Vern is out. Which reminds me, we each need a key. It's demeaning to have to ring the bell to be admitted to a house we now own." Richard leaned on the doorbell.

"Cousin Vern," he greeted when the door opened. "I'm back to stay for a while." Richard pushed past the astonished Vern. "Have you met our cousin, Brian Fisher? Brian, this is your cousin-by-marriage, Vernon Xavier Higgins. He was married for a very short time to your cousin Olivia. Sorry to hear of your wife's death, Vern. Sad thing, death. Both of us with wives who died in this house. Tragic. Absolutely tragic."

Vern had turned pale.

Without pausing a moment longer, Richard urged Brian toward the stairs. "Come on, Cuz," he said. "Let's get you settled in a bedroom so we can rest a while before we head out for dinner."

"Cousin Richard," Brian said. "I'm really surprised that our uncle left such a mess as there is in the dining room. Why would he do that?"

Richard said, "Cousin Vern, what happened in the dining room? All the expensive antique furniture sits in the middle and the Oriental carpet that was under the table is in the study. What's going on?"

"There's an air conditioning problem. I'll explain it later," Vern answered, heading for the kitchen. A bottle of scotch waited on the counter.

Richard and Brian continued up the stairs. "Why don't you take the bedroom on the other side of my bathroom?"

Brian turned to Richard. "Vern didn't know how to answer your question about what he's doing in the dining room."

"I bet he comes up with something damned interesting," Richard whispered back. "See you in a couple of hours."

###

"I finally got that pesky ring off my finger," Myrtle said as Heather joined her in the kitchen.

"Once we stopped eating rich desserts we all did better," Heather said. "I can sit down in my jeans again."

"I made reservations for my trip home. Could you drive me to Portland Friday?"

Heather nodded. "We'll be sorry to see you go."

"I stayed longer than I originally planned, but I've kept my promises to Oliver as well as I could." Myrtle set aside the vegetables she'd been chopping for salad. "His dog is with one of his best friends and they'll get the money Oliver promised them. I didn't do a very good job of looking out for Olivia, but that was pretty much out of my control."

"Are you giving Oliver's ring to his buddies?"

"I think that's where it belongs, even though they have similar rings. I'll see them before I leave. I want to tell them that Mr. Hamilton has their papers and he'll let them know when he needs the originals."

###

Thursday morning arrived with little flair. Vern was quickly out of bed and off on an errand of great importance. It was time he made sure the nice little riverside dumping ground he'd discovered was as perfect as he wanted it to be. With Brian under the same roof and within his reach, there would hopefully be a use for the dumpsite.

Like Vern, there were other early risers on that cloudless Thursday morning. The committee in charge of the riverfront picnic for Sons and Daughters of Oregon Pioneers was at work with portable tables and chairs, balloons and signs, and a canopy or two in case the sun was too hot for some of their older members.

And that's the way Vern found his isolated little dumpsite—decorated with balloons, signs, and an animated group of people welcoming every car that found its way to the area not normally on anyone's beaten path.

Grumbling all the way back to town, Vern stopped for a latte at one of the drive-thru coffee stands. It was while he was waiting his turn in line that the idea came to him. He'd buy lattes for Richard and Brian. What a cousinly thing to do. And from his arsenal of emergency drugs for nefarious purposes, he'd add a little something that would enable him to leave Lewisburg with a somewhat helpless individual who would simply disappear from the face of the earth. No body, no autopsy, no quarter of the estate. With luck he could narrow the field by two cousins and only share the inheritance with Marilyn and her brood. Fifty percent was a number with a very nice ring to it.

Luck was riding with him. He could feel it in his bones.

Brian Fisher awoke to a pounding on his bedroom door in front of which he'd shoved a chest of drawers. When the pounding stopped, he checked his watch. Nine o'clock! What a glorious time to be waking up. Closing his eyes again, he stretched and wiggled his toes, flexed his fingers, and enjoyed the moment. He'd been up late checking for places where a safe might be hidden. If there was one in his room, it was very cleverly disguised.

"Still in bed, I see."

Brian's eyes flew open. Vern Higgins was standing over him, his hands tucked out of sight behind his back.

"Hi," Brian responded, sitting up in bed, wondering what weapon Vern shielded with his body. Would he have a gun? A knife? A rope? Maybe a baseball bat? Brian glanced at his bedroom door where a chest of drawers still blocked the entrance. "How the heck did you get in here?"

"Richard left so I just used my key to come through his bedroom and the adjoining bathroom. I wanted you to have a nice hot latte to start your day. I brought one for Richard too, but since he's gone, I'll drink it. This one," he pushed forward the cup in his right hand, "is decaf and the other is caffeinated. Choose." Vern waited and when Brian chose the caffeinated coffee, Vern handed it to him, pleased that his guess had been right.

"Well, thanks," Brian said, looking quizzically at the drink in his hand. He noticed that Vern had begun drinking from the cup he still held. Morning coffee was as important to Brian as putting on trousers. It was, he thought, a great deal like receiving a blood transfusion and he badly needed one of those.

"I've got other things to do," Vern said, heading back to the shared bathroom. "See you later."

Undecided about the safety of the latte, Brian prepared to shower, nearly missing the note Richard left.

"*Brian,*" the note began. "*I've a couple of legal things to attend to. Enjoy breakfast at the Samuelson's. I'm locking my bedroom door. See you at noon. R.*"

Climbing into the shower Brian argued with himself as he soaped and rinsed. He'd been offered his choice of the two coffees. That must mean they were both safe to drink.

His doubts satisfied, he dried and put on shorts. A moment later he took a tentative sip. The latte tasted all right. Satisfied, he drained the cup.

###

PUZZLES REMAINING

Circle your response, then write the circled letters at the bottom of the
page. If you have answered the questions correctly, the letters should
spell out the name of someone who will save a life.

	Yes	No
1. Is the scrapbook important?	K	W
2. Did Mattie have a lover?	H	A
3. Will Vern get all of the money?	O	T
4. Is Mattie's letter more than a fairy tale?	E	S
5. Will Bender cookies continue arriving?	G	G
6. Will Vern be arrested?	H	I
7. Is Vern's lover guilty of murder?	F	P
8. Is there a safe with money at Oliver's?	F	L
9. Will Vern escape?	C	O
10. Will the missing fortune be found?	R	A
11. Is Brian's life in danger?	D	S

CHAPTER 25

As Vern waited for the latte to have the desired effect, he puzzled again over the air conditioning problem in Oliver's house. The place cooled unevenly. The second floor was cooler than most of the first floor. That made it exactly the opposite of how it should have been. With today's weather scheduled for the nineties, it was time to figure out why there was a problem.

He checked the floor vents in every first floor room. Cool air flowed through them all, except for one in the dining room.

Vern got down on his hands and knees, trying to see why the vent nearest the front door didn't allow cold air to circulate. He wrenched the wooden drop-in vent cover from its place, expecting to find something forgotten during construction. Instead, he found a safe installed in a corner of the slab that had been used to form the top step of the front porch.

"What an ingenious idea," he said. "All I need now is the combination."

But where should he look for it? Vern put the floor vent back in place, making sure the louvers were closed so no one would see any glimmer of metal showing through them. Then he went to the study to look for birthday dates. He'd find out when Oliver was born and give variations of that date a try. Or maybe it was Olivia's birthday he needed. Whatever it was, he'd stick with it until he found the proper combination of numbers even if it was like that old nursery rhyme.

Wow! What if he'd guessed it right off? What if that was it? One-two, buckle my shoe. Three-four . . . Back he went to the vent to try twelve, thirty-four, fifty-six.

###

Richard and the district attorney were discussing charges that would allow them to immediately toss Vernon Xavier Higgins in jail.

"You know as well as I do, Richard," District Attorney Stafford said, "that in order to prosecute Higgins we have to have an airtight case, linking him to at least one of the deaths."

"Then you have your work cut out for you," Richard responded. "He's been too smart for that. The damage to Oliver was done before Vern arrived on the scene, although I suspect he set the wheels in motion. As a pharmacist with access to prescription medicines, I think he supplied Olivia with the anticoagulants she fed her uncle."

Stafford nodded. "The same is true in the case of your wife, Richard. We're still ruling Sharon's death an accident even though the insurance pictures proved the rug she tripped over wasn't outside her bedroom door the evening before. There is no way to lay responsibility for the rug at Vern's feet as opposed to dropping it at Olivia's."

Richard nodded. "Higgins set the stage for Olivia's death by telling her he'd discovered a rare kind of parsley. We can probably prove that as a one-time student of pharmacognosy, Vern recognized poison hemlock. He certainly knew the plant's history which Olivia repeated to me. But he didn't feed it to her; he only made it available."

"It looks hopeless, doesn't it?" Stafford added. "As for Tommy Fuely, there is absolutely no way to connect his death with Vern."

"We can't let that no-good get off scot-free! He's a serial killer."

"He won't get off; not if I can help it."

"I'll help all I can," Richard said. "However, there's one other matter I'd like to run past you."

Stafford nodded. "And that is?"

"Heather Samuelson recently had a visit from a fed by the name of Daniel Elliot. Know him?"

"Slightly. He's local."

"Earlier she asked your trial clerk for a list of juror's from an old case. Elliot showed up to say she couldn't have it."

"I can't give it to you either, Richard."

"You're making it sound like she's right and there's a Witness Protection Program involved. If that's the case, we'll keep out of it, but if that isn't what's going on, then I want to see those names."

Richard arrived back at the Lloyd residence, pleased to be parking in a less crowed carport. He was still puzzling over how they were going to connect Vern with the deaths he'd set in motion. Richard was also wondering what he'd say to Heather about the list of juror's names in the Bishop trial.

He eased his Hummer next to Vern's Lexus, recalling that it had been gone when he left the house that morning. It was the blue convertible Brian rented that was missing now. Where had Brian gone?

"Anyone home?" Richard called, walking into the Lloyd house through an unlocked front door. He checked the rooms. No one was home. Where had Brian and Vern gone? Were they together?

He rushed to the Samuelson house. "Heather," he gasped when she answered her doorbell. "Have you seen Brian this morning?"

"He didn't come for breakfast, but I saw him as he left in his car about thirty minutes ago."

"Was he alone?"

"It didn't occur to me at the time, but he was the passenger. Vern was driving."

"Oh Lord!" Richard said. "Do you have the number for the District Attorney's office?"

"What a pleasant day for a drive," Vern said, heading west on Highway 22. "I'm glad we put the top down." Brian Fisher didn't reply.

Vern continued. "Probably as a newcomer to Oregon one of the sights you shouldn't miss seeing is the Pacific Ocean. It's spectacular with waves crashing against the rocky shoreline. You'll be amazed at how breathtaking that sight is.

"What's that you say," Vern asked when Brian's breathing turned to a snore. "You're exactly right, Cousin. Sometimes newcomers don't realize how dangerous that ocean is. Visitors like to go out on the rocks and watch the wave action right up close. They don't know that the seventh wave is always bigger than the six before it. They get too close and that wave takes them right off the rocks. Gives them a ride they must like a lot, since they don't ever come back to complain about it.

"What's that?" Vern asked as he passed a slow driver on the newly improved section of highway. "You're right again, Cousin Brian. I was wrong. They do come back sometimes, but they never tell how they liked the ride, or how far out to sea they got.

"You still want to see for yourself, you say?" Vern appeared to give it some thought as he approached Lincoln City.

"Well, I shouldn't be so easily coaxed into helping you do something dangerous, but I'm just a good guy at heart. And you do have extraordinary sea-green eyes, and if I wasn't already in a relationship, you might have a chance convincing me that we should team up. Two fourths would give us fifty percent of the loot, and that's a great number. Hang on, Cuz; we're almost there.

"Since you want to see firsthand how that ocean trip goes, I'll help all I can. Sit tight. There's a nice viewpoint just south of the Cape Foulweather headland."

A few minutes later Vern pulled off the road at the deserted viewpoint where minimal parking was allowed. A fence to keep visitors from danger had been constructed between the parking area and the cliff face. Going beyond the fence was dangerous.

"I'm glad you boys could join me for one last get together before I head back," Myrtle said, looking across the table at Jerry Delahugh and Arlyn Jennings.

"We're sorry you're going east again. Any chance you might relocate out here?" asked Jerry.

"We three could have some good times together," encouraged Arlyn. "We could take Max for a few runs. He'd like that. Toss him a ball or a Frisbee and he's one happy dog."

"Sorry. I've really got to head home. I have some dead houseplants that I'll have to apologize to and bury. But before I leave, I wanted to report on what happened with your papers."

"The papers Ollie gave us?"

Myrtle nodded. "Richard Bigelow took them. He's an attorney and one of the heirs. He said they were holographic wills. He thinks the court will honor them, but has to let Chance Hamilton take over on it because Mr. Hamilton is more familiar with Oregon law."

"That's good news, Myrtle. When we get rich, we'll be able to visit you."

"When you do," laughed Myrtle, "bring this decoding ring." She handed Oliver's ring across the table. "I finally got it off my finger."

Arlyn picked it up and cupped it in his hands. "I sure do miss seeing this on Ollie's hand," he said.

"I was surprised to see an inscription inside," Myrtle said. "I didn't understand it."

"Let me see," Jerry said, holding the ring up to the light. "Yep, just as I thought. The old boy put our initials in it."

"In high school we were the three musketeers," explained Arlyn. "We signed everything with A-J-O, then circled the letter that corresponded to the writer's initial."

"Oliver thought highly of you two, that's clear. I hope they find all the money they think is hidden somewhere."

"You mean like banks?"

"No, they've checked the banks. Last I heard they were talking about the possibility of a safe somewhere in Oliver's house."

"They should'a asked us," Jerry laughed, winking at his friend.

"Ollie didn't keep secrets from us, Myrtle," Arlyn added. "He always told us where he put things."

"Do you mean you know where his safe is?"

Two white heads nodded as the waitress came to take their orders.

"Sorry," Myrtle said to the waitress. "We just realized we have something that needs attention. We can't stay for lunch today. Come on, you two. We're going to give the good guys some of the answers they've been searching for."

"What are you doing today?" Chris asked. "And speak up. I can hardly hear you."

"I'm at the beach. The wind's blowing, the waves are crashing, and I've got one of the cousins with me. He's about to take a little ride out to sea."

"What'll that get us?"

"It should bring us back up to a third of the estate instead of a fourth. Better odds, wouldn't you say?"

"Are you coming home soon?"

"I've got one more cousin and one more chance to change the take to fifty percent. As soon as I do that, I'm coming home. We'll wait for the money to show up via the U.S. Mail."

"How soon will that be?"

"It'll take months for the estate to close. We might as well wait wherever we want to eventually settle."

"Can we go back to Hawaii?"

"If you want."

"Should I get tickets?"

"It's a little soon for that. I'll call you in a few days. I'll know then what our time schedule looks like."

"I tell you, Stafford," Richard said. "You're the only one with enough *cojones* to get the state police looking for that murderer. You've got to get hold of the license number of the car Brian Fisher rented at the Portland airport. It's a blue convertible, 1999. Vern's driving and when it comes back from wherever it's headed I'm betting there'll be just one occupant. You've got to notify the state police to '*be on the lookout*' for those two. I'm on my way to your office right this minute. We'll head up the *BOLO* from there."

"Heather," called Myrtle from the living room of the Samuelson house.

"Upstairs, Aunt Myrtle," Heather responded. "I'm just finishing the website for that jeweler. Come on up."

"No, you come down. I have something to show you."

"Aunt Myrt, I'm not at a stopping place."

"It's important, Heather."

Reluctantly Heather pushed away from her desk and hurried down the stairs. "Hi," she said, surprised to see Jerry and Arlyn waiting quietly beside her aunt.

"You remember these two smug individuals, don't you?" Myrtle asked.

"Of course. Nice seeing you again, Arlyn. Jerry. How can I help?"

"It's more of how we can help you," Arlyn replied.

"You folks been looking for Ollie's fortune," added Jerry. "We know where it is."

"I'm sure Mr. Hamilton has checked with all the banks and . . ."

"That's the ready cash. We know where Ollie kept the rare coins and bullion. Want to see it?"

"If I said yes, where would you take me?"

"Just over to Ollie's place."

"Then we better do this legally and get Mr. Hamilton involved."

"If'n you say so," Jerry said.

While Oliver's friends and Myrtle raided the refrigerator and waited for Chance to arrive, Heather called Sally.

"Want to be present at the unveiling of a fortune in gold coins and bullion?" Heather asked.

"Are you kidding me?"

"Looking at the smug faces of the two men who know where it's buried, I'd say it's a sure thing."

"I'll be right there," Sally said.

Heather then dialed Jazz and asked the same question. And got the same answer.

"Here we go, Cousin Brian," Vern said, steering the drugged man around the fence, taking him closer to the edge of the cliff. "Look at that. It's high tide."

"N–no," mumbled Brian. "C–cold."

"Brisk," laughed Vern. "That ocean temperature is *brisk*. This is such a good viewpoint. We need to move a little farther west."

"N-no!"

"You've heard the saying 'go west, young man.' That's what you're doing." Vern laughed

"I thought I heard voices." A young woman crawled from the rocky nest where she'd been painting and watching waves as they splashed against the rocks. She had soft brown eyes and auburn hair.

"Sorry," said Vern. "We didn't mean to interrupt you. This is my Cousin Brian. He's from Colorado and has never seen the ocean before. It's really spectacular. Don't you think so, Cousin Brian?"

Kate Gifford looked at the young man she'd assisted the day before. "Your first time at the ocean, is it, Brian?" she asked. "Are you thinking about going for a swim?" She smiled at the pair.

"C-cold," Brian mumbled.

"It's fifty degrees," laughed Kate. "If you get much closer to the edge of the cliff you'll be testing the water temperature firsthand."

The cliff on which they stood had formed unevenly. On the southern-most length of it was a thirty foot drop to the ocean waves. But to the north the cliff gave way to a six foot drop into a rocky nest protected on three sides by jutting rocks. The area was protected from wind on three sides, and hidden from passing motorists.

"C-cold," Brian repeated.

"What's the matter with your cousin," Kate asked. "He doesn't seem to be fully awake."

"Beats me," Vern said. "He's on some kind of medication that relaxes him. He can hardly stand alone, but he has to fly home tonight so he wanted to see the ocean before he left." Vern studied the woman. Would she serve him best as a disinterested witness to Brian's fall, or should she be included in an ocean ride for two?

Kate said, "Why don't I help. Your cousin has a better chance to see the waves crashing against the base of the cliff if we move a little to my right."

"Th-thanks," sputtered Vern, releasing his vise-like grip. "That does make it easier."

"Is this far enough?" she asked when they'd taken another step or two. "It might not be safe to go closer to the edge."

"What's your pleasure, Cousin Brian?" asked Vern, still trying to ease the drugged man to the cliff's edge.

"N-no" mumbled Brian.

"What's that you say, Cuz? With this lady's help you want to take another step or two?"

"I didn't get your name?" Kate said.

"Everyone calls me *Cuz*," Vern lied.

"Well then! Watch your step, Cuz!" Kate yelled the warning as she twisted Brian's body toward her, taking one more step to her right.

The action threw Vern closer to the southern edge of the cliff where he fought to maintain his balance. A piercing scream filled the air as Kate and Brian disappeared over the jagged, northern edge. They landed on the rocky platform where Kate had been painting.

"I think we'll rest here while we wait for you to sober up," she whispered to the man clasped in her strong arms. "For your first time west of Colorado you certainly manage to get yourself into some pickles."

"P-pickles," agreed Brian, snuggling against her.

Chance, Heather, Sally, Jazz, and an armed guard Chance invited, were following Myrtle and Oliver's friends to the Lloyd house. Chance and the guard lent the group legality.

Oliver's friends led the way into the dining room where Arlyn lifted the wooden vent hiding the safe. "Ollie used our initials for the combination," he explained. "The hard part is the counting."

Jerry had his hand on the safe's dial. "Okay, Linny. Tell me what to do."

"Turn the dial left until number one comes up the fourth time." He turned to the group and explained, "A is the first letter of the alphabet. That's why the first number is a one. It stands for Arlyn."

"Got it," Jerry said.

"Fine, now turn it to the right, but stop when the number ten shows up the third time." He explained, "The ten is for the J in Jerry's name, the tenth letter of the alphabet."

After what seemed like a long time, Jerry announced, "Got it."

"Good, now turn left again, but stop when fifteen comes up the second time. The fifteen is for Oliver's name."

"Got it! Next?"

"Turn right and go past zero until the dial stops in its tracks."

A gentle click sounded from the steel safe in the floor.

"You people interested in what bullion looks like?" Jerry laughed. "Ollie has him some of that, and gold proof sets. There's also several coins he's had appraised at more than $45,000."

"Each?" asked Myrtle.

"Each," answered Oliver's friends in unison.

"A millionaire proposed marriage to me," marveled Myrtle.

"Okay," Chance said. "Let's get that stuff out of there and to a vault until we can get the coins appraised."

"Stamps, too," Arlyn said.

"Okay. Stamps, too."

It was almost dusk when a state highway patrolman spotted Brian's rental car at the deserted viewpoint near Lincoln City. He radioed the finding to the watch captain and was just telling him it looked like no one was around when two figures appeared from the direction of the rocky cliff. One of them was carrying a shoe.

"Does this car belong to one of you?" Sergeant Medford shouted.

"It's mine," replied Brian, walking steadily toward the car. He firmly clasped the hand of the woman at his side.

"We've been looking for it. You want to tell me what's going on?"

"I was kidnapped. By my cousin. He drugged me and brought me here, intending to kill me." Brian looked fondly at Kate. "This lady saved my life."

"Where's the kidnapper now?" the Sergeant asked, ready to phone in his report.

"Kate?" Brian turned to the woman beside him. "I'm afraid I have to leave that part to you."

"Well, officer, I didn't know how to keep the murder from happening, except to get the two men closer to a safe drop-off I knew about. When they got there, I pulled Brian against me and we landed in a protected area. We didn't see what happened to his cousin."

"Do you think he went over the cliff?"

"I guess he could have. When Brian and I tried to figure out where he was, we found this." She motioned to the shoe Brian held. "It was wedged between two boulders."

"I'm glad to see my cousin left my car," Brian said. "I hope the keys are in the ignition."

"Do you think your cousin could have hitchhiked?"

"I really don't know what he might do," Brian said. "I only met him yesterday."

###

Heather was trying to finish updating the Coffman Jewelers website. Abe Coffman employed her shortly after her mother's death in February and here it was July.

Unfortunately Heather was having trouble concentrating. Her aunt was headed back to Massachusetts, but questions plagued her. Why, Heather wondered, was a powerful man like Richard Bigelow denied the list of witnesses and jurors for a trial that had been over for nearly a decade? No one had given her a satisfactory explanation. Once her life calmed down she was going to concentrate on solving her mother's puzzling letter. She thought she was closing in on its hidden message and she was eager to test her theories.

Vern's shoeless body had washed ashore south of Lincoln City, and Oliver's heirs, Richard, Brian and Marilyn, had met. They agreed to send Myrtle the picture she'd once purchased from the Treasure Trove, and make sure Jerry and Arlyn each got ten percent of the estate, just as Oliver intended.

Life at the Samuelson's was beginning to return to normal, except that Sally had gone to work, and the doorbell downstairs was ringing insistently. With a sigh, Heather again abandoned the jeweler's website, and rushed down the stairs.

"Mrs. Bender. Baby." Heather noticed a plate of Danish pastries nearly slipping from her neighbor's trembling hands.

"My Jimmie Joe is coming home from his academy later today," Baby said. "I'm doing a spot of baking. Gotta remember what his favorite pastry is and thought you could help out by taking some of my baking."

"I'm sorry, Baby," Heather replied, having punched some very familiar numbers quickly into her cell phone. "Oh darn," she said when the connection was made and her landline began ringing. "That's my telephone. I need to answer it. You know, Baby, Helen Corbin, next door, was asking how she could get some of your wonderful pastries. I promised I'd send you over the next time you had some."

"I'll take these over," Baby said, pausing to wink a couple of times. "I want you to know that my Jimmie Joe is single." Baby winked again.

"I'm so glad to know that," Heather whispered. "Helen Corbin is single, too. Don't you *love* coincidences like that?"

###

NOT ENOUGH PUZZLES?

More puzzles can be found in the third book of this series. Follow the directions for learning the title.

	1	2	3	4	5	6	7	8
A	M	F	T	E	E	W	L	D
B	D	U	H	B	A	T	B	C
C	K	C	S	S	J	X	Q	P
D	J	E	Z	Y	G	I	R	G
E	M	T	N	S	O	E	N	L
F	R	B	A	G	H	Y	I	N
G	O	C	T	Y	O	O	A	H
H	P	A	I	D	T	L	B	E

B3,H2,B2,E7,G3,H3,F8,F4

G2,G5,F8,C2,H6,B2,E4,H3,G1,E3,C3

—— —— —— —— —— —— —— ——   —— —— —— —— —— —— —— —— —— —— ——

TO BE CONTINUED

PUZZLE SOLUTIONS

Page ix. **LET'S START WITH A BIG CLUE**

FIND ALL THE KILLERS

Page 2. **WHAT SHOULD BE AVOIDED?**

Gore, three, court, scare, there, store = GHOSTS
Prank, four, rain, stalk, board, then   = POISON

Page 10. **DISCOVER A CLUE**

Someone has already been murdered. PAMELA

Page 16. **A BIT OF PHILOSOPHY**

ALL FAIRY TALES COME TO AN END

Page 26. **THE STAGE IS SET**

VICTIMS: Olivia, Stranger, Oliver
MURDERERS: Vernon, Chris
LOVERS: Vernon/Chris
THIEVES: Vern/Chris, Olivia, Stranger
SISTERS: Bender Sisters
BYSTANDERS: Myrtle, Bender Sisters

Page 34. **WATCH OUT, HEATHER!**

YOU ARE BEING WATCHED

SYNONYM FINDER

D	A	N	G	E	R	O	U	S
U	E	G	S	A	O	R	N	D
O	R	S	D	N	U	G	A	E
G	U	A	O	R	D	E	S	N
E	N	D	A	S	G	U	R	O
R	S	O	N	U	E	D	G	A
S	D	U	R	O	N	A	E	G
N	G	R	E	D	A	S	O	U
A	O	E	U	G	S	N	D	R

Page 43. **OH! NO!**

WHERE IS THE FAIRY GODMOTHER?

Page 49. **WHAT'S IN STORE FOR AUNT MYRTLE?**

ENGAGEMENT

Page 53. **WHO IS NOT GOING AWAY?**

CLIENTS, KILLERS

Page 60. **WHAT'S IN A WORD?**

DRAGON   CREATE
SEARCH   HEART
MEATS   NEVER
FLIER   STRANGER
DEATH   EVIDENCE

Page 67. **SILLY SENSE**

1. When unwanted company arrives…(grin and bear it)
2. You may be safe if you…(lock your doors)
3. When discovering a dead body…(Call for help)
4. If you are allergic to the surroundings…(move far away)
5. When there is a thief in your midst…(take inventory often)

Page 75. **WHAT'S GOING ON?**

INTRUDER ALERT WATCH OUT

Page 82. **A LOOK AHEAD (POISON)**

A	C	C	R	I	T	M	U	R	O	I
E	D	I	E	E	D	R	E	D	P	S
N	S	N	H	A	D	Q	U	E	S	O
T	T	I	A	N	T	I	E	T	A	N
S	U	F	F	D	E	S	P	E	R	J
M	A	R	E	O	N	M	E	A	L	E
A	I	R	D	R	A	E	M	I	T	W
G	T	U	N	E	H	M	Y	R	T	E
E	R	P	O	L	S	K	C	O	L	L
F	O	E	C	I	H	E	M	L	E	S

Page 89. **WATCH OUT LEWISBURG; HERE COMES RICHARD**

APPARENT, AUTOPSY, DEVICES, INVESTIGATE, MILLIONS, SPRINGS, DEVASTATION, RICHARDS, CYCLONES

Page 96. **DINNER'S READY**

1. Myrtle
2. Sally
3. Tom
4. Rachel
5. Heather
6. Tim

Page 106. **STAIR STEPS**

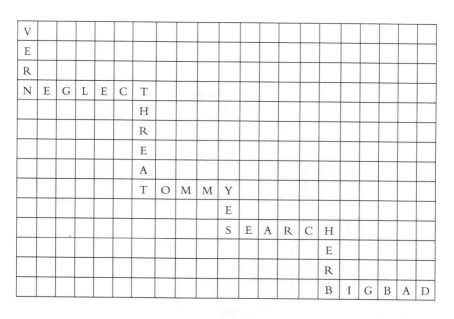

Page 116. **STORY STEW**

ATROCIOUS	CHICANERY	CUNNING
DECEITFUL	FRAUDULENT	HORRIBLE
MALICIOUS	SCOUNDREL	VILLAINOUS

Page 124. **THE SEARCH CONTINUES**

BLUISH____GREEN____GROCER
BONE_____HEAD____LINER
DINNER____RING____TONE
FATHER____TIME____LESS
HATCH____BACK____UP
HEAD_____BAND____SAW
HIDE_____OUT_____LAW

Page 130. **IDENTIFY THE HEIRS**

OLIVIA, MARILYN, RICHARD, BRIAN

Page 144. **ASK THE RIGHT QUESTIONS**

THE KILLER REVEALS CLUES

Page 152. **WATCH OUT, VERN**

THEY ARE COMING AFTER YOU

Page 164. **WHAT TIME IS IT?**

TIME TO FIND THE JEWELS

Page 174. **WHERE IS OLIVER'S MISSING FORTUNE?**

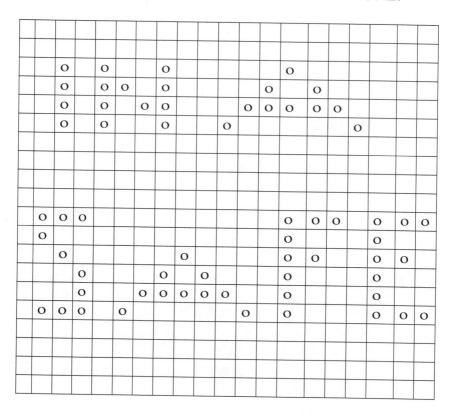

Page 183. **WHAT'S AHEAD?**

Alone, done, four, trace, heat, they, three = another
Drink, here, bead, there, hair   = death

COFFEE BREAK! SHARPEN YOUR WITS

T								H				
W		P	O	I	S	O	N	E	R	A		
I	E							U				
S	R							N				
T	R	I	A	L			G	T	R	A	P	
	S				C		H	I				
	H				R		O	N				W
		S	E	C	R	E	T	S	G		F	E
				C	E		T			H	O	D
			N	P				C		R	D	
		Q	U	E	S	T	Y	J		T	T	I
		D					E	A			U	N
		I				W	A	R	N	I	N	G
	V					E				E		
E	X	P	L	O	D	E		L				

Page 198. **PUZZLES REMAINING**

		Yes	No
1.	Is the scrapbook important?	(K)	w
2.	Did Mattie have a lover?	h	(A)
3.	Will Vern get all of the money?	o	(T)
4.	Is Mattie's letter more than a fairy tale?	(E)	s
5.	Will Bender cookies continue arriving?	(G)	g
6.	Will Vern be arrested?	h	(I)
7.	Is Vern's lover guilty of murder?	(F)	p
8.	Is there a safe with money at Oliver's?	(F)	l
9.	Will Vern escape?	c	(O)
10.	Will the missing fortune be found?	(R)	as
11.	Is Brian's life in danger?	(D)	S

KATE GIFFORD

Page 211. **NOT ENOUGH PUZZLES?**

HAUNTING CONCLUSIONS